DANGEROUS IN LOVE

Leslie Thomas

arrow books

Published by Arrow Books in 2004

5 7 9 10 8 6 4

Copyright © Leslie Thomas, 1987

First published in the United Kingdom in 1987 by Methuen

First published in paperback in the United Kingdom in 1988 by Penguin Books

Arrow Books
Random House, 20 Vauxhall Bridge Road,
London SW1V 2SA

Random House Australia (Pty) Limited
20 Alfred Street, Milsons Point, Sydney,
New South Wales 2061, Australia

Random House New Zealand Limited

Isle of

Papers us   made
from woo   ocesses
conform   rigin

ISBN 9780099474234

Typeset by SX Composing DTP, Rayleigh, Essex
Printed and bound in Great Britain by
CPI Antony Rowe, Chippenham, Wiltshire

To my friend and fellow author
Brian Freemantle
who always buys my books

'Write that down,' the King said to the jury; and the jury eagerly wrote down all three dates on their slates, and then added them up, and reduced the answer to shillings and pence.

Lewis Carroll: *Alice in Wonderland*

1

There were moments when it seemed to Detective Constable Dangerous Davies that mayhem moved into his path, marking him purposefully out, isolating him, and then engulfing him, like those small individual whirlwinds that travelled around in parts of America and which he had seen on television. It was so on this ordinary damp night in early October as he and Mod Lewis, the unemployed Welsh philosopher, were walking to their lodgings at 'Bali Hi', Furtman Gardens, London NW, from an evening at The Babe In Arms public house. They were humming as they walked.

At the Neasden end of Power Station Lane, under the drizzle of the cooling towers, they heard the distant but unmistakable sounds of a fracas. Davies halted like a troubled dog. 'A punch-up,' he said. Mod stood, his face damp and moon-pale in the drizzle. His heavy head rolled to one side as he listened.

'Singing,' he ventured. 'They're only singing. Tuesday's not a fighting night.'

A crash like cannon fire came from the far end of the street. 'Somebody going through a door,' said Davies.

At once, the singing became louder, less enclosed. 'Irish,' he added. 'I suppose we'd better have a look.'

'You're the policeman,' said Mod, standing still.

Davies sighed: 'All right. I'll go. You ring the law. It sounds like a three-dog job to me.'

'Do you happen to have ten pence?' asked Mod.

'You have to ring 999,' Davies said. 'It's free.' Mod went off into the windy drizzle. Tentatively, Davies went along Power Station Lane to where he could see the riot: the light coming through the wildly open door, jostling figures behind the steamy windows.

Spectators had made themselves comfortable in upper storeys across the street, sounding appreciation, *oohs* and *aaahs*, like people watching fireworks. He advanced along broken fences and dripping privet hedges, a short burst at a time, until he was twenty yards short of the battle which occupied the entire terraced house. With caution he fell back into the concealment of an open gate, and was thoroughly frightened by a huge hand on his shoulder. He turned to see a West Indian staring from the night. 'It's the bleeding Irish, mate,' said the man.

'Have they been at it long?' asked Davies, faintly hoping that the alarm might have already been raised and the police on the way. The man's teeth lit up like a window.

'You're Mr Davies,' he said. The hand that had dropped on his shoulder now descended again like a mechanical shovel and, turning him around, grasped his hand and shook it immensely. 'You was very fair to my boy,' said the man fervently. 'Motor Bike trouble. Thompson.'

'Ah, yes, Thompson, Power Station Lane. John Bountiful Thompson,' remembered Davies. 'Taking and driving away. Thirty charges. Six months suspended. How is he?'

'Settled down a treat,' beamed the man. 'You said he ought to take an interest in things, join something. Well, 'e joined the National Front.'

'Oh good,' muttered Davies. He peered further along the street. 'I suppose I'd better go and ask this lot why they're knocking hell out of each other.'

'"Summat to do wiv some bloke wot died in Ireland,"' offered Mr Thompson. 'So they reckoned in the boozer this afternoon.'

'Been going on since this afternoon has it?'

'Since Sunday,' corrected the man. 'After church.'

As he spoke a crate of bottles came out of the open upper window of the uproarious house and crashed into the front garden. 'Empties,' said the West Indian. Davies moved away along the privets. He wondered how long the dogs would take. They were probably in bed. As he moved into the light of a street lamp, someone shouted from an upper window: 'It's Dangerous! Go on Dangerous, mate, sort them out!'

'Never fear,' whispered Davies, timidly raising his hand. He had reached the scene of the fracas now and peered around the dishevelled hedge. The front garden area was a shambles of debris, the just-jettisoned Guinness crate lying like a beached raft on an island. Two dazed men sat in the postures of children in a corner against the house. A boy in a turban appeared. 'It's the Irish,' he said.

'So everyone keeps telling me,' replied the police-man. He scanned the garden area.

'It's always like that, their garden,' said the Indian child. 'Send them back to Ireland where they belong.'

3

As he spoke a man came out of the front door as if propelled by explosives, ejected backwards, arms whirling. His feet became entangled with some bottles on the path, which spun like rollers and capsized him against the low wall. He slid down, eyes flickering, finally closing, and became motionless. 'Mr Phelan,' said the Indian boy. 'He's on the council.'

'Oh God,' muttered Davies. A familiar sense of doom settled on him. His tongue was dry. He looked up and down the street but no help was arriving; no sirens, no dogs. He sighed, straightened up, and walked, as casually as a postman, to the gaping door.

'Now lads, now lads, what's all this about?' he called from the front passage. 'Come on now. You've had your fun.'

A moment later, wide-eyed, the Indian boy saw him coming out headlong. His feet caught bottles lying on the garden path. He staggered as if on skates, tipping backwards over Mr Phelan, striking his head on the brick wall and subsiding with a spent sigh. The child bent and peered into the collapsed face. There was an open cut on the forehead, grazes down the cheekbone. Blood dropped from the lower lip. 'Dumb copper,' the Indian boy muttered. From somewhere distant, beyond the night streets, a police siren sounded. Too late again.

They had put him in his usual bed in the hospital and now, with his head split and aching, swathed like a nun's, lip sewn, he leaned against his pillows and morosely surveyed the grey scene outside the window. It was surprising how swiftly the seasons altered. Only a few weeks ago, during his last stay he recalled, the tree beyond the pane had a cover of gritty leaves, but now there was nothing to cloak its bleakness. He had mentioned this to a Nigerian doctor who had remarked, with a touch of medico-poetry, that it looked like an X-ray photograph of multiple fractures.

The arrival of Mod did little to brighten him. The elliptical Welshman, library books hugged beneath his overcoated arms, shambled down the centre of the ward exchanging small talk with other patients. 'He's back in again, oh aye . . . it's home from home to him.' He arrived beside Davies's bed, the books pinioned by his arms.

'You look like Moses,' muttered Davies.

'Works of power,' answered Mod, piling the volumes on the bed. 'You should read some philosophy or lives-of-the-greats while you are lying there, Dangerous. It could transform your entire outlook.'

'That could only be for the better,' grumbled Davies. 'I've got a half-shut bloody eye and out of it I can just see the swelling of my split bloody lip.'

Mod put his glasses on and leaned closer. 'Boy, that's a beauty,' he observed. 'Exceptional, even for you, Dangerous. Like the spout of a Welsh milk jug. I brought you some fruit.'

From the interior of his commodious overcoat, he produced a sad apple and some dates wrapped in green toilet tissue. He put them on the bedside locker.

'Don't put them there,' said Davies sourly. 'They'll all be wanting some.'

Mod looked around at the other patients and secreted the apple and the dates in the locker drawer. 'Contributions from Mrs Fulljames,' he revealed. 'I nicked them.'

'I thought that might be the case.'

'As usual she wants full rent whether you're there to eat or not. I've fed your dog and informed your wife.'

'Not much reaction from either, I suppose.'

'No noticeable reaction at all,' confirmed Mod. 'But the boys at The Babe once again send their sincere best wishes for your recovery.' He sat on the side of the bed, inspecting Davies's injuries. 'What,' he inquired, 'seems to be the trouble?'

Davies glared under his lowered eyelid. 'I'm in what is called a generally sodded-up condition,' he said. 'Fortunately no fractures. Just what you see, plus a black-and-blue rib-cage.'

'I've seen you worse,' consoled Mod. 'Have you had any visitors?'

'The Coroner,' muttered Davies. 'He was just passing through. The pathologist was with him. They'd been to the mortuary. They gave me a good looking over, and I didn't like the way they did it.'

'Future reference, you think,' mused Mod. His large bald head nodded. 'Well, you never know. You do find trouble, Dangerous. It's a pity you didn't hang on for another fifteen minutes. There were police and dogs everywhere. But everything had subsided by then. You included.'

'Any arrests?' asked Davies.

'Apparently none. One of the dogs wet himself in the house – fear, probably – and the Paddies want compensation.'

'They would,' grunted Davies. 'Kitty is all right, is he?' He did not wholly trust Mod with his dog. 'He's had fresh water?'

'He's had fresh Guinness,' returned Mod. 'The boys from The Babe donated it. Six bottles.'

'Six? How many did Kitty get?'

'We went half and half,' admitted Mod. 'By the way, you've won the pools.'

Davies's eyebrows went up so swiftly he yelped in pain. 'Won them! How much?'

'One hundred and eighty quid between the whole police syndicate. Nine quid each. I'll collect it for you if you like.'

'No thanks,' Davies sighed. His visible eye clouded. Mod leaned privately towards him. 'I don't know why you don't get out,' he said. 'Clear off somewhere.' He regarded his friend painfully. 'Look at you. The embroidered man.'

'The last detective,' acknowledged Davies sadly.

'Exactly. The last detective. The last one they send – unless there's a madman to tackle.'

'It seems to be my fate to look at people with murder in their eyes.'

Mod's fat face softened. 'Why don't you go off and do something else? Open a hardware store.'

Distraught, Davies gazed at him. 'Hardware?' he said, touching his forehead.

'Anything as long as you get out of the police and out of this area,' said Mod. 'Take your accumulated pension and your dog and go. You're not cut out to be a copper. Never were.'

They sat moodily. 'Sierra Leone,' Mod said eventually. 'Anywhere.' A nurse giving out bedpans progressed down the ward. 'Have you got the right time?' asked Mod.

Davies nodded towards his locker. 'It's in there. It must be nearly opening.'

Mod pulled the drawer and took out the watch. 'Half an hour,' he said. 'Could I borrow the ticker? Just while you're in here?'

Firmly, Davies retrieved the watch. 'I like to see the time dragging by,' he said. He put it back into the drawer. Mod rose and took up his burden of books. 'I'd leave one of these for you,' he said. 'But they're a bit heavyweight.'

'I don't want to start reading until both eyes are open,' replied Davies.

Still clutching the books, Mod reached into his pocket and produced a randomly folded newspaper. 'I brought you the local,' he said. 'You're not in it. Nothing about your bravery.'

He shambled off. Davies watched him go down the ward, helping himself to grapes. He revolved at the door and waved royally. Davies lay back, closed his heavy eyes, then opened them as far as he was able and picked up the local newspaper. On the second page he saw that Wilfred Henry Brock, a disordered old man who had wheeled a perambulator about the district for years, had been found drowned in the canal. The news saddened him. Lofty Brock had been a moving landmark, muttering to himself as he pushed his pram, picking up random pieces of paper, as if looking for a lost letter. Nobody knew his story for, it was said, he had himself forgotten it. Davies wondered how he had come to get himself drowned.

He was given sick leave, but after washing his car and attempting to mend some of it, and brushing his dog, he seemed to have little else to occupy him. Cricklewood Snooker Hall was shut while they changed the tables, and there were disadvantages in not having a proper home. He walked to the police station to pay his football-pool stake. Sergeant Bannister, who filled in the coupon, was on duty.

'We hit the jackpot then, Frank,' mentioned Davies.

'Forgot the date of the wife's birthday,' confessed the sergeant, shaking his head morosely over the report book on the counter. 'Always fill in every-body's birthdays for the numbers, Dangerous. I put a cross against seventeen, and it turns out the wife's is the nineteenth. Typical of her. That would have been another draw. Twenty-five thousand quid.'

A furtive woman came in from the street and began to hover.

'Any rewards?' she inquired plaintively. 'Any rewards going this week?'

The sergeant regarded her patiently. 'Not that I've heard of, Minnie,' he said. He turned to Davies. 'You haven't, have you, Dangerous?' Davies pretended to think.

'In short supply these days, rewards,' he said, shaking his head like a shopkeeper. The woman shuffled towards the door and went out silently sideways. Davies said: 'What about poor old Lofty, Frank.'

'Never harmed a fly, Lofty,' mused the sergeant.

Davies began studying the notices on the police

station board. 'Wanted for Terrorism.' 'Wanted for Armed Robbery.' 'Treatment for AIDS.' 'Do You Recognize This Weapon?' It was a wicked world.

'I can never understand these Identikit pictures,' he sniffed, studying the man wanted for armed robbery. 'This bloke's got three different chins.' He felt his own scarred chin. 'When's the inquest on Lofty?' he asked.

'This morning,' said the sergeant. 'PC Westerman's just gone up there.'

'I might look in,' said Davies, glancing down at his watch. He made for the door. A wet-cheeked woman and an old man hugging his leg were coming up the steps as he went out. He wished them good morning and went towards the car compound.

For years he had been the possessor of a seedy but – on account of its antiquity – valuable Lagonda tourer, which also served as a home for his dog, but necessity had ordered its sale. He had replaced it with a venerable Vauxhall Vanguard. It was bulky and plum-coloured with white wheels, obtained at a police auction of misappropriated goods. Kitty, his Yak-like dog, was waiting for him now in the ragged rear seat as he crossed to the vehicle.

Girls in the West Indian hair salon (Pierre of Brent) had recently arranged his tangled hair into dreadlocks. Kitty, pleased with the attention, had sat quietly and ringlets now hung from his large face, his eyes peering between the spiralled strands like those of a prisoner behind bars.

As Davies got into the car, the dog barked provocatively. He frequently had difficulty in accepting him as his master.

10

He edged the bulbous vehicle into the traffic. It was ten minutes to the Coroner's court, a drive through coarse streets: the Rawalpindi Supermarket, The Great Wall Chinese Takeaway, the Halal Butcher, Barbados Groceries, The Jewel in the Crown Curry Centre, and the older-established premises of Smith, Jones, Murphy, the Credit Outfitters and the Queen Victoria off-licence.

The Coroner's court was in a new building which seemed to Davies unnecessarily bright for a place in daily association with tragedy. Some upset people had just come out from an inquest and a man was ineffectually trying to comfort another man who was weeping clumsily into thick hands as he stumbled towards the exit. The first man produced a yellow scarf and gave it to his friend to hold to his eyes. The weeper rubbed at his tears and then blew his nose on it. The first man seemed a little shocked and held out his hand for his scarf.

Davies, soberly observing the pair, moved aside to let them pass. The guiding man whispered: 'His mum took an overdose.' He ran his finger across his throat.

'Sorry about that,' muttered Davies, as if there were some way he might have prevented it. In one ordinary morning there was a lot of small sorrow around. He pushed open the door of the court. The Coroner, Mr Noël Benskin, was perched like an auctioneer on a raised dais at the far end of the neon-lit room, his pen scratching audibly. The next case was proceeding. Evidence had just been given by a doctor who was now descending with pursed lips from the witness stand. A drained woman sat on a front bench watching him dumbly as if she could bear to care no longer. The Coroner looked up from his deathly ledger and said in his low official voice: 'You may go now. You may make the arrangements for the funeral.' The woman said: 'I . . . I don't know how to.' She waited, then added: 'Sir.'

'I'm sure the doctor will help you,' intoned the Coroner, practically. 'He knows the funeral people.'

'I've never had to do it before,' she mumbled, half to the official and half to the doctor who was looking none too pleased. She rose and the Coroner's officer took her arm. Davies sat thoughtfully in the rearmost of the benches. Now the court was vacant except for Benskin, himself, and the officer who was at the distant door. The Coroner looked up at the emptied court as if wondering if he had offended everybody. His rimless spectacles fixed Davies, who smiled uncertainly.

'Ah, Detective Constable Davies. How are the injuries?'

'Getting better by the minute, sir, thank you,' answered Davies, half standing.

'Good, good. Er . . . Why are you here? Are you interested in the next case? Let me see . . .' He examined his ledger. 'Brock, Wilfred Henry. Found drowned.'

Uncertainly again, Davies rose. 'Sort of, sir. I . . . just knew him.'

'Ah,' breathed the Coroner wisely. 'Known to the police, was he?'

Hurriedly protecting the name of a dead man, Davies corrected him. 'No . . . not like that, sir. He didn't have a record. He was just . . . known.'

Benskin looked as if he did not understand why a policeman should know of somebody who was not, in legal terms, known. There was a bellow from the rear of the room, the traditional and unreasonably startling shout of his officer calling those who had some interest in the passing of Wilfred Henry Brock to attend the court forthwith.

Davies was wearing his overcoat. He always changed into that and his long-john underwear when the clocks were altered in the autumn. It was one of his few concessions to regularity. Now he looked around the edge of his thick collar, frayed by London winters, and saw the few people entering the court like the cast of a small play. They were led by Police Constable Westerman, who was subject to massive nosebleeds. He had once had to borrow a set of keys (to put down his back) from a man arrested on suspicion of stealing a car with the same keys. Behind him came an irritated-looking fat man whom Davies recognized as Charlie Copley, the warden of the North West London Refuge for Men, and behind Charlie a fine-looking black girl whom Davies had never seen before. She was tall and relaxed. Her heavy red coat hung about her ankles. She took a seat at the far end of the same bench, never glancing his way but watching the Coroner as she sat down. Davies could see her left eye, deep and dish-shaped, like the eye of an ancient African carving. He kept glancing at her, hoping she would even briefly turn his way, but she kept her face firmly forward. Her only action was to reach down to a briefcase at her feet from which she extracted some papers – a mundane movement which, however, sent a cloud of luxuriant hair toppling forward. Davies swallowed guiltily.

Police Constable Westerman, apprehensively sniffing, climbed to the witness stand. 'I was on duty,' he recited, peering into his notebook as if trying to recall if he was, 'on October 7th, sir, when I received information that what appeared to be a person was floating in the Grand Union at Pikes Lane.'

'A person?' queried the Coroner pedantically.

'A body, as it turned out, sir. In the canal.'

Mr Benskin regarded him as he might someone who could be holding back information. The officer's dubious eyes rose from the notebook. 'Please continue,' muttered the official.

'I went at once to Pikes Lane where two boys were prodding a floating object with some sticks, sir. I told them to desist and with some assistance took the body from the water. It was apparent to me that the man was dead and there was no point in trying any resuscitation et cetera, sir.'

'Was it cold?' inquired the Coroner.

'Cold, sir? The body or the water, sir?' asked the witness timidly.

'The night, constable, the night.'

'On the chilly side, sir.'

The next witness was Charlie Copley, who described himself as the warden of the North West London Refuge for Men. He agreed that he had gone to the mortuary and identified the body of Wilfred Henry Brock. He sounded neither sorry nor surprised.

'He was a . . . habitué . . .?' Benskin thought about

this. 'A frequenter of the hostel, was he?' The rimless glasses fixed the witness.

'A client, sir,' said Copley. 'Regular for years. He used to wander around with an old pram. Everybody knew him.' It was his turn to regard the Coroner. 'Nearly everybody,' he amended. 'Harmless sort of old man. In his seventies, or thereabouts.' He glanced at Police Constable Westerman for confirmation. The policeman began searching his notebook.

'Have you been able to trace relatives?' asked the Coroner, immediately answering the question himself: 'I don't suppose you have or they would be here today, wouldn't they. They usually turn up out of the blue at times like these.'

'They do, sir,' nodded the warden. 'To see if there is anything worth having.'

Benskin raised his eyebrows above his glasses. 'Did you know any reason why he should take his own life?'

'Not as I know of, sir. He seemed all right to me. But I have fifty others to think about. It's a popular place, the hostel.'

Benskin sniffed. 'Yes, I imagine. Call the next witness.'

From the rear of the room sounded a concise tread. Dr Frederick Spilton, the pathologist, took the stand. He was pale and wore tight, sharp suits. Death, he said unmysteriously, was due to drowning. He then stepped down, asked if he might be released and left the court. The handsome black girl stirred in her seat.

'Miss Jemima Duval,' said the Coroner's officer. He nodded at the piece of paper in his hand, looked up and blushed all over his naked head as he met her eyes. Mr Benskin took off and cleaned his glasses, and then replaced them as she went to the witness stand. She turned, and for the first time Davies saw her complete face, the cheekbones, the eyes, the full hair, the soft dark skin, the missing tooth. Every eye in the room was now fixed on the missing tooth, absent in the middle of her otherwise perfect set. 'God help me,' muttered Davies.

Mr Benskin, with a slight squeak, asked her to repeat her name.

'Jemima Duval,' the lady replied quietly. 'I am a social worker.'

'Yes, yes, of course,' nodded the Coroner. 'And what do you know of this sad case?'

She opened a folder and remarked: 'I visit the men's hostel quite regularly.'

'You do?' Mr Benskin looked as if he might go to live there himself. 'Regularly?'

'Yes, regularly.'

'I suppose men talk much better with a lady.'

'So they tell me, sir.'

'And you knew the deceased. What can you tell us about him?'

'He was well liked, sir. They called him Lofty. He was one of those people who just chose to live like that, in the simplest possible way, with little responsibility. He was eccentric. He wandered about talking to himself, picking up pieces of paper at random, but never caused trouble, as far as I could ascertain, and he paid for his keep without any bother. He seemed to me to be quite happy. There was no distress.'

16

'Er . . . when you visited him, what did he talk about?'

'Oh, the usual things. How he was keeping, if he needed any help. He did not remember anything about his past. Apparently he had been in the War but he couldn't recall anything about that either. He was just a poor, sad old man.'

'And you've been unable to trace any relatives, anyone who knows him outside this immediate area.'

'That's correct, sir. He had very few possessions, not many papers, and I was unable to contact anyone who would . . . claim him, sir.'

The Coroner was studying her missing tooth again. He adjusted his glasses quickly, the action of someone pulling themselves together, and asked: 'Is there any reason known to you why he should have taken his own life?'

'None at all, sir. He seemed to me to be a very contented old man.'

Mr Benskin became thoughtful. 'He was a familiar figure in this locality, wheeling an old perambulator, as I understand. What happened to the pram?'

Davies nodded approvingly. The black girl said: 'It has not been found, sir. It's presumed to have gone into the canal with him.'

'*Would* he have taken it with him . . .? I mean, *would* he have plunged into the canal with the pram if he was intent on suicide?' The Coroner mused for a moment and once more answered his own question: 'I suppose he might. On the other hand, if he had fallen into the canal by accident, he is just as likely to have pushed the perambulator in ahead of him.' He looked up at the black girl again. 'How were his drinking habits?' he asked.

'He didn't have any, as far as I know,' she replied. 'He was teetotal. That's very rare in that sort of person, people without home or family. Very rare, sir.'

Davies followed her from the court after the open verdict and caught up with her on the pavement. 'Oh . . . Miss Duval . . . I'm Detective Constable Davies . . .'

Unhurriedly she turned and took him in. He hoped she would not smile because he knew he would not be able to avoid staring. She did and he stared. Until he had seen that missing tooth he had never realized that something could be so potent, even beautiful, by its absence. 'I've heard of you,' she said. 'You're called Dangerous.'

He was abashed. 'Just a nickname,' he said. 'I don't know who started it.' Her smile was reasonable. Encouraged, he said: 'It's just opening time. Would you like a drink?'

'The Dog and Shovel,' she nodded.

His heart had begun to bang blatantly inside his overcoat. He fell in beside her and they walked at a brisk pace along the pavement. She was only an inch below his height, but quite a lot of it was her hair. 'Poor old Lofty,' he said conversationally. 'Never did a soul any harm.'

'Didn't he?' she said curiously. 'Not many go through life without harming somebody.' She shrugged away the moment. 'But that's what every-one says,' she agreed, striding on, looking ahead. He had some difficulty in keeping up with her.

'That pram must be in the bottom of the canal, then,' he said a little breathlessly. 'With all the other junk. And it'll stay there now.'

She reached the public door first, pushed it open and reached for her handbag.

'No, please,' argued Davies, rummaging in his pocket. 'What would you like?'

She regarded him challengingly. 'It's my local,' she said.

'So it is,' he agreed. He smiled directly at her. 'A pint please.'

She came back with a beer for him and a lager for herself. They sat down behind a scarred table. It was only just beyond opening time, and they were the only customers. A waft of street air came in, followed by a man with a dog. His head half revolved in jerks like someone late for an appointment. He grunted and went out.

'How did you come to let them call you Dangerous?' she asked.

'I don't know. It just grew.'

She laughed slightly. 'Some things are like that,' she said. 'They call me Jemma.' As they were drinking, she said casually: 'Funny how they called poor old Brock "Lofty", wasn't it? It was one of those reverse jokes. Like you being called Dangerous.'

'I suppose so,' said Davies thoughtfully. 'I mean, he was hardly an inch over five feet.'

'One inch,' she answered. 'He was five feet one inch.'

He regarded her oddly. He said: 'I get uncomfortable sometimes about things like this. A man is dead, there's an inquest, an open verdict because nobody knows how or why, really nobody cares and that's that. "Rest in Peace Wilfred Henry Brock".'

'An inconsequential death,' she said.

'Exactly.'

2

On the final day of his sick leave, an hour of limp sunshine in the early afternoon provoked Davies into taking his dog for their well-worn walk, along the canal bank and among the stone fingers of Kensal Green Cemetery. He brushed Kitty as much as the animal would allow and set off with him attached to a tough length of rope since he had again chewed through his lead. The dog played awkward games, either tugging him powerfully or lingering so long that he had to drag him. By the time they had reached the canal bank, however, Kitty had become bored by the sameness of the afternoon and trundled along sulkily. The water reflected the pale sun like a trodden flower. There was the usual debris: floating tins and soaked pieces of wood, an armchair like a half-sunken ship, and the evidence of the previous night's sins committed on the tow-path.

It was not cold, but Davies pulled his collar high about his neck as if it might afford some protection from the urban squalor. Even on a good day in that atmosphere buildings that were not very distant became grey silhouettes. Moodily he mounted the steps towards the road bridge. Halfway he looked up and saw Jemma standing at the top.

'Looking for Lofty's pram?' she called down.

He glanced up guiltily. 'No, no, nothing like that,' he said. 'Just taking this beast for some exercise.'

'I saw you walking. Staring into the water.'

'I was thinking I ought to have bought shares in the London Rubber Company, that's all,' he said, reaching the pavement level. 'They're very popular again now.'

She had not moved, and now they were standing quite close to each other at the top of the bridge. She was wearing the fine red coat she had worn at the inquest, but because of the mild day it was open like a door all down her front. For the first time he saw her interior. Even now he tried not to look, although the edges of the coat were kept apart by the accommodation of her bosom. 'We were just going into the cemetery,' mentioned Davies. She began to walk with him. He glanced around, hoping someone he knew might see them together.

'Why don't you walk your dog in the park?' she asked.

'It's too far. Tiredness sets in and then he collapses, and then it's one hell of a job to get home. Anyway, we're not welcome. Last spring he destroyed two-thirds of the daffodils in north-west London.'

'How come the dog is a *he* and gets called Kitty?'

'A drunken Taff,' shrugged Davies. He thought he saw someone staring at them from a bus and he waved. 'A Welsh git. At The Babe In Arms. The Taff said it was a girl dog and it was a few days before I noticed and the name had stuck by then. He's so contrary, he doesn't care anyway. I think sometimes he thinks he's a cat.'

They had reached the cemetery gates. 'Here we

are then,' paused Davies, concluding it was the separation of their ways.

'So I see,' she said. 'I've never been in here. I'll walk with you.'

His eyes grew. 'Oh . . . oh, all right then. It's a good cemetery.'

'I know,' she said. She recited: 'Before we go to Paradise by way of Kensal Green!' They walked through the gates. Jemma's missing tooth showed at its best in the dimming afternoon light. She took hold of his arm. 'I read it all up,' she said. 'The history of this area, including the cemetery, when I knew I was coming here to work.' They walked along the gravel path between the tombs and vaults. 'The roofs make it look like a little town,' she said.

Davies blinked. 'I s'pose it does in a way,' he said. 'Never thought about it like that.'

'It's a good address,' she said solemnly. 'There's all sorts here. Writers, actors, statesmen. Also Blondin, the tightrope man.'

'And Gilbert Harding,' put in Davies. He glanced up. It had begun to rain.

'It would now, wouldn't it.' She looked about them, then said: 'Here,' and moved sideways towards an elaborate vault with a covered marble patio at its front. Uncertainly Davies followed. They crouched under the portico, the dog pushing at Davies's legs for more room.

'Gilbert who? Who did you say?'

'Gilbert Harding.'

'Who was he?'

'He was on television.'

Her face had become very dark, her eyes luminous.

'Before your time,' he said. 'He used to be on quizzes and such-like. And advertised indigestion tablets.'

'When?'

'Oh, I don't know . . . not very long ago . . . in the fifties.' He glanced at her.

'Speak for yourself,' she smiled. She touched the marble column of the tomb as though testing its soundness.

'I wonder who's in here?' Her smile became mischievous. 'Maybe some famous police officer.'

'I doubt it,' he said, examining the sheltering marble roof. 'Not a copper. Bit too ornate. If coppers get memorials they're generally on walls. Donated by a grateful public.'

The rain had thinned. 'We'd better go,' she said. The torn remnants of the day's sky showed between dripping boughs. A bird chirped coldly. They moved off along the wet gravel. Kitty edged across the lawn beside Jemma. She motioned for the rope and Davies, grimacing at the dog, passed it to her. At the gate the cemetery custodian was pacing, sounding his keys like a knell.

'G'night,' called Davies cheerfully. 'Thanks very much. Very nice.' When they were outside he said to her: 'Fancy a cup of tea? And a meat pie or something?'

'It's a little early for me, for a meat pie,' she said. 'But I wouldn't mind a cup of tea.'

They walked together along the pavement to a steamed window with a yellow sign which said 'Texas Café'. He paused, regarded it doubtfully and said: 'There's not much else around here.'

A battery of noises, voices, clanking cups and

plates and the pounding of a juke-box blew out when Davies opened the door. 'You're sure?' he said.

'I'm sure,' she said. She pushed him into the café.

They manoeuvred along the tight aisle between the laminated tables. There were about twenty desultory men in the place, their faces propped on elbows, blowing smoke, lifting heavy mugs of tea, a few biting into meat pies. Some played at a fruit machine, others at a pin table; two thin youths hung languorously over the juke-box.

'Youth,' sighed Davies. 'What d'you do about it? There's not many places they can go like this. Welcoming and warm, between the DHSS and the pub.'

A blotchy boy, so engulfed by a greasy woollen sweater that he looked trapped in a hole, passed them and said: ''Ello, miss.'

'One of my clients,' said Jemma.

'And mine,' grunted Davies. 'Grievous Bodily Harm.'

'Not him. It must have been an accident.'

'It often is. Accidental GBH.'

He rose heavily. 'Alfie's busy,' he said, looking towards the counter. 'I'll get them. Hang on to Kitty, will you.' He looked down threateningly at the dog. 'Behave, or no pie.'

Jemma watched him pull his overcoat collar up symbolically around his neck, and he pushed towards the counter. A man with smarmed hair and an earring regarded her speculatively.

'Can't they play that row a bit quieter,' Jemma remarked to him, nodding towards the juke-box.

'Stone bloody deaf, they are.' He opened a cave of

a mouth and bawled: 'Order! Order! – Leave it out, will you?'

'Finished anyway,' sniffed one of the youths who had been hanging over the machine. 'I notice no uvver fucker puts any money innit.'

'Less of the verbals,' threatened the smarmed man, 'in 'ere.'

Davies returned and set down the teacups and the plate supporting the meat pie, a single curl of steam ascending like a signal or a prayer. His troubled eyes were on the juke-box youth. He moved clumsily between the tables. 'Like the man said, watch the verbals,' he said.

'All right, all right,' sniffed the youth. 'We was just going, wasn't we?' He glanced at his companion who nodded minimally. They moved towards the door.

Davies turned back towards Jemma. A cold stream of air caught his neck. The door was swinging open. He put the cups down and went to the entrance. 'Hey,' he called up the street. 'Hey, Robert Redford. The door.'

He returned to the table. A figure returned past the misted window and the door was shut heavily from outside. Davies divided the meat pie. Steam gushed out. Jemma was regarding him with deep amusement over her thick cup. 'Sure you don't want one?' he said.

'You know, Dangerous,' she said quietly, 'I think I will. All the excitement has made me quite hungry.'

By the time they left, the five o'clock darkness had closed in; the little shop windows, the windows of the buses and homeward cars, all squares of illumination. In such an unpicturesque place it was often the best time of the day.

'Where,' inquired Davies after some hesitation, 'do you come from?'

He asked around the corner of his overcoat collar and she replied likewise. 'Forty-two, Westwood Road, NW6,' she recited deliberately. A vivid eye rose to observe his reaction.

'No . . . no, I mean . . .' They sidled through some Sikhs heading home to Willesden. 'No . . . where . . . originally . . . if you see what I mean?'

'I was born in Martinique,' she told him.

'Ah, Martinique . . .' he nodded, striding alongside.

'You know it?'

'Well, I know *of* it.'

'French West Indies.'

'Yes, well of course. Naturally.'

'How about you?'

'Me?' said Davies. 'Here. Well, Kensal Rise. Born, went to school, and nicked my first bike driver without lights all within a couple of yards. I've not been that much further since.'

'I went to school in Paris and London,' she said. 'My father was in the Consular Service. Then I went back to Martinique. That's where I was married.'

His face came from his collar. 'You're married then, are you?'

'I have a son,' she said. 'He is seven now. He is with my mother.'

'In Kilburn?'

'Martinique. I had to leave him. Some day I'll go back.'

'Oh, I'm sorry about that,' said Davies genuinely. 'I bet you miss him.'

'I do. He's called Anthony.' Her head dropped into her coat again. He lowered his also and they walked silently through the homing people and the traffic. Davies gave bogus orders to the dog.

'You married?' she asked eventually.

'In name only,' he admitted.

'Where is she?'

'In the same house as me. It's only digs, lodgings . . . in a boarding house. But we don't speak. Separate rooms and all that. I'm closer to the dog than I am to her – and you can see how close I am to the dog.'

'Why don't you move out? One of you?'

'God knows. It's getting around to it. And one not going to move to spite the other.' He regarded her woefully. 'I'm a nineteen fifties' man, I suppose,' he shrugged.

'Like Gilbert . . .'

'Harding.'

She halted. 'I can get my bus here,' she said. There were people hunched like stones at the stop.

Davies said, 'Right. Number fifty-two.' She stood, all at once a little awkward. He said: 'Thanks for coming, anyway. It made my day. Sorry it wasn't quite Maxim's.'

Jemma laughed freely. 'It certainly wasn't.' She leaned forward and touched his hand. 'I've been on some dates,' she said. 'But a walk through the cemetery followed by a meat pie . . .'

'I know,' he mumbled. 'It wasn't all that good, was it? That café's the sort of place you wipe your feet when you come out.' He looked up. 'Here's your bus,' he said with regret and relief. 'Fair amount of room.'

He remained standing on the pavement, feet splayed. She boarded the platform of the bus. She was the last one. The conductor called: ''Old tight!' and rang the bell. Abruptly she leaned out and kissed Davies on the cheek.

'It was lovely, Dangerous,' she said.

The bus jolted and groaned off. Speechless, he stood and slowly raised his hand after it. The dog looked up to see who he was waving at. The bus joined the traffic. Through the diminishing windows, he saw that she had gone on the top deck. He waved again and then, with a suddenly soaring heart, he started out with his dog towards home. 'God help me,' he said, so loudly that people turned. 'I'm in bloody love.'

3

'Nomenclature,' mused Mod. 'Names, terms, appellations. Fascinating, fascinating. Why are Clarks Nobby? How intriguing to know that Bert Pollard's agricultural ancestor cut poles and Nicky Fletcher's fashioned arrows.' He peered roundly over the verge of his beer. Davies said: 'I'm sure it's of great interest to you academics. It was poor old Lofty I was thinking about.'

It would be difficult to force Mod to desist now. 'You are probably not aware,' interpolated the rotund philosopher, 'that the word "tawdry" emanates from Audrey. Tawdry Audrey. Derived from St Audrey's Fair held annually on the Isle of Ely, I believe. The shoddy goods were called "tawdry".'

'That,' admitted Davies, 'is something which somehow seems to have slipped my attention.' He rose, the only method he knew of stemming Mod's flow. Mod's tankard swung out in his extended hand like a weight on the end of a crane jib. Davies went to the bar and returned with the replenishments. It was early evening at The Babe In Arms.

A concerned expression now moved across Mod's large face. 'As I have told you previously, Dangerous, I have a major disability. Everything I glean from my studies, no matter how intense, has gone in a couple of weeks. It seeps down inside me somewhere.' He ran an untidy finger down his front.

'Like sediment,' suggested Davies, putting down his glass. He habitually drank without a handle, Mod drank with one. He described it as a safety measure to prevent spillage. 'Sediment,' he nodded. 'If you like.' He rubbed his stomach. 'But it's all there inside me, somewhere. Piled up, fact upon fascinating fact.'

Davies surveyed the mufflered figure. 'I can imagine that,' he said.

Mod let his hollowed eyes travel around the bar. 'One day it might all explode,' he forecast theatrically. 'Right here in The Babe. Like a bursting atom, shattering the bar stock, making staff and customers duck for cover! An explosion of knowledge.'

They left and trudged through the damp dark of the autumn streets, the pavement padded with leaves. 'It's funny,' said Davies, pushing his toes through the vegetation. 'You hardly notice the trees in this place until they're under your feet.'

'Until they descend to our level,' nodded Mod massively. 'And then, of course, it's too late. So many things are, Dangerous.'

They walked along the large and shabby Victorian house-fronts. 'Bali Hi', Furtman Gardens, in the better part of the borough and with a monkey tree at the front, was a ten- sober minutes' journey.

'If you were going to commit suicide . . .' began Davies, 'what would you take with you?'

Mod sniffed the clammy air. 'It's always been my understanding that you can't take *anything* with you. No matter which way you go. We brought nothing into this world and it is certain we can carry nothing out.'

Davies said: 'Why should Lofty suddenly do himself in? He didn't have much of a life but he'd had the same life for years and he was apparently content. But, even if he did drown himself, would he have taken his pram?'

Mod paused and with his foot made a runic pattern in the leaves. 'It's a nice thought. Operatic. Charging into the Grand Union pushing a pram in front of you. But I don't think Lofty was operatic. If he had been, he'd have altered his act once in a while.' He scraped the side of his shabby shoe across the figure he had fashioned in the leaves. They walked on. Lights yellowed the windows of the bulky houses, lending even to the most pessimistic of them a gloss of welcome.

'I wonder what was in that pram, anyway?' said Davies.

'Perhaps a baby,' suggested Mod. 'Perhaps Lofty was a secret male nanny. Over the years he may have cared for many concealed infants. As far as I remember, whatever was in there was hidden below an old blanket.'

'Now we'll never know,' said Davies.

'You seem to have got one of your occasional bees in your bonnet about this one,' said Mod. They opened the creaking gate of 'Bali Hi' and went up to the stained-glass front door. The front hall light illuminated a pattern of glass flowers in the door with the virginal face of a young girl peering innocently through them. Davies bent gently and gave the glass face a kiss. 'Good evening, darling,' he whispered. 'I'm home.'

Mod had produced a key and opened the door.

'You've had too much time to think lately,' he said. 'After your sick leave, when you're back investigating big-time crime, stolen bicycles, vandalized bus shelters, knocking-on-doors-and-running-away, you'll soon forget Lofty.'

Davies hung his coat on the grim hall-stand. There was an unfamiliar garment, a good grey coat. Davies touched the lapel. 'We've got a new lodger,' he said.

'I'm not sure this is the time to bring it up,' mentioned Davies when they had sat down to the suet pudding, potatoes and two vegetables. 'But my bed was wet this morning.'

Eyes lifted from plates. The suet was heavy and hot, and Mrs Fulljames, who had just put some in her mouth, juggled with it painfully. She fanned her hand in front of it. 'I beg your pardon?' she said as haughtily as she could at that moment.

'My bed,' repeated Davies. 'Wet. The leak in the ceiling has reappeared.'

The landlady sniffed. Mod read the folded *Guardian* at the side of his plate, his fork, like a tuning fork, poised near his ear. 'You're supposed to *eat* suet pudding, not listen to it, Mr Lewis,' Mrs Fulljames remarked tartly. Mod swung the food to his mouth and continued reading the paper. 'So sorry,' he mumbled. 'I was absorbed in the Higher Management Vacancies.' Doris, Davies's estranged wife, regarded her estranged husband with everyday displeasure. Mr Smeeton, the Complete Home Entertainer, was memorizing jokes from a book in preparation for a professional engagement. He privately placed a

Groucho Marx combination – nose, eyebrows and spectacles – on his face and then took them off, continued eating and reciting under his breath. Minnie Banks, a distraught schoolteacher, stared through the steam at some approaching fate. Only the newcomer, a pale pipe-like young man, looked uncertainly around the table.

'Mr Tennant,' said Mrs Fulljames. 'Perhaps he can help. I can't keep the rent at the present level *and* have the roof repaired every time it leaks. Mr Tennant, as it happens, works in water.'

'I'm an aquatic engineer,' said the young man. Minnie Banks gave him a skinny smile.

'Have you got a diver's suit?' inquired Davies.

The new lodger looked unsurprised. 'Not of my own but I use one at the subaqua club,' he answered. 'At work I'm usually concerned with tanks and suchlike. I'm working at the power station for a couple of weeks.'

Davies balanced a dripping sprout on his fork like a projectile. 'If you hear a lot of noise in the next street, it's the Irish beating somebody up. Usually me,' he said.

'I've never known anybody spend so much time in hospital,' tutted Doris. Her nose curled. 'A burden on the National Health.'

Davies studied the loaded sprout but dropped it back to the plate. 'Mrs Davies,' he said coldly, 'I don't end up in the casualty department out of a sense of fun. I get there through my attempts, sometimes misguided, I agree, to keep law and order. So that the streets are safe.'

'Well, they're not,' complained Doris. 'I had a man followed me today.'

'I shouldn't complain about that,' he muttered.

'I wish someone would follow me,' sighed Minnie Banks. She blushed. Mod's brooding eyes moved like twin planets to her stick-like face. He said nothing.

Mrs Fulljames got up to clear the plates. 'Lovely, Mrs Fulljames,' enthused Davies. 'That suet was a real treat.'

She eyed him maliciously but went in silence to the kitchen. Davies leaned towards the new lodger.

'I'd like to get something out of the canal,' he confided.

The lamps along the bank of the Grand Union Canal were among the oldest and most sombre in London, and they cast a Victorian gleam on the oily water. They were spaced out at fifty yards so that the three slowly walking men progressed from one aura of dubious light into another.

'Body found at eleven-forty,' said Davies. 'Night-time, that is. October 7th. Been in the water twenty-four hours or more. Corpses tend to go unnoticed down here.'

They paused in the grisly glow of one of the lamps. Mod tugged his muffler closer. 'The body,' said Davies, pointing, 'was found about here. By some kids.'

'At eleven-forty?' murmured Tennant.

'They're allowed to stay up late around here,' said Davies defensively. He disliked amateur detectives. 'But where he was found is not necessarily the same place as where he went in.'

'Fell in or jumped in,' put in Tennant.

'Or was pushed,' Davies said defiantly. 'The towpath varies in width.' He pointed. 'It's narrow and close to the edge along here, but back there it's yards distant.' They retraced their steps. The ragged asphalt path backed away from the water almost against the dark wall of one of the neighbouring factories. Davies paced the distance to the edge of the canal. 'Six yards – eighteen feet,' he said. 'If Lofty had been pushing his pram along this piece then he could hardly have gone in by accident. Even if he'd been drunk, which is unlikely because he didn't drink, he would have had plenty of time to pull up.'

He led them back along the bank. 'Not so, further on,' he said. 'The path is narrow and runs right against the edge of the canal. He could easily have stumbled and pushed the pram over the edge.'

They climbed the wet stone steps to the street and walked silently to The Babe In Arms. Three pale youths from Cricklewood, wearing tartan shirts and waistcoats, were nasally singing a country-and-western song: a lament about a wife who had gone off for a good time leaving her husband with four hungry children and a crop in the field. 'It's a fine time to leave me, Lucille,' they howled.

'Who could blame her?' said Mod pensively.

Jemma came in smiling her spectacularly split smile. Davies introduced Mod and Tennant. She winced at the singers and sat down. 'In surrealist painting, of course,' Mod said, looking at her absent tooth, 'it's so often what is *not* there that makes the work so riveting.'

Jemma bent forward confidingly. Her hand, like

velvet, dropped across Davies's wrist. She whispered: 'I've found something out. Lofty had a secret.'

It was only ten-thirty when they arrived at the North-West London Refuge for Men but the warden was disgruntled.

'These chaps need their sleep like everybody else,' Charlie Copley grumbled, leading them through the snoring dormitory. 'It's heads down at ten, you know.' He had switched on a bleak light and as they trooped through, spectral foreheads rose over bedclothes and there were protests, inquiries and onsets of coughing. Someone, asleep, shouted plaintively that he wanted to go home.

Mod's eyes flickered with melancholy in the half-dark. Davies whispered: 'Better pick your bed-space now.'

'I'd go to hell first,' muttered Mod. 'Or work.'

Charlie led them to a small brick room. 'Lofty's,' whispered Jemma. 'He had a room of his own because he was a regular.'

The abrupt opening of the door disturbed the man in the single iron bed. Uncomprehendingly he stared at them. 'I left the stuff in here,' said Charlie. Brusquely he turned to the occupant: 'No need to wake up, Barker.' Barker dropped beneath the blanket like a soldier ducking into a trench. Charlie bent down and began to move a small grating in the wall at floor-level.

'Lofty's own personal safe deposit,' said Jemma.

The grating came away with a sound loud enough to cause half the head of the room's occupant to emerge again. 'It's the police, Barker,' said Charlie. The ashen forehead and the disturbed eyes slid away. The warden put his hand into the aperture and brought out a dusty shoe box. 'Barker found it when he was nosing around,' he said.

'I found it,' confirmed a padded voice beneath the blanket.

'You'll have to sign for it,' said Charlie. 'I can't take the responsibility.'

'We'll sign,' Jemma told him. 'Detective Constable Davies will.'

Charlie took the box and they went out of the room. A ghostly 'good-night' followed them.

They followed the warden through the shadows of the dormitory once more. Faces, white blotches, appeared, for the men were awake and as excited as children now. 'It's Dangerous,' whispered a croaky voice, 'and that darkie lady.'

'Settle down,' ordered Charlie sternly. 'I won't be responsible for any refusals tomorrow.'

The threat was a dire one because the inmates dropped at once to silence. The party went down some stone steps and waited on a bleak landing while Charlie turned, with three distinct keys, the locks of a heavy door. It opened and the switching of a single light revealed a room used as an office, piled untidily with papers and with unkempt files leaning in a corner. There Charlie tore a page from an account book and wrote crudely on it: 'Box and contents, property of Brock, deceased.' Davies signed it.

'What's refusals?' he asked as he did so.

Charlie regarded him narrowly. 'Refusals?' he inquired.

'Like you just said in there,' Davies explained. 'About not being responsible for any refusals tomorrow.'

'Oh, *those* refusals. Well, if they don't behave, toe the line, we can refuse them a bed. You have to have rules when you're dealing with DMs.'

'Distressed Men,' put in Jemma. Decisively she took Brock's box and put it under her arm. Charlie looked at her with doubt, as if he would have been happier if the person who had signed for the box had taken charge of it, but he said nothing. They went out into the dripping night and the warden closed the door massively behind them. Mod sniffed the air. 'It smells positively luxurious out here,' he observed.

'Let it be a warning,' said Davies as they shuffled along the pavement with Jemma between them. They were crouched against the weather but she strode on purposefully upright and had to pause to allow them to catch up. 'You could end up as a DM,' Davies added to Mod.

'Or worse,' put in Jemma. 'You might be a VDM, a Very Distressed Man, or even a UDM, an Utterly Distressed Man. When you have to be looked after officially, you are reduced to initials.'

'Where are we going to look at Brock's box?' Davies asked suddenly. The Babe In Arms was now shut and he did not want to go to the police station because it would have aroused interest, even suspicion. There were few places that Jemma could go unnoticed.

'It's your place or mine,' the black girl said.

'It's not ours,' Davies told her. The trio had paused

on the rainy pavement. 'Women aren't allowed. Mrs Fulljames wouldn't have it.'

The girl laughed in disbelief. 'What a place to live! You'll be telling me next that she wouldn't have blacks.'

Morosely Davies glanced at Mod. 'I wouldn't be at all surprised,' he said.

'It will have to be my house, then,' Jemma said. 'It's not all that far. When Charlie told me about the box I only had a quick look because he was looking over my shoulder and I prefer not to get too near to him. His colour prejudice dissolves at close proximity.'

She wheeled around a lamplit corner and they followed. 'It's just here,' she said, stopping outside a frowning house. Her voice lowered. 'Don't wake the babies.'

Davies was aware of his eyebrows going up. He sensed Mod's glance. She unlocked the door and they crept in. The house had been divided into flats. There was another door which Jemma unlocked to let them into a tight but bright hall and then into a sitting room where a skinny black boy was moodily watching a football match on television. Jemma said his name was Danny. 'Are we winning?' asked Davies, glancing at the screen.

'We just did. Three nil,' said the boy. He stood thinly and turned the set off.

'Any noise?' asked Jemma.

'Not that I heard,' shrugged Danny. 'I was cheering.'

She gave the youth some reward and he sloped away. Jemma opened a darkened room and said: 'Come and see my babies.'

With no enthusiasm Davies and Mod moved towards the door. 'You didn't mention . . . you had babies,' stumbled Davies.

'Take a look,' she invited seriously. She opened the door wider so that it admitted a slice of light and they looked down into a cot cosseting two infants, one black and one white. Both slept deeply.

'I sometimes – unofficially – bring my work home,' Jemma said. 'Their mothers have flown the coop.'

'Too bad,' muttered Davies inadequately as she ushered them from the room. 'Too bad,' echoed Mod.

Without asking them she poured three glasses of neat Scotch and they sat around the table looking at the grimy shoe box. It was parcelled with string which Jemma, taking responsibility, began to unknot. Her fingers were long and loose, with unpainted nails. She opened the box.

'All sorts of stuff in here,' she said.

Davies looked at the creased papers and envelopes in the box. On top was a linen bag which he turned sideways. Out slid a dull medal with a faded maroon and purple ribbon. He held it in his palm and, turning the medallion, read: '"For distinguished conduct in the field."' He turned it again. 'It's got his name on it. "Wilfred Henry Brock, May 29th, 1940."'

'Lofty, a hero!' said Jemma. One of the babies in the bedroom began to cry. Davies handed the medal to Mod. The second baby joined in. Jemma rose and went into the bedroom. They could hear her hushing. Soon the crying ceased.

Davies returned his attention to the box, picking up each item with a care that suggested there might be lingering fingerprints. Jemma returned and watched him intently. 'It's like opening somebody's forgotten present,' she said.

'Forgotten past,' he replied absently. She watched him extract the papers, dirty and creased, spreading them out and studying each one for a few moments before passing to the next. 'All stuff from the War,' he muttered. 'Lofty was in a prison camp, Stalag 62 in Germany. Letters, notes. Very odd. Scribbled bits about his fellow prisoners. Traitors, informers, even gangs. And I thought they were always digging tunnels or playing chess.'

He continued through the box. 'He kept everything,' he said. 'Here's a laundry list. And here . . .' he paused. 'Here is another list. And Lofty Brock's name is on it. Wilfred Brock. It's marked with a cross. So are some of the others. And there's a skull at the top. It looks like a death list.'

4

On Sundays there were invariably some desperate fishermen mustered on the canal bank, dolefully eyeing the glutinous water where nothing but the most primitive life had wriggled for many a year. These men looked up, as monks might when disturbed at their devotions, and studied the arrival of Davies and the frogmen with unchanging expressions. Theirs was not a pastime for displaying emotions.

'Morning lads,' called Davies with heavy cheeriness. 'Big ones biting today?'

Tennant, who appeared even thinner in his rubber suit, sniffed above mildewed water. 'The only thing you'll catch in there,' he forecast gloomily, 'is cholera.' He glanced round carefully as if anxious to ensure that the two other divers had not gone hurriedly home. 'I didn't tell them it was quite like this,' he confided in Davies.

'They'll probably like it once they get in,' suggested Davies unconvincingly. He looked back towards the steps climbing to the road. Jemma was descending towards them with his dog lolloping and falling before her.

'I brought him down,' she said breathlessly. She was wearing a brilliant green dress with a suede coat and a bright headscarf which scarcely contained her hair. 'He was making a fuss in your car. Trying to get out to attack some small children.'

'He's very fond of small children,' said Davies. 'Can't get enough of them.' He regarded the dog who stared back insolently between his dreadlocks.

The two other divers were unhappily surveying the scene. 'This is *it* then?' asked one, a neat and aggressive youth. Savagely he butted his head at the water. 'This?'

'Yes, it is. More or less,' admitted Davies. He glanced for help towards Tennant. The second diver who had a pinched nose and watering eyes, as if he had recently trapped his face, wandered along the tow-path staring down like someone trying to peer through glass darkly. ''Ow deep is this lot then?' he asked.

'Usual Grand Union depth,' answered Tennant briskly. 'Canals don't generally go up and down.'

'I'll put it up to thirty quid,' whispered Davies urgently. 'The contribution to the subaqua club. It's not from official police funds, you know.'

Tennant said: 'Done.' He walked to the others. They still grumbled but set about readying their equipment. Davies stood back beside Jemma. Kitty rested his head against the black girl's suede thigh. Davies eyed the dog. Jemma said: 'He's smitten.'

'Not with me,' said Davies. 'You ought to come around and bath the brute, or try to comb his coat. He's not an easy dog.'

There was a call from the bridge. Mod was coming down the steps. 'Your philosopher friend,' observed Jemma. 'Why is he called Mod?'

'After Tchaikovsky's brother,' said Davies.

'Oh.'

Mod descended from the road at his customary waddle, the Sunday newspapers clutched in front of him like a breastplate. 'Terrible situation in Africa,' he said breathlessly as if it had just occurred. 'What the answer is I really don't know.'

'What chance have the rest of us got?' shrugged Davies.

Mod surveyed the divers. 'Have they come up with anything?' he asked.

'They haven't been in yet,' grunted Davies. 'We were waiting for you.'

Jemma said: 'They want somebody to go first.'

Mod regarded her patiently. 'The world is dark enough,' he replied heavily, 'without looking for darkness.' Tennant called that they were ready. The short, aggressive one, who was called Archie, was going down first at the point where the body was found.

'He could easily have just gone in and then floated around in that vicinity,' said Tennant professionally. 'They do sometimes. And the pram, of course.'

'Right then,' said Archie, preparing to adjust his mask. 'We're looking for an old pram, right? I bet there are a few in the bottom of this lot.' He pulled his mask down, stood on the bank, legs bent and, like a large tadpole, leaped feet first into the canal.

Concentric circles of sludgy water spread. The clutch of anglers on the other bank angrily withdrew their lines. 'That's right!' bawled one. 'Go on, disturb the bloody water! Very bloody nice, I must say.'

'In the season,' added his nearest companion, staring at the mud.

'Police operations,' Davies called out.

'You won't find Lord Lucan in there, mate!' one bellowed back.

Davies glared across the water. 'I thought fishing made you a philosopher,' he said.

Mod said soberly: 'The essence of philosophy, surely, is the facility to order your thoughts, to categorize them, to collate them if you like, and to publish them, put them into action, or, at the very least, speak them. These persons squat for hours and reach no conclusions whatever. Anyway, it's wet.'

Jemma said: 'He's coming up.' The displacement of the surface heralded Archie's return. He broke the water and then descended once more making a hand signal to Tennant as he did so. Tennant said something to the other diver, Charlie, who once more began to grumble. Tennant gave him a short, hard push towards the canal and his involuntary momentum became another graceless leap. He glugged down into the murk. Both divers reappeared several times and eventually came out of the water and were hauled to the bank by Tennant and Davies with Mod hovering in support.

''Orrible,' announced Archie. 'Never seen so much shit in my life. No prams though.'

The second diver said firmly: 'I want to go home.'

Tennant pursed his lips and tutted. 'Quit,' he threatened, 'and you won't come on the Bognor trip.'

Charlie appeared crushed. 'Oh, all right then,' he said. He tapped Tennant's dry rubber suit. 'But you're coming down too?'

'I haven't got into this to work up a sweat,' said Tennant haughtily. 'I'm next in.' He told Davies he was going to try a hundred yards further along the bank where the tow-path was wider. They watched while he prepared to leap into the canal. He returned their looks as though embarrassed. Then he pulled his mask down in a finalizing way and performed the ungainly, feet-first jump into the water.

'That scores nil for elegance,' observed Jemma.

'It's the flippers that spoil it from an aesthetic point of view,' agreed Mod. Davies half turned. The fishermen, muttering like gnomes, were trudging away with their gear and baskets. He saw that beyond them spectators had gathered on the bridge that took the road across the canal.

Tennant surfaced, waved what appeared to be an excited hand, and submerged again. They gathered at the edge of the grim water. Globular disturbances were followed by a waving arm. 'What's he got, I wonder?' said Jemma.

'Cramp,' guessed Archie, standing with them.

They hauled Tennant out, backing away from the ordure that ran from his wet-suit. 'Stinking,' he said, when the mask was off. 'Foul. But it's down there. A pram. It hasn't been under there long. It's on its nose. We could hook it up.'

Archie and Charlie went to get some rope and tackle from their truck which was parked on the road. When they returned, a small shifty man came with them. 'Hello, Shiny,' said Davies.

'Hello, Dangerous. What you up to then?'

'Sponsored salvage dive, Shiny.'

The newcomer nodded, turned and walked back towards the crowd on the bridge. 'They was all wondering,' he mentioned.

Tennant was preparing to go into the canal again,

taking the ropes and a metal hook. 'Shiny Bright,' said Davies to Jemma with a nod at the small man's departing back. 'Did a housebreaking once and wore a pair of mittens so he wouldn't leave fingerprints.'

Tennant went into the water, this time with a mildly triumphant splash. He surfaced once, went down and surfaced again. He threw the rope ashore to Archie. He held up two hands in a signal and then submerged once more. Archie began to count, wagging one finger. When he reached fifty, he nodded to wedge-faced Charlie and they began to heave studiously on the rope. It tightened. Davies moved forward to help and after a hesitation, so did Mod. Davies motioned him aside. 'You stand there and think,' he said. The other three men began to pull. Kitty, sensing the excitement, barked. They heaved until the smooth, once-white handle of the perambulator surfaced.

'Hold it, hold it,' muttered Davies anxiously.

'Keep hauling,' contradicted Archie. They hauled. Tennant's seal-like head appeared almost alongside the pram and he began to swim in small rings, guiding it with his flippers. Gradually, it cleared the surface, the brown-grey water cascading from within.

'Now!' snorted Archie and with a final haul, they brought it clear of the water, the wheels cutting into the mud of the bank and on to the flat surface. The stench was appalling.

'Is that it, then?' said Archie.

Davies said defensively: 'That's it.'

Archie and Charlie helped Tennant from the water. 'You won't find anything else,' he forecast. 'There's too much gunge on the bottom.'

Jemma moved forward and put both hands into the well of the pram, located and turned the four rusted clips. 'There's always a little trapdoor in the bottom,' she said. 'You can put a potty in it.'

Davies put his hands into the cavity and brought out a large oblong biscuit tin, its lid strapped to its body by over-layers of sticky tape. '"Jacob's Cream Crackers,"' he read aloud.

At Jemma's place the black and white babies had gone but had been replaced by a sprawling woman who occupied an armchair, knitting frantically at a nebulous garment that spread itself about her like a ceremonial robe. 'Edeee!' she bellowed. 'I'm Edeee!'

'That's Edie,' said Jemma. She placed Lofty's sealed biscuit tin on the table.

Tentatively, Davies and Mod greeted Edie. 'What did she say her name was?' asked Davies. Jemma glared at him. Davies put his hand to his ear.

'Edeee!' bawled the woman, 'it's Edeee!'

'Edie is staying for a while until they find a place for her,' said Jemma.

'Somewhere isolated,' suggested Mod.

Jemma regarded him sternly. 'There's no need to have your fun at her expense,' she reproved. 'She's got nowhere to go.'

Mod looked shamefaced. Davies studied the spreadeagled stranger. Solicitously he leaned over the knitting. 'What is it?' he asked.

'Edeee!' hooted the woman. 'It's Edeee!'

'You're upsetting her,' warned Jemma seriously. 'It's *knitting*. It's therapy. She's not knitting anything in particular. Don't you think we had better look in Lofty's box?'

Davies agreed. Mod was smiling inanely at Edie, nodding encouragement for the needles clicking like a two-stroke engine. They turned their attention to the biscuit box. It was scratched and scuffed. '"King Edward the Eighth",' Davies read on the design. '"Coronation".' There was a figure in robes below the scratches, like someone standing behind a gauze curtain. Jemma produced a pair of scissors and deftly cut the blackened tape which sealed the tin. She nodded, passing the authority on to Davies. He pulled at one of the severed ends. Edie ceased knitting and creaked forward. 'Is it biscuits?' she shouted.

Jemma turned to calm her. Davies had pulled the binding away from the box. He eased the rusted lid free. Within was a further box, well-made wood, with good brass hinges and a brass lock, which was open. Davies turned back the lid. The water had scarcely penetrated the sealed tin and the wood was only damp. Inside, packed closely with yellow news-paper, was a collection of elderly utensils, an ancient safety razor and a packet of blades, a stained bottle of Doctor Collis Browne's Mixture, a thick penknife, a mirror dimly blinking at the unaccustomed light, a cream jug in the shape of a cow with the words: 'A present from Clacton-on-Sea' on its flank, a hair-brush, a tin picture frame surrounding the faded face of an unhappy woman, and a single pearl in a worn ring box. Davies picked it out. 'I wonder if it's real?' he said. Jemma held it in her fingers. 'It's warm,' she said. 'It's real.'

She handed it back to him and he opened his hand flat and let it lie there. 'Look at that,' he said quietly. 'Now what was Lofty Brock doing with a pearl?' They regarded it in silence, the stone rocking slightly in the palm of Davies's hand, until Mod said: 'Edward the Eighth didn't have a coronation. They made all these biscuit tins for nothing.'

One by one Davies took the items from the wooden box. The mottled face of the woman blinked from her tin porthole. She was regarding the camera with suspicion, as if she feared something might jump from it. Davies turned it over and opened the stiff clips at the back. The little metal door opened. 'Nothing,' he said, turning the photograph over. 'No name. Nothing.'

He took the creased newspaper packing and spread it out. 'August 13, 1936,' he said. 'The *Daily Express*.'

He surveyed the unpromising hoard. 'Well, we've got a photograph, a box, a biscuit tin, a cow, a penknife, some medicine, a newspaper, a razor and a hairbrush . . . and a pearl.' He began replacing the articles in the box, packing them in the newspaper. As he did so he paused and read a headline from the sere pages. '"Masterly Century by Hammond",' he read aloud. 'Good old Wally,' he said.

The Vauxhall Vanguard in which his dog lived was in its turn lodged in a railway-arch garage only a minute's walk from 'Bali Hi', Furtman Gardens. On Thursday, his day off, Davies fastened a new rope to Kitty's collar and took him along the rain-smeared streets, down the steps from the road bridge and along the canal tow-path. It was a poor day, the sky the same sludgy hue as the water, the only specks of brightness coming from the early-afternoon lights in the small factories and warehouses on the banks.

There were a dozen of these close premises, three with their outer walls facing the canal. Shurrock Industrial Clocks, Blissen Ltd Pharmaceuticals, and Security Plus Safes were each housed in an identical building: two-storey brick under a flat roof, with offices on the upper floor and working or storage space on the floor below. Each had a double loading door leading out on to a concrete road that ran at right angles to the canal tow-path. At the end of the road, at the tow-path end, there was a metal-grid fence with a door at its centre. Clocks and Pharmaceuticals faced each other across their joint access with the Safes on the left of the Clocks, nearer the town and the road bridge. The businesses closed simultaneously at five each evening, but the Safes' employees were first in the bus queue.

George Williams, the manager of Security Plus Safes, was a stiff-faced, busy man, chairman of the Rotary, the town sports committee and the ex-servicemen's club. He shook hands with Davies and his eyes flicked to his watch. 'I won't keep you,' Davies reassured him. 'I've left my dog on a double yellow line.'

Williams laughed emptily like someone who has heard every joke ever told. Despite the season he was in his shirt-sleeves. 'What's it all about?' he asked, sitting on the last two inches of his desk. He had a pointed moustache like miniature buffalo horns. He motioned Davies to one of the two chairs in the small office. The walls were covered with samples of safe doors, like a burglar's dream. 'Is it about the licence?' he asked, this time looking frankly at his watch.

'What licence is that?' asked Davies.

'For the club. The Ex-Service Club. We've had trouble with the magistrates.'

'Different department,' corrected Davies firmly. 'At the moment, anyway. No, I was wondering – do you have any night security here?'

'Not much. I mean there's not much to steal except the safes. Most of them weigh a ton.'

'You did have a break-in though, if I remember. A couple of years ago.'

Williams thinned his lips, the buffalo moustache see-sawed. 'Don't remind me,' he sighed. 'It got in the newspapers.'

Davies nodded. 'Petty cash, wasn't it?'

'Right. Well-known safe company and some idiot leaves the petty cash lying on the desk and it's nicked. Funny story for the papers.'

Consulting his notebook Davies said: 'Five hundred and three quid.'

'Was it? I can't remember the exact amount. We must have needed it for some reason.'

'More than just stamps,' added Davies.

'We must have needed it,' Williams said again. 'But we don't have any big deal security. It's damned expensive. All the businesses here share one security company and they're no great shakes.' He regarded Davies challengingly. 'Anyway, that's why we've got a police force.'

'Ah, the good old days,' mused Davies. 'The bobby on the beat.' He shifted in the chair. 'No, the only reason I asked is to find out whether anyone here might have seen or heard anything, any commotion, along the tow-path on the night of October 6th.' Williams glanced at his desk calendar. Davies continued: 'An old chap fell . . . went into the canal. Got drowned.'

Williams nodded. 'I read about it. He used to trundle along with that old pram. Plastered, I suppose.'

'Never touched it,' said Davies. He stood up. 'It was about eleven at night. There wouldn't have been anyone here then, on the premises?'

'No way. This is not the sort of business where there's a call for much overtime. It's just steady. So there'd be no one here. Not at that time of night.'

'Thanks,' said Davies. 'I just thought I'd ask.'

Mr Harrison, of Blissen Ltd Pharmaceuticals, was on holiday in Las Palmas, his lacquered secretary informed Davies proudly. It was his fourth visit. They had received a card only that morning. Would Mrs Harrer do? Davies said he thought she might. He waited in the narrow reception area, boarded with pine like a sauna, with some arty lighting and a cornered palm. The receptionist, a wan, desultory girl, wore green fingernails. 'It's all right for him,' she said. 'Las Palmas. I wish I was in Las Palmas.'

'So do I,' agreed Davies, studying her slothful posture. 'We could have a good time.'

'Cheeky bugger,' she said in almost a whisper. She returned to watching her nails. The secretary clipped back, her thighs like rods under her pencil skirt. 'Mrs

54

Harrer will see you,' she said, as though he had won a prize. 'This way.'

They tuned a couple of plywood bends up a flight of stairs and Davies was confronted with an office door which framed, but only just, the form of a huge woman. 'Ah, so,' she said thickly. The Germanic was compounded by a nasal American tone. 'You are the police. Tell me what it is.'

Apparently as an afterthought, she held out her hand. Davies was shocked at her height: one of the biggest women he had ever seen. Her great fingers enclosed his.

'We have security?' she said when he told her why he had come. 'But of course. This place is for the storage of pharmaceuticals, and pharmaceuticals are expensive. You, perhaps, are on National Health Service.'

Davies bashfully admitted he was. 'What sort of security do you have?' he asked. 'A night-watchman?'

'They sleep,' she shrugged. 'We have a security company. They visit every hour in the night.'

Diffidently, Davies took out his notebook. 'Could you tell me who they are, please?' he said. 'I am just inquiring so that we can clear up the death of this old man.'

'So he fell in the water? Is that not cleared up? Already there was a police officer here, the day after. A man with a bloody nose.'

'Ah, yes. PC Westerman,' nodded Davies.

'There is a treatment,' she confided professionally. 'He can go on the National Health.'

'I'll tell him,' promised Davies. 'Now . . . could I have the name of the security people.'

'Ah so! Ja.' She went to a filing cabinet, rising as Davies imagined a volcano might rise from the sea. The great globe of skirted backside was spread before him. She returned with a surprisingly soft smile. 'There. I have,' she said. She handed the headed notepaper to him. He copied it laboriously into his notebook, muttering the words: 'Keystone Security, Edgware Mews, London W1.' When he looked up, her face had set hard with impatience. 'Sorry,' he said. 'I must be going.'

'Yes, I suppose you must. We are busy, you are busy.'

Massively, she moved towards him and he backed away before the oncoming chest, then went out of the office, down the stairs and into the narrow corridor. Mrs Harrer only just fitted. 'Do you make, manufacture, stuff here?' asked Davies, as they reached the reception area. The receptionist had slotted her magazine between her knees.

'Not at all,' said the big woman. 'We are part of a larger European operation, you understand. This place is for distribution only.'

He saw she was frowning through the glass of the door at Kitty who was tethered outside. 'What is that?' she demanded. 'That dog?'

'Oh,' apologized Davies. 'It's mine.'

'What a gross thing. It is so big,' she said.

'Gross,' agreed Davies.

Davies was certain he had seen Mr Adrian Shurrock, of Shurrock Industrial Clocks, in different surroundings.

The wispy young man agreed. 'I do amateur dramatics,' he said.

Davies sat in the office. On the desk stood half a dozen time-pieces. 'What's this one for?' he asked, picking up a dial in a brass housing.

The man looked confused. 'It's a bit of a secret,' he said. 'But as you're the police . . .'

'Don't tell me,' said Davies, holding up his hand. 'I couldn't bear the responsibility.' He opened his notebook and unnecessarily referred to it. 'There was a man drowned in the canal on the night of October 6th, and we're just trying to work out how he came to get in there,' he said. 'Was there anybody on these premises that night?'

'I thought that was all over,' said Shurrock. 'There was an inquest.'

Davies said uncomfortably: 'These things sometimes drag on, you know.'

'Oh, I imagine. And you want to know if there was anybody here who might have seen something. Well, we do have security.'

'I suppose,' suggested Davies, picking up the brass-bound dial again, 'that clocks like these could be used for timing devices. For bombs, maybe.'

Shurrock appeared shocked and shook his head. 'We keep all our sensitive time-pieces at our other premises in Maidenhead. These would be a bit big and clumsy for that sort of thing. But we do employ a security company – Keystone . . .'

Davies recited: '. . . Keystone Security, Edgware Mews, London, W1.'

'That's them. We share the service with the other businesses on this industrial estate. They patrol all the time. Or they're supposed to.'

Davies closed his notebook. Shurrock looked

relieved that he was going. He accompanied him to the main door. 'Is that your dog?' the young man asked.

'Yes. His name's Kitty.'

'He's ever so big, isn't he,' said the young man.

They shook hands. After Mrs Harrer's big paw, the young man's grip was damp and limp. 'You've never had a break-in here, have you?' Davies asked, as he was about to untether Kitty.

'Oh no. Never,' said Shurrock. 'Thank goodness.'

That night when he returned to the railway-arch garage to feed the dog and put it to bed, there was a scrawled note fixed under the windscreen wiper of the Vanguard. It read: 'Be at 143a, Maida Crescent, tonight for a surprise. Come alone.' It was signed: 'A well-wisher.'

He did not like scrawled notes fixed to windscreens any more than he liked keeping solitary appointments with persons unknown. In the past he had been set upon and half murdered. As a precaution he left the address with Mod and went alone on the bus.

It was in Maida Vale, a half-oval of Victorian villas ripe for developers. Some already had a grid of scaffolding and notice-boards. One of those being gutted was number 143, a threatening place, caged in iron, dark and windowless. He was not going in there.

As he searched for an annexe or separate entrance marked 143a, he was startled by organ music and a burst of choral singing. Next along the crescent was the lit and open door of a church hall. The voices rose strongly. He moved cautiously towards them.

You never knew with religion. He did not want to end up being baptized. There was an iron gate, on it the number 143a. He stepped towards the reassuring doorway.

There was a lobby and beyond this a further pair of doors, these closed. The singing ceased and was replaced by brisk applause. The doors half opened and the lively face of a silver-haired woman emerged. 'Late!' she admonished. 'You're quite late.'

'Oh, sorry,' mumbled Davies. 'I didn't know.'

She pushed the door and let herself out. 'It's fifty pence,' she announced, producing a coil of tickets. He fumbled for the money and took the ticket. 'Quickly now,' she warned. 'You'll have to sit at the back. It's jam-packed.'

As if released by his push on the door, there came a sudden burst of voices. He hesitated but then went in with the door lady behind him, nudging him in the small of the back. He sat on a chair immediately inside and looked over the heads towards the platform at the far end. The choir was ranged in a semi-circle: men in bow ties, ladies in long black dresses. At one side was a small orchestra with a stumpy conductor standing on a box. Davies looked about him. Who wanted to meet him here? One of the singers stepped forward and with a full, lovely contralto began to sing:

> He shall feed His flock
> Like a shepherd . . .

It was Jemma.

Davies felt his mouth fall open and he sat back, his

eyes riveted. She looked so magnificent in her long black dress, her neck and face warm in the lights. A deep smile snaked across his tired face.

'So. You were surprised?'

'As much as I've ever been.'

She put her thickly coated arm in his as they walked towards the bus stop. 'It's so angelic,' she said. Softly she began to sing again: 'He shall feed His flock . . .'

'Tum-tum, tum-tum, tum-tum,' mumbled Davies.

'You didn't bring your car, Dangerous? Mine wouldn't start.'

'Nor mine. Kitty wouldn't let me get in,' admitted Davies. 'He's in a bad mood. I took him down by the canal this afternoon and he's tired.'

They had reached the bus stop. It had begun to rain gently and darkly. No one else was at the stop. They stood below the shelter. 'You're still on the trail then?' she said. 'Lofty.'

He shrugged. 'It niggles me. I talk to people, like I did this afternoon in those industrial units . . . I just wanted to know if anybody had seen anything . . . I talk to them and I *know* sometimes they're lying. I can *see* they are. But about what? Anything almost. People are always lying, especially to the police.' Traffic was sizzling by. The yellow lights of a bus materialized in the distant drizzle.

'Everyone's got a past,' she pointed out. 'Lofty was no different.' She still had her warm arm in his. The bus splashed alongside the kerb. They boarded it and went to the seats at the front, on the top deck. Apart

60

from two chewing girls in the rear seat, there was no one else.

The conductor appeared, an Indian, not pleased at having to traipse to the front of the bus. 'Sorry, mate,' said Davies. 'I like pretending I'm the driver.' He made a mime of turning a steering wheel. The man smiled dispiritedly.

When he had gone, Davies said: 'There's one basic thing that doesn't make sense. How that old man came to go into the canal, at the particular place he did, and take the ruddy pram with him.'

'Where's the pram now?' she asked.

'In my garage.'

She stood up. 'Next stop,' she said. 'D'you want to come home? I'll make some coffee.' He was still sitting.

'Is Edie still with you?' he inquired defensively as they went down the bus stairs.

'She's gone,' said Jemma. 'Poor woman. You should try some compassion. It doesn't cost anything.'

Edie had certainly gone but her place had, to Davies's deep disappointment, been taken by an old man who sat in the same chair and scratched.

'I didn't realize he was coming here tonight,' Jemma explained. Her eyes came up with a suspicion of an apology. 'Betty, one of the other social workers, must have brought him around after I'd left. I understood he wasn't going to be homeless until tomorrow.'

'Why,' asked Davies moodily, 'didn't Betty take him home with *her*?'

'Betty's got problems at home,' said Jemma, going into the kitchen. 'Social workers frequently have problems.'

Davies followed her to the kitchen door. It was a small space and he stood close to her. 'I can believe that,' he said. He turned to study the old man who was busy scratching his chest but then changed his attack to his legs and after that, with a reach like a spider, over his shoulder to his back. 'He's quiet anyway,' he observed. 'Just the sound of his fingernails.'

'You're a very hard man,' she said quietly. 'Life's full of people who need help.'

From behind he put his arm around her waist. 'I'm one of them,' he said. He eased his chin forward, touched her neck with it and then kissed her on the cheek. She eased her cheek more firmly against his mouth. 'You're a funny old-fashioned thing, Dangerous,' she said. There was a ring at the doorbell. Davies's face dropped. 'It's probably a few lepers,' he sighed.

She went out and returned with Mod, who appeared pleased. 'Tracked you down,' he beamed.

Davies regarded him irritably. 'So you have,' he agreed. 'Did you get lonely?'

Mod sat in the remaining armchair and agreed to join them for coffee. 'What's wrong with him?' he inquired, looking at the scratching man.

'He itches,' sighed Davies. 'All over. What brings you here?'

'A splendid bit of deduction. I sometimes think I'm a better detective than you.'

'Who isn't?' shrugged Davies.

'I decided to come after you,' said Mod. 'I thought

you might be walking into one of your customary traps, be beaten up, maimed, killed. I just missed you at the church hall. I just missed the bus too.' He looked smug.

'All right,' said Davies. 'Tell us.'

'I had a phone call tonight. I've been making inquiries, as you say, and I've found Lofty Brock's old commanding officer from the prison camp. And his sergeant major.'

5

Both Davies and Mod were parochial men, rarely straying from their gritty patch of north-west London, and the long journey to Yorkshire was an adventure. There was, even before they embarked, the uncertainty of whether the Vauxhall Vanguard would get there. It was like an elderly elephant, large, ragged and impressive, but for many years untried over distance.

The garage mechanic was dubious. 'It could crumble,' he said. 'If I were you, Dangerous, I'd leave well alone.'

A further problem was Kitty. 'You'll have to come with us,' Davies informed the dog as he wiped its eyes. 'Yorkshire – where the terriers come from. You could do with a bit of fresh air.'

They set out at dawn, a measly sky moping on the house-tops. Early people, almost senseless at bus stops, eyed them as they drove off to the north.

Mod had armed himself with facts about their route, filleting through the library guidebooks and marking the information on cards. As they drove up the motorway, he read aloud: 'St Albans. Cathedral city. Hertfordshire. Population – 52,470. Early closing – Thursday. Named after Alban, the first English martyr.' Kitty had begun howling at the unaccustomed duration of the journey and the unfamiliar scenery, but he had now settled into a tangled pile and was snoring in the wrecked rear seat.

The car was coughing at intervals but otherwise behaving well. Davies kept it below forty miles an hour, steadfastly in the middle lane of the motorway, provoking a series of horn blasts and signs from antagonized drivers.

They stopped at a service area to let the car simmer down, have a cup of coffee and walk Kitty on his rope through the surrounding ornamental copse.

It took them all day and half the next to reach Topling-on-the-Moor. They stayed overnight at a bed-and-breakfast house in Derbyshire, with Kitty sleeping in the car.

As they journeyed, the dog began to take an increasing interest in the wide white flocks of moorland sheep. He pressed his massive head against the car window and sounded grunts which became growls and finally howls.

'Stop him for God's sake!' shouted Mod, covering his ears.

'How? I can't stop him,' bellowed Davies. 'He's never seen sheep.'

Kitty had to be released from the car at intervals and eventually, at a bleak and misty place, with no livestock in view, they stopped.

'Now don't go far,' warned Davies, getting out of his car and opening the dog's door. 'You'll be falling down a hole.'

Kitty projected his hairy bulk from the back seat and with a manic barking pounded over the nearest brown hill, disappearing from their view. 'Kitty! Kitty!' shouted Davies hopelessly.

To his astonishment the dog at once reappeared, heading in their direction at speed. Behind him came a dirty white cavalry charge of fierce sheep, led by a rampant ram, head down.

'Let's go,' said Mod. He jumped into the front seat and slammed the door. Davies bellowed: 'Run!' at the dog and threw open the rear door. Kitty came down the slope at a gallop, and flung himself heavily into the back of the car. Davies slammed the door and ran for the driving seat. He started the engine, making the snorting ram and the sheep swerve. As the Vanguard roared away, they ran beside it. Gradually, they dropped back and Davies saw them in the driving mirror, grouped in the road, glowering. Kitty looked up and barked defiantly from the rear window.

It was almost midday when they reached the higher moor, which rose like a brown blanket, and Davies pointed the Vanguard's sturdy nose on the final upward track. Mist came down, then drizzle within the mist, while the road curved and canted. Mod saw a long drop over his side of the car and fell silent. Eventually they reached a sign which said 'Topling-on-the-Moor', and beyond that the broken silhouette of a long building. 'Topling Hall,' read Mod from the gate. He peered through the drizzle. 'Toppling it seems to be,' he said.

The house was half demolished, one wing lying in grey rubble, rafters and beams standing out like bones. They left the car and doubtfully walked towards it. Only the front portion was complete, its windows staring apprehensively, with the expressions of condemned men. A notice, like a personal warning to Davies, said: 'Keep out – Dangerous.'

Within the stone porch was a bell-pull in the shape of a nose. Davies pulled it. A dull dong echoed within the house, followed eventually by the squeaking of metal and the scraping of the door. As it opened pulverized plaster showered from the lintel. A stout untidy man stood there, debris on his black overcoat. 'This place gets terribly dusty,' he said, attempting to brush it off. 'Come in, will you.'

He led them through a giant hall, pillars and vaulted ceiling, with half-concealed portraits peering out like spies. 'This part of the building's all right,' he assured them. 'It's the middle portion that's unsafe. The back's already fallen down, as you probably saw. I was going to have it double-glazed, but it scarcely seems worth it now.'

They followed him into a big and chilly chamber. A single-bar electric fire stood balefully in the void of a grand fireplace, an armchair drawn close to it. A dog like a dinosaur glanced up at their arrival but collapsed back to its prostrate place before the meagre warmth. 'We squabble over the fire,' said the man. He smiled surprisingly brightly through his dust. 'I'm Robin Ingate,' he said, revealing a hand from his overcoat sleeve. 'I'm so glad you came. I don't get many visitors. How about a drink?'

Davies introduced himself and then Mod. 'It's good of you to agree to see us, Colonel Ingate,' he said. His eyes travelled about. 'I expect you're kept pretty busy.'

The old officer was pouring long measures of

sherry from a decanter. 'Bloody good stuff, this is,' he said, handing it to them. 'All that's left, the cellar. I've still got ten or fifteen years to get through down there.' He went to the chair and motioned them to a threadbare six-seater sofa. Davies rummaged behind his back and produced a massive bone from a crevice. The colonel leaned forward and took it from him. 'We wondered where that had gone,' he said amiably. He raised his glass and they raised theirs.

'Just marking time, now,' he said, as if he owned them an explanation. 'Just trying to synchronize what's left, so that when I die the rest of the damn place will fall on top of me. Make rather a grand tomb, don't you think?'

They laughed uneasily. The colonel said: 'I was delighted with your call. Not many people telephone me these days. In fact, I'm surprised the blessed thing still functions. I can't recall paying a bill for some considerable time.'

Davies regarded him with sadness. 'Do you,' he ventured, 'live here by yourself?'

'Absolutely!' exclaimed the colonel cheerfully. 'Except for this bloody dog.' He prodded the sprawled animal with his carpet-slippered toe. 'Only way, old boy. Wife passed on ten years ago and, frankly, I didn't want to live with anyone else. Perfectly happy. Can't stand staff around the place. Anyway, can't afford the blighters now. So here I am. Just waiting, really.'

Mod coughed awkwardly. 'I discovered your whereabouts from the Stalag 62 Ex-POW Club, sir,' he said. 'They send their best wishes and asked me to tell you that you would be an honoured guest at the annual dinner.'

'I know, I know,' sighed Colonel Ingate. 'But I won't go now. I'm not going down to London to hear a lot of museum pieces talking about dead men and dead battles.' Regret crossed his strong face. 'Being a soldier is like being in a club,' he said. 'And being a prisoner too. Nobody else is interested. So I don't go. It was all such a long time ago.'

Leaning forward, Davies said: 'We were hoping that you would be able to recall something of it for us. About the prison camp.'

'The old Clickety-Duck,' smiled the old man.

'Pardon, sir?'

'Clickety-Duck. Stalag 62. Housey-Housey, you know. Played a lot of Housey-Housey, there. The Boche used to love it.'

'You let them . . . er, join in then?' asked Davies. 'Play . . .? The Germans?'

'Oh, gracious yes. They weren't so bad, you know, and we were all stuck there together. And the Boche were the only means we had of getting prizes, apart from the stuff we'd saved from Red Cross parcels and so forth. Cigarettes mostly. But you didn't come to talk about that.'

Davies smiled. 'It's all related. We wondered if you could remember a British soldier called Wilfred Henry Brock.'

The old man started to shake his head. 'There were three thousand British in the camp . . .' he began.

'Known as Lofty,' prompted Davies.

The colonel's face brightened. 'Ah, yes . . . Lofty Brock! Deuce, I *do* remember him! Yes, young Lofty.'

Davies leaned forward. He felt the thin firelight touch on his face. 'Anything you can remember might be useful. He died a couple of months ago . . . in rather odd circumstances . . . and it may have a long history . . .' From his pocket he took the small bag and slid from it the medal they had found with Brock's papers. 'He won this,' he said.

'Ah, the DCM,' said Colonel Ingate. He held the medal in the palm of his hand, tenderly, it seemed. He turned it over and read the name. 'Fancy that,' he said. 'I don't recall it. Won just before Dunkirk. It's a long time ago now.' He handed the medal back. 'So he came to a bad death, did he? What a shame,' he said. 'Now let me see. He wasn't there all that long, because, I seem to remember, he was one of the contingent shipped off to Silesia.'

'Oh, they moved?'

'Half the camp. Went off early in 1945, as the Russians were advancing. It was very bad. Some of them died, not always at the hand of the enemy. There was warfare within the camp among the prisoners of different nationalities. But I remember young Brock, right enough, when he was with us in Stalag 62. You could hardly miss him . . . He was the camp goalkeeper.'

Davies felt his mouth drop. 'Goalkeeper?' he said. 'Brock?'

'Indeed, very agile too for his size, as I recall.' On a thought he rose. 'Wait a moment. I might even have a picture of him. In the team. I've got a whole lot of rubbish from those days in the next room.' He put down his sherry glass and stumped off towards the adjoining room.

Davies eyed Mod. 'A goalkeeper?' he muttered. 'He must have worn springs.'

'Or they had small goals,' said Mod.

From the other room came a muffled crash, a shout, and a low discharge of dust through the open door. They rose anxiously but the colonel appeared, newly coated but triumphantly carrying a bound album. 'Got it,' he said. 'Put my hand on it at once. Unfortunately it was half-buried in there. Holding up a part of the wall, actually. Thought the blessed lot was coming down.' He brushed himself ineffectually and handed the album, opened, to Davies. 'That's the team,' he said. '1944. That's Lofty Brock at the back. See, his name's underneath.'

Together Davies and Mod peered at the browned photograph. The man standing at the rear of the team, wearing the roll-necked jersey, was all of six feet six inches.

6

The journey to Botfield was less demanding. They left The Babe In Arms at noon, to the incredulity of drinkers and staff, and drove down into December Hampshire.

'"The New Forest",' read Mod aloud as they travelled. '"Established by William the Conqueror in the eleventh century as a hunting ground . . ."'

'Fascinating,' mumbled Davies, narrowly watching the unaccustomed motorway ahead. They rarely overtook anything. 'And there, in the Forest, is former Sergeant Major George Bing. Late of Silesia.'

Mod grunted: 'About forty years late of Silesia.' He returned to his information cards. '"King Rufus met his untimely end at Stoney Cross, near Lyndhurst",' he recited. 'Arrow in the eye. Was it an accident? Now, there's a real mystery for you, Dangerous.'

'I'd rather find out who shoved Lofty in the canal.'

Mod sighed. 'Has it ever occurred to you that he *fell* in . . . accidentally, I mean, *really*. He *fell*. Splash! The official version. Don't you think that sometimes these little whims of yours get a bit out of hand?'

The lines deepened on Davies's face. He knew Mod had been waiting to say it. 'No, I don't,' he said.

Kitty, who had so far slept through the journey, woke with a gaping yawn and blinked out of the window. They were chugging past trees and fields with red roofs showing between winter branches. The dog began to moan.

'Shut up, you,' ordered Dangerous in the direction of the dog. He glanced acidly sideways at Mod. 'It's not a bloody whim.'

'Dangerous,' insisted Mod. 'All I'm saying is that you might be wrong. When you get one of these bees in your bonnet nothing will stop you. But, there are times when the most *obvious* explanation is the *right* one. Lofty Brock *fell* in the canal. How, we don't know. But he just *fell.*'

Grimly, Davies said: 'So you think all this investigation is just a waste of time?'

'Not at all. It gets us out in the fresh air. Away from the pub . . . Yorkshire . . . Hampshire. It's very interesting.'

'Like a hobby,' muttered Davies.

'If you like. You've said yourself that everybody's got a past. Ordinary people have secrets. Dig into their history and something murky can turn up, a skeleton in the cupboard. Perhaps you're reading too much into Lofty's past.'

'In 1944,' grunted Davies, 'Lofty Brock was six feet six inches. How come he was five feet one inch when he died? He didn't just shrink.'

'That doesn't mean somebody *killed* him for his past. What you're doing, Dangerous, is getting all the circumstances and *trying to make them fit the crime*, which may not have been a crime at all.'

The cracks in Davies's face grew darker. 'All this is the mad imaginings of a frustrated copper then . . .'

'No, no. Now wait a minute.'

'. . . A copper who gets all the miserable, shitty little jobs that nobody else wants and which never get in the headlines. The last detective. So he's trying to make his own headlines. He's making up a crime to suit himself.'

Kitty began a renewed howling in the back seat. 'And you can shut up too,' snapped Davies over his shoulder. 'There's sod-all you know about it.'

Former Sergeant Major Bing had gone to the golf club, his pink-pinafored wife said from their cottage door. 'I don't know why,' she complained inadequately. 'He can hardly drag one foot after another. But he goes every day, rain or snow or shine. He says he likes to get out.'

It was not far. They parked the Vanguard and the dog among the few vehicles in the gravel car park and went into the modest wooden club house. It was mid-afternoon and the early dark was moving in. There was a robust fire in the grate reflecting in the glasses polished by the steward. 'He'll be in soon,' he told them. 'He won't be able to see his ball. You'll hear him.'

After ten minutes, they saw a cambered figure coming alone through the trees in the dripping dusk, stumbling and tugging a golf trolley as if it were a field gun. 'You'll hear him in a minute,' forecast the steward. 'He won't let a soul help him. He'd drop first.'

They watched from the bay window while the man stumbled closer. The steward went to the bar door and opened it, and then the outer door. Now they heard Mr Bing moaning as he limped up the incline. 'Oh . . . oh . . . oh God . . . Damn it . . . to hell with it . . . Oh, oh . . . nearly there . . . nearly there.'

He arrived in the room, apparently close to collapse, and Davies and Mod rose to assist him. Clay-faced he motioned them away. 'No, no thanks. Don't need anybody. I'll manage.' His golf trolley had fallen over outside the door and the clubs, like arrows from a quiver, had spilled. He ignored it and staggered towards a chair. Even easing himself into it was a torture. They winced at the cracking of his bones. 'Jesus,' he said eventually. 'It's good to get some fresh air, you know.'

The steward brought them a tray of tea. Bing had managed to get out of his muddy golf shoes and was in his stockinged feet.

'They don't mind here,' he said, waving a hand around the bar. 'It isn't a very posh club, thank God. Well done, son.' The steward had picked up his shoes and carried them out to the locker room. 'A good chap,' he confided, leaning forward. 'Ex-Royal Marine.'

'Were you playing alone?' asked Davies.

'I have to. No other bugger will play with me. Nine holes and they have to carry me back. Anyway, this club is geriatric. The flag seems permanently at half-mast. Top half of the pole has hardly been used.' He half laughed, half coughed. 'That's why there's nobody here now. Not in this weather. I *make* myself. Once I'm trapped, I'm finished. My missus knows that.'

The steward came to the low table and poured some more tea. They surveyed the soaking grey countryside through the window with the four o'clock darkness sliding into every knot and crevice of the golf course. A dishevelled blackbird was sitting on the muddy putting green under the window. 'But it suits me,' the old man said oddly. 'There are worse places.'

Davies said: 'As I explained on the telephone, we came to ask you to try to remember anything you can about the prison camp days.'

'Right. So you did.' A momentary wistfulness came to his eyes. 'Seems like yesterday,' he said. 'How has all this come up then? With the police?'

'An old chap died in somewhat odd circumstances, drowned in a canal in London,' Davies told him. 'A few weeks ago.' He glanced at Mod before continuing. 'We're not altogether satisfied it was an accident. One or two things have come to light which make us think that his death might *just* have some connection with something in his past.'

'And you said he was in Stalag 62,' said Bing. 'There were a lot of blokes there, mind you. About three thousand. What was his name? I might just remember him.'

'Brock,' Davies said quietly. 'Wilfred Henry. Also known as Lofty.'

Bing was taking a drink of his tea and he choked over the cup, spilling it in all directions. The attentive steward brought a napkin across and the old man thanked him for it. He stared at Davies and Mod. 'Lofty Brock? It couldn't be. Lofty Brock's been dead forty years or more. I saw him die.'

*

'They carted us off to Silesia,' related Mr Bing. 'It was terrible. Cold as hell. They had us building defensive systems and air-raid shelters because the Russians were on their way. It was only the winter holding them up. In the old Stalag 62 it wasn't so bad. Just whiling away the time until the War finished, we were. None of this escape stuff you see on your television or read in books. If anybody tried it, the Germans would come down like a ton of bricks on the rest. Short rations, everything. So it wasn't encouraged. There were all sorts there, all nationalities and types, half the time falling out among themselves. But it was bearable. The old man, Colonel Ingate, kept the British more or less together, kept up morale and discipline . . .' His cup was empty and he stared into it as if trying to read what the tea leaves said.

'What happened when you went to Silesia?' Davies inquired.

'Well, we knew that the War didn't have far to go, six months at the most. The Russians were coming one way and the Yanks coming from the other. But we didn't even know exactly where we were. We were taken east by train and then told to get off in the wilds. It turned out to be about sixty miles from Nysa, but we didn't know then. And the guards were bastards. Ukrainians mostly, fighting for the Huns. They knew when the Reds caught up with them, they'd be for the high jump, and they weren't overjoyed about that. All sorts of things went on in that camp and not always after dark either. There was a lot of in-fighting, personal some of it, some of it political. But, by any standards, it was a pretty unhealthy place. You could never tell who your enemies were.'

'How,' asked Davies, 'did Lofty Brock die?'

'Somebody put a knife in him. He was just about a goner when we found him. Never said a word. Looked like somebody crept up on him because there were no signs of a fight and he was a great big bloke. But it was in the last days there. The Russkies were on the way and there was panic everywhere. We didn't feel all that smug about it because they were reckoned to be not all that particular who or what they shot. The Ukrainians ran away and we more or less followed them, going west, back into Germany to try and join up with the Americans. Eventually most of us did.'

Davies asked: 'Would it have been an easy matter for somebody to take over Brock's identity? Even somebody who didn't look remotely like him? Who was seventeen inches shorter, for a start.'

The elderly man began to work his hands. The knuckles were knotted. 'It gets me there,' he said. He returned to Davies. 'It wouldn't be all that difficult,' he replied. 'It was a shambles. You could easily alter identification papers, such as they were, give yourself a new name. God, some of the ruddy Nazis did it, didn't they? Just took over somebody else's name and got clean away. Some of them lived in prison camps for months before sliding out scot-free.'

'So a man could have taken over Brock's identity without much of a problem?'

'No problem at all. Most of our lot, the British, ended up in Vienna. Thousands of them. As I say, it was a shambles. And nobody wanted to know. The

War was over and that was all that mattered. Everybody wanted to bugger off home and forget it. Men just disappeared. Some with good reason.'

'What about his family? Brock's?' put in Mod.

'I don't know about that,' said Mr Bing, shaking his head. 'I can't remember anything about his circumstances. But having a family didn't prevent people vanishing. Sometimes they were only too glad to.' He looked up at them. His eyes, as Davies now saw, very pale and hopeless. 'Sometimes I wish I had myself,' he said.

7

Jemma had placed the tank of goldfish on the table where Davies regarded them sternly. 'At least they don't scratch,' he observed. 'Or yell like Edie.' The fish were crowding against the wall of the tank. 'They stare,' he said. 'Look at them staring.'

'Tomorrow,' said Jemma, 'they'll be going back. Once the man is out of hospital.'

'Who,' wondered Mod, eyeing the fish, 'would want to do a smash and grab on a pet shop?'

Davies, his own eyes widening with those of the goldfish, said: 'Maybe someone with a craving for hamsters.'

'He stole three pounds fifty and put a poor man in hospital,' said Jemma firmly. 'I just hope you catch him.'

'Oh, we'll get him,' forecast Davies. 'We've had sniffer dogs down there. They've noshed a couple of tons of biscuits between them and one of them swallowed a white mouse.'

Jemma went into the kitchen and came back with some toasted bacon sandwiches and three mugs of coffee on a tray. Gratefully, Davies smiled at her. 'At least we're getting decent rations on this case,' he said. He bit into a sandwich and felt the bacon fat roll warmly down his stubbled chin. He had – in the pursuit of his official duties – been on a case dealing with unrest among vagrants and had gone among the down-and-outs trying to look like one, but most of them had recognized him.

'I think we ought to recap,' he said eventually. 'Get everything into order and see where we are.'

'Go to jail,' muttered Mod. 'Do not pass Go. Do not collect two hundred pounds.' He caught Davies's eye.

'All right,' Mod agreed, his mouth bulging with sandwich. When he had finished it, he immediately began to look as if he had been left out. Davies put the remainder of his sandwich in his mouth. Speaking at first through the bread, he went carefully over the known history of the person they still called Lofty Brock.

The goldfish were still congregated at the glass as though hardly able to believe what they saw. 'Incidentally,' said Davies, 'I called in on the security company, Keystone, who are supposed to keep an eye on the industrial estate. Keystone is a good name. Like the comedy cops. Nobody heard a thing that night. They're supposed to patrol regularly through-out the night, but I bet they don't. One of the blokes had holes in his socks.'

Jemma went to a cupboard and from it took two cardboard boxes. 'The file of papers from the hostel,' she said, putting the first on the coffee-table. 'And the things from the pram.' She placed the second box alongside the first.

She sat down and the trio became motionless, three pairs of eyes on the two containers. Eventually, Davies opened the flaps of the box from the hostel.

An odd expectancy came over them, as if the answer might be miraculously revealed. Nothing happened. On top of the folded papers was the linen bag which contained the medal. Davies picked it up, the maroon and purple ribbon lying across the palm of his hand. He turned the medal over. 'I wonder,' said Mod, 'what the penalty is for impersonating a holder of the Distinguished Conduct Medal?'

'Or for stealing it,' added Jemma.

'Or for murdering the recipient,' suggested Davies. He balanced the medal in the palm of his hand. 'Somebody killed the real Lofty Brock in the prison camp. There's a cross beside his name on the list in this box,' he said doggedly. 'Sergeant Major Bing must have been right. Perhaps it was the man who stole his identity. Lofty Brock Mark Two.'

'I'll be glad when he's got a name,' said Mod.

Davies nodded: 'It's difficult investigating some- body nameless. Half the time you never know who you're talking about.' His eyes went to Jemma. 'Haven't got any more bacon, have you?' he said.

Jemma rose. 'There's three rashers left. Don't continue without me.'

When she had gone into the kitchen, Mod said quietly: 'I wonder how she came to get that tooth knocked out.'

'I don't know,' replied Davies. 'I don't like to ask. Maybe she fell off her bike.'

He got up and went to the bookshelf. '*Aspects of Social Behaviour*,' he read aloud. '*Applied Psychology. A Plan for Social Realignment, Patterns of Deprivation, The Thinking of Children, Decisions in Cities*.' He sniffed and turned away. 'If you read stuff like that you could make something of yourself,' he said to Mod.

'Aye,' nodded the philosopher, 'and have somebody else's goldfish to look after.'

Jemma returned with the bacon sandwiches and coffee. 'Wipe your fingers before you start picking up any more of Lofty's things,' she said. Before taking hers from the plate, Jemma opened the biscuit tin and took out the wooden box. She laid out the contents on the table, first opening the ring box in which the pearl sat like a small bird's egg, then came the hairbrush, the razor and the blades, the bottle of cough mixture, the penknife, the cow creamer, and finally, the stained and faded photograph in the metal frame: a woman staring out, possibly from the dead.

She placed the picture on the table and as they chewed they fixed their eyes on it, like hungry spiritualists hoping to raise a ghost. 'If those lips could only speak,' Mod recited.

'She'd probably ask for a bacon sandwich,' said Davies. He wiped his hands and picked up the frame. He opened the back as he had done before. 'No name, not even a photographer's trade mark,' he said. 'Nothing.'

'But it's not the original size,' said Jemma carefully. She examined it more closely. 'It's had a piece cut off to make it fit the frame. At the bottom, done with scissors by the look of it. It's not as level as the other edges.'

Davies picked up the frame. 'You're right,' he said. 'It's top-heavy – and it's not centred.'

'She looks grim, doesn't she,' put in Mod. 'Years

ago, people didn't use to smile at the camera. There was no shouting "cheese". You had to be dead serious.'

'You're right as well,' mused Davies. 'She looks *so* miserable. Fancy having your picture taken looking like that. And the way she's staring like she hated having her photograph taken.'

'Perhaps she did,' suggested Jemma slowly. 'You know . . . Dangerous . . . it looks like . . . it looks . . .' Davies realized.

'Say it,' he said.

'. . . like a prison photograph,' she finished.

8

The early weather that winter had been the usual desultory grey, often mild and often wet in the streets (the inhabitants of the area only considered the weather at street-level; it was not a place where people looked much at the sky). The lights of the shops and houses provided the sole visual warmth; the power station sent up its personal white clouds while working chimneys and traffic fumes added to the wintry grit. Then, like an order miraculously delivered on time, a few days before Christmas, it began to snow. The nuisance and ugliness of the underfoot slush was more than compensated for by the lambent white of ordinary roofs. On the first night of moonlight factory chimneys glistened like candles.

'Somebody's got to work over Christmas,' said Davies in The Babe In Arms. 'As usual, it's me.'

'There won't be much serious crime,' forecast the little man Shiny Bright. He looked almost too frail to lift his Guinness.

'Staying at home are you, Shiny?' said Davies convivially. 'In the warm.'

'Footprints,' answered Shiny, looking down at his tiny feet. 'footprints, Dangerous. In the snow.' He left his stool and walked pigeon-toed to the bar.

Engulfed in her vivid red coat Jemma arrived, new snow speckling her thick hair. The men in the bar turned from their drinking to take her in. Davies felt a warm flush of pride. Mod rolled his eyes as if he could see no good coming of it. She was going with Davies to the Divisional Christmas Party and, after one drink, they left the bar. Shiny Bright stared at his Guinness and said fervently: 'That was my sort of woman, that was.'

Her car was parked on the next junction. It was small and Dangerous had difficulty climbing in. She started the engine but did not put the car into gear, waiting for the wipers to clear the windscreen. 'You look very nice in the snow,' he said awkwardly, looking away from her and peering out of the window. 'It's the contrast.'

'Thank you. I'm not sure how to take that.' She still did not engage the gear lever. Davies said: 'I would have liked to have taken you to the pictures one night when there was something decent on, but we've been too busy.'

To his intense pleasure she leaned towards him and gave him a kiss on the mouth. His hand went up around her warm neck and he pulled her towards him for another. As they parted her face remained close, her dark eyes very full. 'How many beers have you had?' she asked.

'Two or three. If I'd known this was going to happen, I'd have put on some scent.'

Smiling privately she eased herself back behind the driving seat.

She started the car and they drove through the slushy streets towards the Mafeking Hall where the

Divisional Christmas Party had been held every year since the time of the famous siege. (A few years before, several trapped bank robbers had barricaded themselves in a council house in nearby Mafeking Street and the Christmas Party had been swiftly transferred from another part of the division to the adjacent hall so that officers taking part in the siege should not altogether miss out on the social side of things. Eventually, an inspector eating a mince pie had persuaded the malefactors to give up their pointless defiance.)

As Davies and Jemma went into the hall, a musical group of young constables, The Cellmates, with a woman traffic warden vocalist, were playing. The singer, professionally called Dolly Parking, wearing orange wig and sundered dress, was bawling into a hand mike. The hall was filled with drinking policemen and their ladies. At the bar Davies was greeted by a broad ginger man. 'Hello, Affie,' Davies said. He looked around. Jemma was conversing with the Coroner's officer. 'How's prison?'

'I reckon it's more difficult keeping them in than getting them there in the first place,' grumbled the man. 'Sometimes I wish I'd never transferred, Dangerous, stayed in the force. When you're a copper, you're dealing with the criminal classes only part of the time. In the Prison Service you live with them.'

Davies said: 'What d'you know about women's prisons, Affie?'

'Not a thing. Don't know much about women, come to think of it.' He looked about the crowded room. 'There's an old dame who's here tonight, mind you. I saw her come in. She gives lectures on women's prisons, history and everything. When you do your training course she bores the ears off you.' He indicated with his glass. 'I saw her over there somewhere, talking to my boss. Miss Gladstone, she's called. Like an old bag, they used to say on the training course. But she's over there, Dangerous. Why did you want to know?'

'I just thought I'd take an interest in them,' said Davies affably. 'Thanks, Affie.'

Almost with stealth he made his way through the drinking and talking people, murmuring apologies as he nudged elbows. He heard Jemma's voice just behind him. 'Take it steady, Dangerous, you're too big to be a rattlesnake. Where are you heading?' She rubbed his ear with her glass.

Davies paused and spoke quietly over his shoulder. 'There's an old lady here, she knows all about women in clink. I'm wondering if she can shed a bit of light on that photograph.'

'She'd have to have a photographic memory. And a long one.'

'I know. But she's the expert. Gives lectures. I thought it would be worth a try.'

'You've got it with you?'

Davies patted his pocket. 'I took it to Watkins, the photographers, to see if they had any idea about it, you know, by looking at it. How old it is, what sort of camera. I also got them to copy it. It's called clutching at straws.'

He had turned to face her and because of the crush in the room they suddenly found themselves in very close proximity. The bust of her dress was touching his lapels. He swallowed hard and shuffled back a pace. She smiled. 'You're lovely, you know,' she said to him. 'Bloody lovely.'

'Thanks,' he croaked. The colour of her eyes was amazing, even allowing for the time of year. He took a deep drink and regarded her over the edge of the tankard. 'You're fairly bloody lovely yourself.'

'When we've got time,' she said seriously, 'we've got to have a proper talk.'

'I'd better get going,' he said awkwardly. 'Will you be all right for a couple of minutes?'

'Don't worry about me. I'll soon find company. I'll just smile at some nice chief inspector.'

'Not a word . . .'

'. . . about Lofty,' she finished for him.

Davies regarded her steadily. 'I don't want the police involved,' he said. He stopped himself looking at her and turned into the crowd. As he went he felt her touch the nape of his neck with her finger. He pushed on through the people, searching, like an explorer through undergrowth.

'Who are you looking for, Dangerous? Santa?' A portly probation officer smiled as Davies emerged from the drinkers. The Cellmates launched into another frenzied song.

'Listen, Ronnie,' said Davies. 'You know all these theoretical law-enforcers. I'm looking for a lady, an old girl, Miss Gladstone, Prison Service.'

'Know her well,' said the other man. 'Makes your ear ache. A bit like this band.' Like many fat men he had small eyes and he swivelled them around the room like a sniper looking for a target. 'There,' he pointed out. 'Over there, see. In the dress that looks like a bit of our carpet. Talking to that chap from the fingerprint department. D'you know him?'

'Dabber Donnelly,' nodded Davies. 'Right, thanks, Ronnie. Keep keeping them on the straight and narrow.'

'I try, Dangerous. I can only try.'

As Davies approached the elderly woman and Donnelly, the man turned to take two glasses from a passing colleague who had been to the bar. 'Hello, Dabber,' said Davies. The lady regarded him with reserve. Donnelly grinned and introduced him. 'Miss Gladstone, this is Detective Constable Davies. One of our more interesting officers.'

Miss Gladstone extended a hand so soft that, at first, he thought it must be enclosed in a glove. It was not. 'Why are you so interesting?' she demanded boomingly. Her eyes were indistinguishable behind dense spectacles. 'You don't look very interesting.'

'I'm not,' agreed Davies hurriedly. 'It's just that Mr Donnelly spends all his time in his fingerprint laboratory. Lives in a world of whorls. He thinks that anybody who gets out of doors is interesting.' He paused. Donnelly asked him if he would like another drink. Davies guessed it was the escape route the fingerprint man had been seeking, and gave him the excuse. He took it gratefully.

'I wondered, Miss Gladstone,' said Davies, 'if I could pick your brains. I know you're an expert on women's prisons.'

Her ragged face took on a glow. 'The Incarceration of Women,' she boomed, 'has been my lifelong work.' Her voice was so penetrating that all the nearby people turned. 'Have you, young man, read my autobiography, *In and Out of Women's Prisons*?' Shamefacedly, Davies admitted that he had not. 'Published 1949,' she said. 'But there are still copies to be found. Get it and enjoy it.'

'Oh, I will, right away.' Davies tried to look as if he would like it for Christmas. 'I need to get to know something about the system, pre-War that is.'

She looked slightly displeased and drank her gin at a gulp. Donnelly had just returned with Davies's pint so Davies took the glass from the old lady and handed it to the fingerprint man. 'Another for Miss Gladstone, please, Dabber,' he said.

'Of course, I was only a gel,' said Miss Gladstone, a little mollified. 'Doing my pioneer work. It was 1937 before I wrote my first book *Girls in Confinement*.'

'That's about the period,' said Davies hurriedly. 'What were women's prisons like then?'

'Healthy,' said Miss Gladstone firmly. 'Jolly healthy. Far far better than the environment from which most of the prisoners emanated and to which, unhappily, of course, they returned.'

'Oh,' said Davies. 'Healthy . . .'

'Quite a number were farm prisons, you see,' she continued. Her enthusiasm was warming. Donnelly came back with the gin and she again despatched it at a gulp, in mid-sentence. 'The inmates worked in the fields. Good fresh air, hard labour, tired their bodies but brought roses to their cheeks. Wonderful experience for them. And they were always imprisoned close to their homes. Upon release some of them couldn't wait to get back in. They enjoyed their incarceration.'

Clumsily, Davies was reaching inside his pocket. He

took out an envelope and from that, like a conjuror doing a small trick, he produced the photograph which had come from Lofty Brock's wooden box. 'This lady,' he said, 'doesn't look very happy. But then it must have been taken on her first day.'

'Hmmm,' said Miss Gladstone, holding the picture at arm's length and lifting her glasses. 'Before she started enjoying herself. She does look a bit downcast.'

'I'm trying to ascertain who she might be,' said Davies. He had dropped his voice and now he glanced about him.

'Why are you whispering?' she demanded astutely. She looked around. 'They're all policemen and the like here.'

'I don't want the police to know,' he said, trying to make it sound like a joke. 'They'll all want to be on the case.'

She examined the picture again. 'Her prison number's been cut off,' she observed. 'Without that you haven't got much hope, have you?' To Davies's consternation, she decisively pushed the photograph into her huge handbag. She hushed him by wafting the great bag at him. 'I shall take good care of it, never fear, Mr Davies. You have a copy I take it?' He admitted he had. 'I shall have to consult my files,' she said. 'Perhaps I may be able to discover something.' The challenge in her eyes was not to be denied. 'And now,' she said, 'I'd like another sizeable gin.'

Later that evening, Davies began singing softly, not to himself but not quite loudly enough for anyone at a distance of more than a few feet to hear, as if the tune were a secret.

'Is that a moan or a song?' demanded Jemma as they walked along the winter-night pavements.

From The Babe In Arms came after-hours lights and voices. Poised uncertainly on the kerb, Davies looked at her askew.

'Louder,' he said, 'and it could be a breach of the peace. Anyway, I prefer to sing to myself. When you have a voice like mine, singing becomes confidential.'

'It's after closing,' said Jemma, taking his arm. Davies was looking wildly up the street, one way then the other, like a soldier about to advance under fire. 'Extra Yuletide drinking time,' he explained vaguely. 'Mod will be standing there with a miraculously empty glass.'

She helped him across the empty road. 'Thanks,' he said sweetly as they reached the bar door. 'There were times when I didn't think we were going to make it.'

Few people had left the bar, despite the ringing of a bell, as forlorn as a buoy out at sea, and unhopeful exhortations from the various Irish barmen. Mod saw them enter and swiftly swallowed the remainder of his beer. He had been entertaining a girl who appeared to have two footballs under her thick grey sweater. Without speaking Davies took Mod's glass. The girl declined his brief offer, saying she had to return to her boyfriend.

Davies was quickly back with the drinks. 'Just in time,' he commented, handing one to Jemma and the other to Mod. 'Who was that?' he said to Mod.

'Works in Woolworths,' smiled Mod with late-middle-aged wickedness.

'She looks like Woolworths,' said Davies.

'Wait, wait,' cautioned Mod. 'Within that large bosom beats a large heart.' He smiled with a little bliss. 'Things that go bump in the night,' he murmured.

Davies drained his beer. 'I've got to go to the station. I'm officially on stand-by,' he said.

'I'd better come with you,' said Jemma, regarding him doubtfully. 'In case you're kept in.'

They went out into the sharp night once more, leaving Mod in the bar where unrequited bells were still sounding and barmen hoarsely calling for time.

'Look at the stars, all blinking,' pointed Davies. Her gaze followed his finger. 'All up there. Blotto and . . .'

'Pluto,' she pointed out. 'Blotto is what you are.' Suddenly she said, 'It's my son's birthday today. I telephoned him.'

Davies glanced at her and saw her eyes were glistening. 'Oh,' he said. 'It makes you sad. I'm sorry about that.'

'Next year, end of next year maybe, I'm going to have him back. His father won't let him come now. But I'll see him some day. It's three years since I was with him.'

'Don't cry,' said Davies, clumsily putting his arm about her. 'I'll show you our new cells.'

'He hardly ever saw his father,' she complained, putting her face against his shoulder. 'It wasn't fair. That man was months, years away, and never setting eyes on his little kid. One day, you've got to believe this, Dangerous, one day the priest came to the door

94

and I said "Hello, Father" and . . . and my little boy went crazy because he thought it was *his* father.'

'That's a bad mistake,' agreed Davies with sombre wisdom. 'No wonder you got a divorce.'

'I didn't. We're still married. Like you are.'

She hung on to his arm and blinked her eyes towards the stars. 'Never mind,' she said almost to herself. It sounded as if she had said it many times before.

It was midnight when they reached the police station. The night sergeant had just come on duty and was unpacking his lunch from a fine old wooden case. It had brass corners, a brass lock and a polished handle with brass fittings. In regular rows around its sides, small bright screws glimmered deeply, like bulkhead lights.

'Nice piece of furniture, Lew,' said Davies. Jemma ran her finger over the line of inset screws. The sergeant looked momentarily pleased and wished them good evening.

'My old dad made that, donkey's years ago,' he said, patting the box. There was distant Welsh in his voice. 'He was a cabinet-maker. I wish I'd been now.'

'Got you on the red-eye trick again, have they?' said Davies. 'They've lumbered me with most of Christmas too. They reckon I haven't got anywhere better to go.'

'Exactly,' emphasized the sergeant, pointing his finger at them. 'Just because I'm Lewis Emmanuel, they put me down as Jewish, so I don't qualify for Christmas off. Every year it's the same. I keep telling them I'm bloody *Welsh*.'

'Rotten luck,' said Davies sympathetically. 'We haven't got any prisoners, have we? Not staying?'

'No residents, Dangerous. Few drunks but they've been bailed. All quiet otherwise, thank God.'

'I'll just check the CID room,' said Davies, moving away from the front desk. Jemma went with him. 'See if there's any messages. I'm only stand-by tonight.'

'Right you are, Dangerous,' said Sergeant Emmanuel, continuing the exploration of his box.

They walked along the corridor and into the CID office. Jemma's nose wrinkled. 'Doesn't anyone come and clean up in here?' she asked.

'Well, they do,' answered Davies doubtfully. 'But it only gets filthy again. It's the cells that are the posh part of this building. They've all been refurbished. All mod cons.'

'Show me,' she suggested suddenly. 'You promised you would.'

He looked up in surprise. 'Oh, right you are, then.' He took a bunch of keys from the wall. 'They're really homely. Better than *my* home.'

She held his elbow and they walked to the rear of the building down a resounding flight of steps and through a corridor. Davies pressed a light switch, illuminating a row of six barred cells. 'Warmest place in the nick,' he said.

'What's through that door?'

'Maximum security,' he told her with a hint of pride. 'For real baddies.' He began opening the locks. 'They've only just finished them.'

He motioned her into a thickly padded interior. There were two cells, each with a bed, a chair fixed to the floor and a basin. To his surprise, Jemma sat on the bed.

'Pretty comfortable,' she said quietly, looking up into his face. Davies swallowed so violently he almost choked. 'We . . . we aim to please,' he said.

'So do I,' said Jemma. She took his hand and coaxed him down beside her.

'This is likely to be the most private place we'll ever find, Dangerous,' she said seriously. She pulled his bemused face towards her. He was so mesmerized he forgot to kiss her. She kissed him. She had lovely lips and he could feel the gap in her teeth. His uncertain hands eventually located her breasts. Her coat was wide open and he stroked them as they stood out under her dress. Jemma half pulled away and looked beyond him. 'The door,' she said. Dragging herself clear of him, she walked the three paces to the main door of the Security Wing. At her touch it swung closed with a soft clang.

'Now we're locked in,' mentioned Davies from the bed.

'We've got the keys,' she murmured, walking back towards him.

'It doesn't open from the inside,' he pointed out. 'It would be silly if it did, wouldn't it.'

She turned to face him with a frank grin. 'So we're stuck,' she said mischievously.

'Stuck until Sergeant Emmanuel does his rounds, or wonders where we've gone. He probably thinks we've gone out the back way.' He spoke, even then, without realizing the possibilities. 'There's a red light outside the door,' he continued. 'If we press the switch it will go on. But it's still got to be seen.

They didn't fit anything noisy in case the villains in here disturbed the honest peace of the police station.'

He stood and made towards a light switch high on the wall. His raised hand was almost there when her long brown fingers fell calmly across his wrist. Davies regarded her with near-alarm. 'Not yet, Dangerous,' she suggested. 'We're okay here for a while. It's quiet and warm.' She sat on the bed and patted it. 'And this is quite comfortable.'

'We look after our villains very well . . . in the circumstances . . .' His voice tailed off. He stood stupidly while she took off her coat. 'That's better,' she said, examining one of the big buttons. 'It really is close.'

Davies did not believe what was about to happen. He half moved forward to help her with the coat, then halted. Still without looking at him, she began to undo the square buttons of her dress, moving upwards from the hem. It fell open like gradually parting curtains. Davies remained transfixed. His eyes alone moved, blinking twice. She stopped at the waist and looked up at him. The opening slipped to its widest extent, the side of the dress falling away, revealing the dark lengths of her stockinged legs and, like the sail of a small oncoming ship, a triangle of white between them.

'Let me help you,' blurted Davies, stumbling on to his knees, striking them on the concrete floor. He swallowed his cry as she seized his head with both hands and fiercely once more brought their mouths together. Half suffocating, Davies clawed his way forward, forcing his knees up from the floor and almost bulldozing her back on to the low, top-security cell bed. He clambered above her, heels kicking. Again they kissed frantically. His head hit the wall at the back of the bunk.

'Wait, take it easy,' she pleaded. 'Down, Dangerous, down.'

Perspiring, Davies lowered himself away from her. 'Sorry,' he mumbled. His knees hurt. 'I got carried away.'

'So you did,' she replied sweetly. She leaned over and kissed him at random on the face. 'Me too.' She sat up. 'Let's take it easy. Forget the wrestling. Nobody is hurrying us. Maybe we'll stay here until Boxing Day.'

'You're quite right,' said Davies, smiling broadly through his sweat. 'What shall we do next?'

'Well, I think you ought to take some of your clothes off. That overcoat reeks of The Babe In Arms.' She regarded him teasingly. 'You take some off, and then I'll take some more off, and then it's your turn, and so on. But nobody touches anybody until we're finished, naked. All right?'

'I'll try my best,' promised Davies. He rolled off his overcoat and then his jacket and pullover. Sitting in his braces, he studied her challengingly.

'My turn,' she agreed. Her hands returned to her dress buttons, and without rush she undid them to the neck. Davies stood, then sat down heavily on the prisoner's chair. 'More?' she inquired.

'A bit more,' he suggested croakily.

'Okay,' she agreed. With a delicious flick of her dark body, she wriggled out of the dress. It fell to the bed, leaving her naked shoulders glimmering in the lamplight. Her eyes moved up to him. 'Your deal,' she invited.

Instead of unlooping his braces, Davies undid each button separately, causing the elastic to fly dashingly over his shoulders, striking the wall behind. Now he became uncertain. She merely nodded for him to continue. He unzipped his fly at the third attempt, and began to peel back his heavy trousers. Then he changed direction and took off his boots.

'Your deal now,' he muttered.

Without leaning down, she kicked off her shoes.

'Go ahead,' she said.

Closing his eyes, his face colouring, Dangerous pulled down his trousers, revealing his white, woollen long johns. Jemma fell at once into hilarity. 'Oh, Dangerous!' she laughed. 'Look at you! I've never . . .'

'They go on in October when the clocks go back,' said Davies doggedly. 'And they stay on until March when the clocks go on again.'

'Not . . . not the same pair?' She was looking over her hands.

'No, not the same pair,' he said, hurt. 'I've got four pairs.' She still couldn't stop. 'Listen,' he said in an upset voice. 'I didn't expect all this . . . I'd have worn my Union Jack jockstrap.'

'No, no. I'm sorry,' she pleaded. Wiping her eyes, she stood and in her stockinged feet stepped towards him. He remained in the chair. She pressed his face to her naked stomach. Then she bent at the knees so that his trembling nose travelled up to the folds of her breasts. Her hands moved down and she pulled the heavy long johns from him. His hands slid around her waist and then down over her buttocks, pulling her pants with them. 'You don't wear a lot considering the weather,' he said.

'Enough,' she mumbled. Her fingers were on his thighs now, stroking them. Davies began to groan. He rose from the hard chair and pushed her, gently this time, towards the bed. After several bungled attempts to undo her bra, he took his hands away and she did it for him. Her glimmering breasts lolled forward. He kissed them.

They stretched out to enjoy each other. She urged him to take his time and he did. When they were lying quietly afterwards, her head in the crook of his arm, he said, looking at the ceiling: 'This is HM Government Property, you know.'

'Is it?' she mumbled dozily. 'I take it what I've just had was yours.'

There was no more conversation. Davies remained happily awake, but Jemma quickly slept. After a while he began to think about Sergeant Emmanuel's brass-bound box.

9

'Rhubarb—' said Davies, making it sound like a long word. The remark was the first for some time above the lonely noise of the cutlery. Dinner at 'Bali Hi', Furtman Gardens, was often a muted feast. '—is at its best, I always think, at this time of year.'

Mrs Fulljames's mantled eyes came up from her plate. The eyes of Doris, his estranged wife, followed obediently. The schoolteacher, Minnie Banks, examined her rhubarb as if something had eluded her. Mod ate another spoonful of his.

Davies regarded in turn each half-person exposed above the table. 'A touch of frost, a bit of sooty London rain and a few slugs,' he continued, 'and what do you get – perfection.' He examined the length of rhubarb on his spoon, its strands hanging like the lifeboat davits of an abandoned ship.

'It's a shame it has to be cooked in such long dishes,' put in Mr Smeeton, the Home Entertainer. He guffawed silently above his pudding. Mod examined him with loathing.

'And the custard,' continued Davies, rolling a yellow avalanche from his spoon. 'Thick and glorious.'

'I hope you mean what you're saying, Mr Davies,'

102

muttered the landlady. 'Anybody who's not satisfied can move on at a week's notice.'

Davies appeared slowly shocked. 'I was most sincere, Mrs Fulljames,' he said.

'He *should* like the custard,' chortled Mr Smeeton. 'He's a policeman. He takes people into custard-y!' He almost choked on that one. Mod said: 'Good God.'

Davies finished his rhubarb and wiped his mouth on his handkerchief, a Christmas present from the cleaning lady at the police station. Leaning over the table he said: 'I bet you've wowed a few over Christmas and New Year, Mr Smeeton.'

'Thirteen separate functions, ten for the old folks,' replied the entertainer with brisk pleasure.

'Had them laid out in the aisles, throttled by their own corsets, I bet.'

'Mr Smeeton,' put in the landlady stonily, 'does wonderful work for charity.'

'Hmmm,' said Mod. 'The Euthanasia Society.'

'Really!' exclaimed Doris. 'It's a pity some others don't get off their backsides and do some good.' She glared at Mod. Miss Banks said: 'Back to school next week. Another term.'

Nobody had anything to add to that. An armed silence dropped over the table. Doris, like someone who had been lying undecidedly in ambush, broke it. 'You've been seen,' she said up the table towards her husband.

His eyebrows went up over the custard. 'I wouldn't argue with that,' he said. 'I'm not The Invisible Man.'

'Let me finish,' she said tartly. 'You've been seen – with a dark woman.'

103

Davies looked askance around the table. 'What other revelations are we going to have tonight?' he inquired. He leaned again across the cloth. 'Women, Mrs Davies,' he said heavily, 'come either dark or fair, with a few ginger ones thrown in.' He concentrated his gaze on his wife's starved head.

'Mine is Titian,' she replied haughtily. 'And the dark woman was dark all over – a darkie in other words.'

Davies thought he heard the eyelids of Mrs Fulljames click up once more. He continued to look in the direction of his wife. 'That,' he said, 'is enough to have you nicked under the Race Relations Act.'

'She's a darkie,' said Doris defiantly. 'No Race Relations Act is going to alter that. It won't whiten her.'

'I don't know why I should bother to reply to this slander,' Davies said. 'Let's say she's a friend.'

He left the table. Mod rose and went with him from the room.

'Going to The Babe?' he asked casually.

'Inquiries,' said Davies, 'of a certain nature.'

'Oh, I see. Well, give her my regards. I'm busy tonight anyway. Radio Four. Ibsen. *Peer Gynt*.'

'Oh good,' said Davies. He went out of the front door and walked along the echoing street. Christmas and the New Year had emptied them. When he reached Jemma's door he rang; she called through and released the safety lock. The deep aroma of cooking filled the passageway. Jemma came to the inner door and kissed him.

'Where's Mod?' she asked. 'Gone to the pub?' Sizzling came from the kitchen.

'Not Wednesday,' he said, his nose wrinkling. 'There's something on the radio he wants to hear.'

'*Peer Gynt*,' she nodded. 'I was going to listen but somebody turned up. A fugitive. Mrs Wan from the Chinese take-away. Her husband's threatened to chop her head off.'

'So she's staying here.'

'Just for tonight. Tomorrow, she says, her brother will come and he'll chop her husband's head off.'

'Better examine your next take-away,' said Davies. He took off his overcoat and kissed her properly. 'You're lovely,' she said. 'Lovely.'

'You're not so bad yourself,' said Davies. He sniffed. 'She's certainly doing something miraculous.'

'Have you eaten?'

'Well, eating at "Bali Hi", Furtman Gardens, doesn't count. We had rhubarb. Like eating firewood.'

'There'll be plenty,' said Jemma.

He looked at her. 'I came to have another peep at Lofty's things,' he said, almost shamefaced.

'Now?' she asked.

'I'd like to.'

'Right. I don't think she's ready yet.'

'Not ready yet,' Mrs Wan called from the kitchen.

Jemma fetched Lofty's belongings. From the biscuit tin Davies took the wooden box. 'This,' he said. 'This is what I was thinking about. After seeing Sergeant Emmanuel's box. Remember?'

'Not while . . . you know . . . we were . . .?'

'No. God no. Afterwards. Post-coital.'

She smiled. 'We should do it more often. If it helps you think.'

'Depends how full the cells are,' said Davies. He

held the box, turning it lightly in his hands. 'All that work in Emmanuel's box made me think of it. The brass and everything. Have you got a screwdriver? These screws are buried right down.'

'Several,' she said. 'When you live alone you find you need screwdrivers.' She went into the kitchen and returned with a plastic cutlery tray from which she took three screwdrivers. Davies selected one. His eyes tightened as he pushed it into the rounded recess. 'It's a lovely bit of work, this box,' he said. 'Made by a craftsman.'

As he eased the screw away from its burrow the Chinese woman came from the kitchen and watched him. 'Good box,' she said.

The screw gradually came free. 'Look at that,' said Davies. 'Just look at that – it's made of wood.'

Walter Pitt, the undertaker, was busy, as he often carefully phrased it, with a customer. As Davies came through the street door and the bell jangled, Walter called out: 'With you in a minute.' His small businesslike face quickly fulfilled the promise.

'Ah, it's you, Dangerous,' he said. 'Come on through.'

Davies did not enjoy going into the back of the premises, but Walter solicitously closed a coffin lid as he did so. Then he opened it again to retrieve his glasses. There was the overwhelming sweetness of French polish and flowers.

Walter had a long reputation for decency and fair prices. He was absently polishing the casket to which he had been attending and now, disconcertingly, he half-lifted the lid as if to be assured that the occupant was still there. To Davies's relief he closed it again. 'Lost my pen now,' he explained. 'I'm always doing it. Between you and me, Dangerous, there's quite a few of my ball-points gone where I'll never be able to get them back. And three pairs of glasses.'

There was a small green-clothed table in the room, at the side, upon which was a tray set with cups, a teapot, sugar and milk. The undertaker poured two cups. 'We're pretty busy,' he said. 'You'd be surprised how many people hang on for a few more days over Christmas and the New Year. First and second week of January, it's quite lively.'

'Bit like the sales,' suggested Davies.

'In a way,' said Walter. 'People sometimes struggle into another year, anyway.' He looked up. 'Is there anything I can do for you, Dangerous, or did you just drop in?'

'There is, actually, Walter,' said Davies. He rummaged in his overcoat pocket and brought out an envelope from which he took the screw from Lofty Brock's box. 'Ever seen one of these?' He handed it to the undertaker.

A small light came into Walter's face. 'Now just look at that,' he said, turning the screw in his fingers. 'Wood, and beautifully made.' He turned it happily just below his nose, emitting little hums of approval. He looked up. 'Lovely job,' he said.

'Ever seen one before?' asked Davies. 'I thought if anyone would know it would be you.'

'Thank you, Dangerous,' said Walter graciously. 'But I can't say I have.' He held out his palm and rolled the screw to and fro. 'It must be for a very special purpose,' he said. 'Or it *was*, because it seems to be some years old.'

'Not just to use in keeping a box together?'

'Well, if it were a very special box, I suppose so. But it's finely made, turned, and it's good as new. You could use it now.' His fingers tested the screw. 'It's very hard,' he said. 'Well turned.' He looked up at Davies. 'Is finding out a matter of urgency?' he inquired.

'The sooner the better,' said Davies. 'It came from a small cabinet. A box. There were twelve used altogether.'

'Well, if you don't mind me keeping it for a short while, I could make some inquiries in the wood-working fraternity. Someone might know.' Once more he rolled the screw on his palm, beginning again his pleased hum. 'They don't make things like this,' he said. 'Not these days.'

Miss Honoria Gladstone, late of HM Prison Service, lived in Bedfordshire, a small castellated building with tight windows and a heavy studded door.

'It was the lodge once,' she explained. 'The gatehouse to the estate, but it looked so much like a minor prison that I purchased it at once. After a lifetime's work in places of confinement, it's rather appropriate and comforting.'

Davies ducked below the threshold of the front door and followed her, almost at a crouch, along a damp and diminishing corridor to a cell-like room piled and lined with books and papers. A desk towards the lancet windows was contained in a crater between the overwhelming paraphernalia.

'The work continues,' enthused the old lady. '*Girls Behind Bars* is my current labour.' She put her surprisingly gentle hand on his sleeve and her powerful eyes gleamed through her dense spectacles. 'There are not many people doing this work today, you know,' she said with a fierceness that made him blink. 'Fortunately,' she added.

She pushed her way towards the desk, advancing through the alleys of literature like someone in a maze. A tower of periodicals slithered to the ground and Davies bent ineffectually, first to stop the avalanche and then to pick it up.

'Don't bother, don't bother!' exclaimed Miss Gladstone. 'Next year's work, that is – *Paying the Price: The Crimes and Punishments of Women*.' She pointed vaguely: 'There's a chair somewhere under that lot.'

Davies went to the area she had indicated and burrowed below books until he unearthed an upright wooden chair. On the chair was a flat tabby cat.

'Ah,' said Miss Gladstone. 'That's where you got to.' She waved a satin hand at the tabby. 'Come on, Holloway,' she urged. 'Move your rump.'

The cat yawned and slithered away. 'Sometimes,' mentioned the old lady, 'even food won't bring her out of hiding. She's a born fugitive.' The remark provoked her to jot a note on a pad. Davies, pushing aside further books, eventually sat on the chair.

'I cannot think what further use I may be to you,' said Miss Gladstone, looking like an eagle over the desk. 'I kept your photograph, of course, and I've given it thought, but although I am an authority, *the* authority, on British Women's Prisons, that does not mean to indicate an ability to recognize individual denizens.'

'As you know I had some copies of the photograph made,' he said, 'before I gave you the original picture at the Christmas party. I've had one copy blown up.' He took it out from an envelope. 'There's one thing that has come to light with the enlargement, although it's not very much.'

He produced the picture, now eight inches by twelve, and passed it across to the elderly lady. 'Hmm, she's no beauty, is she,' commented Miss Gladstone. 'She would never have been a member of the sewing circle.' She glanced up. 'A special clique of prisoners,' she explained.

Davies leaned forward. 'The thing that has come out by enlarging the photograph,' he said, his finger pointed to the top right-hand corner, 'is this bit here. If you look carefully, there is faint sunlight coming through some sort of leaded window, in the shape of a curve. You can just make it out.'

'Chelmsford,' said Miss Gladstone firmly. 'Circa 1935–37. They took the prisoner pictures in the chapel.'

He pushed the door of the CID Room open with such bad-tempered force that he knocked Detective Constable Sanderson off a chair he was using to reach his tennis racquet, which he kept hidden on top of a cupboard.

'Oh God, sorry, Sandy,' said Davies, righting the chair and then the policeman. 'I'm bloody livid, that's all.'

'Your two villains,' guessed Sanderson, examining a broken string in the racquet. 'They got off.'

'They might as well have done,' growled Davies. He picked up three darts and hurled them violently at the dartboard. 'Mag . . . i . . . bloody . . . strates!' he said, flinging each one with emphasis. All three missed the board. He sat down bulkily. 'Six months – suspended,' he said. 'Six months is bad enough. When the silly old sod said "suspended", I nearly ran over and throttled him.'

'You'd have got fifteen years for that,' forecast Sanderson. 'They conjured up a defence, did they?'

Davies's eyes bulged. 'A defence? Jesus Christ, listen to this. They said the old lady attacked *them first!*'

That smote even Sanderson. 'Attacked *them!*' he said unbelievingly. 'How old is she? Seventy-five?'

'Seventy-eight,' said Davies, grinding his teeth. 'Two bleeding eighteen-year-olds, and they say that she attacked them first.'

He put his head in his hands and, looking down, saw for the first time the note on his desk. 'Oh, I took that,' remembered Sanderson. 'Hampstead nick. They've got Shiny Bright. He wants to speak to you. Says he has information, whatever that may mean.'

'Hampstead? Shiny?' wondered Davies. 'Bit rarified for him.' He looked up the number and dialled it.

'Bright,' said the sergeant at the other end. 'Know him?'

'Fairly frequently,' said Davies. 'What's he nicked for?'

'Breaking and entering. Trod on the watch-dog.'

'That sounds like Shiny. And he wants to see me?'

'Wants to grass about something or other. Thinks he'll get off with a smacked hand. Are you interested?'

'I'll come over. Don't let him escape.'

'That won't happen. Somehow the cell was left open and he managed to lock himself in.'

Bright looked like an apprehensive boy seated behind the table in the charge room.

'Now, Shiny, what's all this?' asked Davies, pulling a chair to the other side of the table. 'I hope you haven't brought me all this way to say you're sorry.'

'I'm sorry, all right, Dangerous,' said the small criminal. 'Sorry I trod on the bleedin' dog. Bit the arse out of my trousers.'

'Hard luck. You shouldn't break into people's houses. They'll put you away again, and the nice weather is coming.'

'I got information, Dangerous.' Bright sat up hopefully, his eyes shining. 'Maybe I'll get off light.'

Davies leaned forward. 'You know I can't make promises, Shiny. Not of that nature. On the other hand, I know a few magistrates who'll give you a few quid from the poor box and have the dog destroyed.' His head thrust further over the table. 'What information?'

'Well, you know when you was fishing the pram out of the canal. Couple of months ago. Lofty Brock's pram.'

112

'Yes,' said Davies slowly. 'What about it?'

'Well, I got some information about that.'

Davies leaned further. 'What, Shiny?'

'The night Lofty went into the canal . . .'

'October 6th,' said Davies.

'Right you are. Well, I was trying to do a little job in one of them workshops along there, by the canal. The place where they do the clocks.'

'Yes . . . Shurrock's . . .'

'That's it . . . Well, I nosed about for a bit. It was all quiet. About eleven-thirty, I know because I got 'ome in time for the *Open University*. For a start, I couldn't get into the place. Locked tight and barred. Then on the off-chance I tried the front door and, blow me, it opened. Just easy, like that. So I'm in, ain't I? I reckoned they might have some loose around in the desks, so I 'ad a rummage but I didn't find nothing.' He looked questioningly at Davies.

'No break-in was reported, Shiny,' said Davies, as calmly as he could. 'Now, you saw something, didn't you?'

'You're right, Dangerous, and that's what I want to tell you about. Will all this be taken into consideration when I come up, Dangerous?'

'Tell me what you saw, Shiny.'

'Cars. Two or three cars on that bit of road and lights. Doors opening and suchlike. I couldn't tell exact where. I was in a state because I thought it was the law. I don't know how many people either, because I was keeping low, wasn't I. Then I heard a gurgling.'

Davies felt his eyebrows go up. 'A gurgling?'

'Like somebody being strangled. I looked out and

113

saw this bloke bash another bloke on the 'ead with summat. Blimey, I nearly wet myself. What have I got myself into now, I thought.'

'Did you see them? What were they like?'

'Only like shadows, Dangerous. I couldn't see much. Then there was another sort of row going on. Voices, but not English. You know that wire gate at the bottom of the little road, by the canal. I'd climbed over that myself. But now I 'eard it bein' opened, and then some running and a shout like somebody was dead scared. After, when I 'eard about Lofty Brock I thought it could be 'im. Because there was a splash, Dangerous. Somebody went in the water . . .'

Davies stared at Bright. 'Honest,' said the small man. 'I ain' making it up.'

'What happened next?'

'I 'id. I 'id like I've never 'id before. Cor, I reckoned they'd 'ear my ticker banging. I was dead scared. I just got down and stayed there under the window until I 'eard the cars drive off. It was only about five minutes. Then I waited a bit more and poked my 'ead up. They'd all gone. Everything was dark and all quiet. So I got up, shut the door locked behind me and climbed over the fence and went 'ome.'

Davies said: 'And you failed to report this to the police?'

Bright's hurt little eyes came up from the table. 'I'm telling you now, Dangerous,' he said.

'Hello, Mr Shurrock. It's me. Back again.' Davies sat down heavily at the desk. Adrian Shurrock, startled as a rabbit, regarded him from the other side.

'Mr Davies,' he said. 'So you are. What brings you to these parts?'

'Same old thing,' said Davies. 'What the police call "certain inquiries". How's the dramatics?'

'Oh . . . the amateur dramatics. Well, funnily enough, we did *An Inspector Calls* just before Christmas. It was very well received.'

Davies laughed bulkily. 'Can't say I've risen to the heights of inspector yet, Mr Shurrock, but I've certainly called.' He leaned forward. 'It's about the old man who died in the canal,' he confided. 'October 6th last year, remember?'

'Yes, of course. But . . . you're still on that?'

'Some cases, unfortunately, make slow progress. A meagre little bit at a time.' He produced his notebook and importantly licked the end of a thick pencil, bringing a glint of apprehension into the eyes of the wispy young man.

'I told you all I know,' he said like a plea.

'Did you, now,' said Davies. 'Have you got a couple of minutes to go over it again?'

'We're very busy,' said Shurrock. He looked sideways and rose to make certain his office door was closed. 'But if it helps.'

'I'm sure it will,' said Davies, trying to read his own writing in his notebook. 'Now, when I came to see you before, you told me that you'd never had a break-in at these premises.' Shurrock's underfed moustache began to quiver like the whiskers of a mouse.

'I told you we have a security watch,' he said nervously.

'That's not the question,' pursued Davies. 'Have you had any break-ins? You told me you hadn't.' He

115

bent confidingly. 'Now, I don't think you were telling me the truth. I think you had a break-in on the very night we're talking about – to wit, October 6th. I even know what time it was – eleven-thirty, because the burglar was home in time for *Open University*.'

Shurrock's white face became blotched with pink. 'All right, all right, there was,' he said. 'But to start with, I didn't even know it was a break-in. Things had been disturbed, drawers left open, but there were no signs of forcible entry.'

'That's because you left the front door open,' Davies pointed out.

Shurrock put his fingers to his face. 'Oh, God, did I?' he said. 'That's what happened. It was all locked up in the morning.'

'The burglar locked up after him.'

'Yes, yes, I see now.' He looked over the thin tops of his fingers, a little defiantly. 'But there's no *law* which says you have to report a break-in, is there? Not if you don't want to?'

Davies wasn't sure. 'Why didn't you want to?' he asked instead. 'Why did you lie to me when I asked?'

'I had my reasons,' said Shurrock. He got up and looked out of the bleak window like a prisoner. 'My father owns this company and he thinks I'm useless. He once referred to me in public as a whining shit and then said he meant a shining wit. Everybody pissed themselves laughing. I'm only here because he *has* to employ me – my mother says so.'

Davies rocked his head and tutted. 'So when you made a mistake, like letting burglars in, you daren't tell him.'

'He'd crucify me. I'd be out on my neck.' He looked weak and lost. 'I'd have nowhere to go. Not at anything like the money I get here. I couldn't tell him. God, we had a fire here and he put that down to my carelessness, which I suppose it was, and then a whole consignment of stuff went missing, vanished, never to be found again, and that was down to me too. This time would have been the last.'

Sighing, Davies stood up. 'You might like to know that omitting to report the crime, and covering up when I asked you, has set back my inquiries several months.' Loudly he shut his notebook.

'I'm sorry, Mr Davies. Life gets very difficult, doesn't it?'

'I'll say it does.' He went towards the door.

'That's it then?' said the young man. 'I won't hear any more?'

'I'm not promising anything,' Davies told him. He went out. 'Don't forget to lock up,' he said.

At Blissen Ltd Pharmaceuticals, there was a different girl at the desk. She was arranging her eyebrows before leaving for the day.

'Just off home?' said Davies.

'Five o'clock,' she replied firmly. She was plump and plain. Davies tried to see what she had been doing to her eyebrows.

'Is Mrs Harrer still here?' he inquired.

'Oh, I'll say,' said the girl contemptuously. Davies thought she was probably leaving at the end of the week. 'And him, Mr Harrison.'

'Good. Could you tell them Mr Davies is here?'

'Can't,' said the girl. 'She's on the phone. She grunts away for hours. I'm off at five.'

'You said.'

'Why don't you just go up. He's up there. Old half-baked.'

Davies thanked her gravely and wished her well in her new job wherever it was. 'Who told you?' she asked.

He went along the corridor. At the foot of the stairs he paused and called up politely. A grey man with an oblong jaw appeared. 'Who is it?' he inquired sharply. 'We are closing.'

'Mr Harrison?' said Davies, heavily mounting the stairs. 'How was Las Palmas?'

The man was nonplussed. 'Las Palmas? It's months since I was in Las Palmas. Who are you?'

'I'm a policeman. Detective Constable Davies,' said Davies, showing his warrant card like a conjurer showing an ace of spades. 'I won't keep you long.'

He heard the telephone replaced in the next office, and the huge Mrs Harrer loomed in the corridor. She seemed even bigger than when he had last seen her. She had to move sideways along the passage.

'Good evening, madam,' said Davies. 'You remember I called previously, when Mr Harrison was in Las Palmas.'

'Ja, of course,' said the woman suspiciously. 'And now you are here again. Something else this time?'

Davies shook his head. 'No, no. Same old thing.'

'What's it about?' asked Harrison. He turned from

one to the other as if expecting a simultaneous answer.

'It was a drunk man fallen in the canal,' said Mrs Harrer. 'I told you.'

'Oh, that.' He peered at Davies. 'That was months ago,' he said. 'You'd better come in. It gets crowded in these corridors.'

Davies caught the fat woman's scowl as she lumbered into the office. When the three of them were seated there was no room for another person.

'It takes the English police a long time to solve their unimportant mysteries,' said Mrs Harrer. She had rolled herself behind the desk and Harrison had sat in a chair beside it.

Davies spread his hands. 'Ages, sometimes,' he agreed.

'What did all this have to do with us, this company?' demanded Harrison. 'I can't remember anything about it, except that it was a tramp who fell in the canal.'

'Nothing,' admitted Davies, 'except that it happened just outside.'

'But wasn't it at night?'

'Yes it was.'

'There is no person here at night,' put in Mrs Harrer thickly. 'So I told you before.'

'Quite so. But do you have deliveries here late sometimes? Vehicles arriving after dark.'

Harrison was astonished. 'Not at all,' he said. 'Our deliveries always arrive in daylight. We don't have staff to unload otherwise.'

'If I remember . . .' said Davies. He paused to study his notebook. 'You mainly act as a distribution centre for deliveries of pharmaceuticals from the Continent.'

'That's almost all we do.'

'How do they get here, these deliveries?'

'All sorts of ways they come,' put in Mrs Harrer impatiently. 'Across the Channel or sometimes by air.'

'Generally Heathrow?'

'Not at all,' said Harrison. 'Heathrow, Gatwick, Birmingham.'

'And the ferries?'

Harrison was beginning to show ill-temper. 'Dover, Weymouth and others. But I don't see what this has got to do with a tramp falling in the damned canal.'

Davies shut his book. 'Neither do I, frankly,' he confessed. 'Well, I'll be going.' He stood up. 'It's just that we had a report of some vehicles in the service road, just outside, on the night in question.' He regarded them both. 'But you wouldn't know about that?'

'Not at all,' said Harrison. 'Business is done in business hours here. If there were vehicles outside, then they had nothing to do with this company. I'm afraid you're wasting all our time.'

'It looks like it,' said Davies. He got up apologetically.

'That's not to say there weren't vehicles on the road,' said Harrison. 'For all I know there may have been. There's supposed to be a security man on duty. Ask him.'

'Ha,' said Mrs Harrer. 'He is stupid.'

*

Davies had rarely seen – even in an era of traffic wardens and British Rail porters – a body more unsuited to uniform than that of the security man who had just appeared for duty at the gatehouse of the industrial area. He was young, short and scant, with a shining chin and round, rimless glasses. He had a big hat and a brown tunic. He looked, Davies thought, like a member of the Hitler Youth.

His manner, however, was inoffensive. 'I always wanted to be in the police,' he confided. 'Unfortunately, the height wasn't there.'

'Yes,' said Davies vaguely. 'There is a minimum.'

'You wouldn't think I was perfect for *this* job,' the man went on. 'Physically, I mean. But I can *shout*. My voice carries.' Outside the gatehouse, it was the end of the February afternoon, damp and calm. Lights streamed along the road.

'Let's see,' said Davies, opening his notebook. 'According to your employers, you were on duty here on the night of October 6th last year.' He read from his notes: 'Edwin Francis Curl.'

'That's when the old man went into the canal,' said the security man without hesitation. 'Yes, that's me. They asked me about it when you were making inquiries before.' He squinted through his glasses. 'Taking a long time to find out about it, isn't it?' he said.

Davies sighed. 'It's on the steady side,' he answered. 'But we've established that you were the man on duty here.'

'Right. It was a weekday, so I must have been. I've been on this job since August.'

'You get here at five.'

121

'Yes. Straight from work.'

'And you leave at eight in the morning . . . What d'you mean, *straight from work*?'

Curl looked embarrassed. 'I shouldn't have said that, should I,' he admonished himself. 'Silly thing to say.' He looked pleadingly at Davies. 'Do you have to tell them?'

'I don't see why,' shrugged Davies. 'What's your day job then?'

'I'm a security man,' answered Curl. 'For another firm. Blue uniform. A better lot than this. Naturally, you have to keep awake all day because it's mostly what we call scrutinizing – keeping check on people going in and out of buildings and that.'

'So you get some sleep at night?'

'Well, I have to. This job is a bit of a steal. Once the gate's closed. I can get my head down after midnight. Look . . .' He reached into a canvas holdall. 'I bring my own Lilo.'

'Aren't you supposed to check in every hour or so?' asked Davies.

'And my alarm clock,' said Curl, producing it in a pleased way.

'Oh, yes. I see.'

'They're not much of a security firm, this bunch,' confided the small brown-shirted man. 'Some very unsuitable types working for them. People with criminal records . . .'

'Have you got one?' asked Davies swiftly.

'Me? Oh . . . well, I used to have a bit of trouble . . . horses and greyhounds and that. I might as well tell you because you only have to look me up on your computer, don't you?'

'It's easy,' said Davies. 'When do you get time to eat?'

Curl spread his neat hands. 'When I can,' he said. 'I have to admit I do sneak off to the fish and chip shop.'

'What time?'

'Oh, usually about nine.'

'Did you that night? October 6th?'

'I can't remember, but I probably did. I have a different sort of fish every night.'

'On that night could you have been absent between say, ten-thirty and eleven-thirty?'

'The fish shop shuts at ten.' His hairless face became abruptly wrinkled. Behind the bare glasses, his eyes pleaded. 'Don't tell them if you don't have to. I need the money, Mr Davies, I've got three women.'

'Three!'

'You know how one thing leads to another.'

There was a movement at the door. Davies turned. Williams, the manager of the safe company, was handing over a key from the window of his car. His expression solidified when he saw Davies. 'More trouble?' he said.

'Same lot,' said Davies.

'Christ! Not the old man with the pram!'

'Still him. I was going to come and see you. But you're off home now.'

'Yes, I am.' The security man took the key from him and operated the rising gate.

'Could I have your home number? I'd like to give you a call some time.'

Williams scowled. 'Well . . . I don't see . . . oh, all right. It's in the book anyway.'

Davies wrote down the figures as he dictated them. Williams turned without saying anything further, and drove through the gate.

'He wasn't all that pleased, was he,' observed Curl. Another car drew up outside the gatehouse. Davies could see Mrs Harrer glinting at him through the passenger window. Harrison was driving. He went down the two steps to them. The big woman lowered the window. 'Overtime you work,' she observed sourly.

'Devotion to duty,' Davies smiled brokenly. 'I wonder if I could bother you both for your home telephone numbers.'

'Why is this?' demanded the woman. The German in her voice thickened. 'What is this business?'

'I might need to call you after hours,' he said pleasantly.

'Mine's here, on my card,' said Harrison impatiently, handing the card across. After a moment's hesitation, Mrs Harrer gave him a card. 'Mine also. Do not ring when it is not convenient.'

Curl operated the gate and waved as the car jerked out into the traffic. 'You really upset people, don't you,' he observed, returning to the gatehouse.

Confidingly, Davies said: 'Let me give you a professional tip, Edwin lad. It might come in useful. People don't like being asked for their home phone numbers. It worries them, upsets them.'

'I see,' said Curl. 'I wouldn't mind that Mrs Harrer's number. I really fancy her.' He looked a little ashamed at Davies. 'All my women are big,' he mumbled.

Davies said: 'I'd like to take a wander around all the premises on this site.'

'Now?'

'Now. By myself.'

'Yes, well, it's all right, I suppose. I mean, if I can't trust you, who can I trust?'

10

The many colours, creeds and cultures wedged into that north-western corner of London had over the years borrowed a little of each other's life, and nowhere was this more apparent than in the restaurant owned by Monsieur François Ramchand who came from Auroville near Pondicherry in what was once French India, and who had been trained as a chef in Calcutta, Paris and Hendon. It was called Côte du Ganges.

It was Monday night and there was a table available, big enough for eating the house curry and for spreading out the cards which Mod had brought with him. They were library index cards and upon each of them Mod had printed the scanty clues.

'It's like Happy Families,' summed up Davies pessimistically. Jemma said: 'Except nobody fits anywhere.'

They shuffled and tried again, and again, but no sequence emerged; no connection was apparent. 'Unless,' said Mod ponderously, 'we put this one with this . . .' He rearranged the sequence. '. . . and this one with this. This gives us the story that Mrs Harrer had a father who was a guard at the prisoner-of-war camp in Silesia . . .'

'She's like a mountain,' said Davies thoughtfully. 'The Jungfrau.'

'And her father,' continued Mod, 'murdered the real Lofty Brock, and became a bosom pal of Sergeant-Major Bing and then lived happily ever after at Clacton-on-Sea, curing his coughs with Doctor Collis Browne's Mixture.'

Moodily, Davies tapped the card upon which was written: 'A present from Clacton-on-Sea'. 'The cow cream jug and Chelmsford Prison, thirty miles apart, are the only links of any sort. The rest . . .' He scattered the cards over the table. '. . . don't add up at all. We've got the prison picture of the nameless lady. But all the records of Chelmsford Women's Prison were destroyed by a German bomb in the war . . .'

'. . . Dropped by the Jungfrau's Luftwaffe uncle,' mentioned Mod.

Mod gathered up his cards, they left the restaurant and went into the windy street. It was March now and moonlit, and the steam from the power station cooling towers blew like long silver hair in the sky. Mod trundled to The Babe In Arms and Davies walked Jemma home.

'Have you thought of the possibility that none of it *does* add up?' suggested Jemma, putting her coated arm into his.

'You mean that I'm *making up* a mystery, a case with no crime; I'm playing at being a big detective when I'm only a small one,' he said gloomily. 'You've been talking to Mod.'

'Since the art of detection is logic,' she pursued, 'would you not agree that Lofty Brock might have had an interesting, even a criminal past without it necessarily catching up with him on the canal tow-path that night? Perhaps, for all his secrets, he just fell in.'

'He *wasn't* Lofty Brock,' Davies pointed out grumpily. 'He was somebody else. He became Lofty Brock in the prison camp – for reasons of his own.'

'That, as you were told by the old soldier, happened in any number of cases. Men took advantage of the confusion to disappear and reappear as somebody else.'

'Shiny Bright,' said Davies doggedly, 'saw and heard something by the canal that night.'

She pouted. 'Shiny Bright,' she observed, 'is scarcely reliable.'

'Somewhere,' said Davies, plodding on at her side, 'there's an answer. There's something smelly in that trading estate. I had a good look around.'

'People don't like being investigated,' she pointed out firmly. 'They get anxious, they do odd things, they look at you in a funny way. That doesn't mean they're murderers. What would happen if Harrison and Harrer, or Shurrock or Williams, went to your superiors and complained about harassment?'

'Don't,' mumbled Davies, closing his eyes. '*Don't.*' He stumbled on a broken paving stone. They were almost at her door. She turned and quietly wrapped her arms about him. 'You're like Don Quixote,' she said. 'Perhaps fighting imaginary wrongs.'

He glared at her, but his expression melted at her smile. 'Maybe you're right,' he sighed. 'I'm really cut out for the detection of petty pilfering.' His head went against her chest. 'Have you got any lodgers?' he asked.

'Not tonight,' she smiled. 'There is a vacancy for bed-and-breakfast.'

They kissed and he said, 'Thanks.' They went into the passage as the telephone rang. She picked up the receiver. 'Okay,' she eventually said. 'If I can help . . .'

She turned to see him crestfallen. He stood against the wallpaper in the passage. 'It's all right,' she assured him. 'I think it's being taken care of. It's a gypsy family.'

'Oh,' said Davies. 'Perhaps they'll bring their horse.'

'Shut up,' she laughed, walking into the room. 'Why don't you get us a drink.'

He watched her go into the bedroom. There was half a bottle of Scotch on the sideboard, and he poured out two glasses and added water. She came back in a pale robe. He handed her the Scotch and they drank and embraced. 'It's getting towards bedtime,' she said.

'Right,' he agreed. 'The gypsies may turn up any minute.'

She giggled again and turned into the bedroom. Putting her glass down, she began to take off his pullover, shirt and tie. 'I'll do the next bit,' he said, unlooping his braces. 'Get an eyeful of these.'

He let his heavy grey trousers fall and stood posed in his long johns.

'Blue!' exclaimed Jemma. 'And not baggy.'

'Skiers wear them,' said Davies proudly. 'So the man said.'

He sat on the bed and, pushing her away a little, he provocatively began to peel down the elongated underpants while whistling the refrain of 'The Stripper' through his teeth, revolving his eyes, rolling the blue flannel down each ashen leg until he finally flicked them off with his big toe.

'Oh, Dangerous!' Jemma collapsed laughing across the bed. Her pale robe fell open as she arched one of her legs. He climbed up beside her and embraced her. 'You're so funny, Dangerous,' she said, her voice trailing off.

'And you,' he said seriously, 'are so beautiful. You're like winning a gold clock.' Their arms went about each other. The telephone rang.

'The raggle-taggle gypsies-o,' chanted Davies.

'Leave it,' she said. 'Let them ring back.'

He kissed her softly. 'Answer it,' he sighed. 'They'll hate being kept waiting.'

Keeping her eyes on him she picked up the receiver from the bedside table. 'It's for you,' she said, handing it across. 'It's Mod.'

'Dangerous,' said Mod. 'I'm in The Babe. Are you busy?'

'No, not at all,' answered Davies. 'I was just getting bored.'

'The undertaker, Wally Pitt, has been in looking for you. He's found out about the wooden screw.'

Davies sat up. 'He has? What does he say?'

'He didn't. He wants to tell you.'

'Right. I'll . . .' He glanced at the naked Jemma. 'I'll ring him in the morning. Thanks, Mod.'

He replaced the phone. 'Wally Pitt . . .' he began.

'I know, I heard,' said Jemma. She began to laugh again. 'God help me,' she said. 'The last thing I want to hear about now is a wooden screw.'

*

130

'Wally?'

'This is Walter Pitt, Funeral Directors.'

'Is Wally, Mr Pitt, there? It's Detective Constable Davies.'

'From the police?'

'Er . . . yes.'

'I'll get him. He's with a customer.'

Davies was alone in the CID room. A thin shaft of spring sun sidled through the dusty window. Davies moved his backside to meet it, manoeuvring until it fell wanly upon his face.

'Dangerous, it's Wally.'

'Oh, hello Wally. Sorry to call when you're busy.'

'It will wait, Dangerous. It often will in this business. I think I've had some joy about that strange wooden screw.'

'So I hear. What is it?'

'I still don't know myself. But there's somebody who can certainly help you out. We had one of our quarterly get-togethers, just the trade. We have a sort of quiz – a question-and-answer session – and I took the wooden screw with me, showed it around, and asked if they'd seen anything like it before. Now I thought, naturally, that if anyone knew the answer, it would be on the cabinet-making side of things. But a burials chap from Paddington, Ben Phipps, said he remembered his father, who was in the business before him, having several of these screws. As far as Ben remembered, they fell out of a corpse.'

Davies felt his own mouth fall open. 'A corpse?' he repeated. 'They fell out?'

'That's what he said. He couldn't remember much more about it. It was years ago.'

131

'Thanks,' said Davies. 'It's something anyway. I'm not sure what.'

'I had a think about it when I got home,' went on the undertaker. 'And I believe there's a chap who might give you some more on it. He came to one of our meetings too. Last year. Gave us a talk on the Black Death. His name is Kinlock, Dr Christopher Kinlock. He's a medical historian. He lives somewhere in the docks area – the bit they've all smartened up. You should be able to find him all right.'

Dr Kinlock himself answered the door. There was an oddly shaped knocker. 'This house,' he said, 'was used by an apothecary two hundred years ago. I'm very pleased to have it now.' He indicated the curved steel knocker. 'That,' he said proudly, 'is a third-generation artificial hip, a prosthesis; makes a wonderful bit of door furniture, don't you think?'

Davies said uncertainly that he did. The doctor led the way through a panelled hall, beyond glass doors into a room where a gas fire was burning boldly.

Around the walls were showcases containing items of human anatomy. Davies could see a library through another door with an encased skeleton grinning at nothing. There were other skulls, bones and nameless things in jars. The death mask of a bald man occupied another container. 'Unusual room,' mentioned Davies, accepting the doctor's Scotch.

'An unusual facet of Dockland development,' smiled Kinlock. 'It's not all fancy former warehouses.' He was a small Scot with ginger eyebrows.

'It's been a fine opportunity to gather interesting specimens from medical history. I'm adding to it all the time. The death mask is of Mikhail Bakunin, the father of modern anarchy, one of only twelve made. One day, I would love to buy Napoleon's testicle.'

'That,' agreed Davies vaguely, 'would be worth having.'

'Now, you had a little poser for me,' said Kinlock. 'Not much of one because, even from your telephone conversation, I think I know what we are talking about.'

'These,' said Davies. He had taken a further two screws from Lofty's box and reclaimed the first from Walter Pitt. He held the three wooden screws out in the palm of his hand.

Kinlock picked up one with a musing smile. 'Cunningly made, aren't they,' he said. 'You'd have a job having something like this turned today. They needed to be the hardest wood, and of course, non-toxic.'

'What,' asked Davies, 'were they for?'

'Orthopaedic,' said Kinlock brightly. 'Screwing together bones.' He twisted one of the screws as he turned and led the way into the further room. From a shelf he eased a heavy red book and, perching a pair of rough glasses on the ridge of his nose, turned the big pages. 'Developed,' he paraphrased, 'in the nineteen twenties. A revolution in orthopaedic surgery.' Once more he twirled the wooden spiral. 'Cunning,' he said again.

Davies asked cautiously, 'How . . . common were they, at the time?'

'Not so very. It wasn't long before a stainless steel

133

screw was developed, obviously an advantage because this little lady was very finicky and very costly to make.' He looked quizzically at Davies. 'I have, incidentally, only a very vague idea why the Metropolitan Police should want to know. Is it very secret?'

'Not at all. I'm sorry. I could have explained it first.'

'Would you like another Scotch?'

'I would. I don't get down to the docks often.'

They returned to the other room and while they drank, Davies told Kinlock of Lofty and his box. The doctor shook his head: 'I've never heard of them being used in carpentry, I must say, but why not. It would be a somewhat expensive box, that's all.'

'Unless,' said Davies, 'you had the screws available and there was no further use for them. And you liked making boxes.'

'Ah, agreed. As I say, the practice was not wide-spread because the period of their use was relatively short and it was an expensive operation. Let's see who was in the bone-business at that time. Someone prominent who would be likely to be an innovator.' He rose again and Davies followed him once more to the library room. 'There were also fewer orthopaedic specialists in those days,' he said. 'Let us see.'

He took the same volume from the shelf. He read the entry again. 'There are some names here: Mr Bernard Helmer, Mr John Cope – Cope was a great character – Sir Thomas Hands, Sir Cyril Linder, Sir John Stanton.' He wrote the names in a pad as he said them. 'Now, let's cross-check in the medical *Who*

Was Who. They'll all be in there. I imagine they're all gone by now. You don't get to be Sir Cyril Linder until you're fifty – at least they didn't in those days.' He turned the pages. 'Cope,' he read. 'John Grey.' He moved the heavy book towards Davies. 'You read them,' he said. 'Something may occur to you.'

It was ten minutes before he reached the entry for Sir Cyril Linder. Then he read: 'Residence: Cape House, Frinton-on-Sea, Essex.' Then, later: 'Hobbies: natural history and archaeology, antiques, cabinet-making. President: Eastern England Archaeology Society. President: Essex Conservation Association. Life-President: The Prisoners' Rehabilitation Scheme.'

'That's him,' said Davies quietly. 'I think.'

'Splendid,' said Kinlock. 'I'm glad we found your man.' He left Davies to make detailed notes. Then they had a final Scotch. As they went to the door, Kinlock said diffidently: 'I wonder, when you have completed this matter, if I could have one of those wooden screws for the museum. I've never actually seen one before.'

'Take three,' said Davies, handing them to him. 'There's others in the box. You've been very helpful. You might as well have a set.'

A new singing season had begun and Jemma was rehearsing for a performance of 'Zadok The Priest' at an Easter choral festival in Cricklewood. She agreed to Kitty being moved temporarily into her flat and the great dog was soon sprawled contentedly across the armchair previously occupied by Edie, the scratching man and other itinerants. There had, however, been a rash of mini-burglaries and other time-consuming investigations in the division, and it was ten days before Davies could take enough time off to visit Frinton-on-Sea.

'Old-fashioned but exclusive,' recited Mod from the guide-book as they motored eastwards in the Vanguard.

'A bit like you,' said Davies. On the rear seat was a valise containing Lofty Brock's wooden box.

Cape House, the pre-War home of the surgeon Sir Cyril Linder, was now, according to telephone inquiries made by Mod, a small hotel. One of the family, however, Bernard Linder, Sir Cyril's son, retained a flat there.

The hotel was closed for the winter but Mr Linder had instructed them to persist with the doorbell. After they had been doing this, hunched in the spring rain, for several minutes, a long dressing-gowned figure could be discerned moving like a wraith among the interior glass doors.

There was a series of doors to unlock, and they watched him through the wet front panes as he did so. Eventually, he arrived directly before them, a blanched figure in a tall paisley dressing-gown. 'Sorry, sorry,' he said quite heartily once he had opened the door. 'Been waiting long? I normally don't get up until Easter.'

They followed him into the damp and empty reception area of the hotel. Last summer's postcards were curling in a rack, keys hung in dead rows. Most of the furniture was covered with drapes and the chairs in the glass-doored dining-room were standing on the tables as if they were afraid of the mice.

'You're seeing it at its best,' said Bernard Linder, waving his hand at the desolation. 'When the damned people arrive it's spoiled.' He grunted, almost to himself. 'Tennis racquets and brats.' He led them up the resounding main staircase.

'How long has it been a hotel?' asked Davies.

'Thirty years now,' said Linder with a shrug. 'At the beginning you did get a better type, but it's deteriorated sadly. I dread the coming of Easter. These days, I get out, away to France, as soon as I can. And I don't come back until October.' He opened a heavy panelled door. A thoughtful smile then crossed his face. 'After that, I have the place to myself.'

He led them into a large untidy flat with generous bay windows overlooking the expressionless sea. 'Sometimes in January,' he said, 'I sit in bed and just look out of the window for hours. I can't see any land, just sea, empty grey sea. Not a boat, sometimes. All I can hear of the outside world is the occasional traffic on the road, the bus that goes every hour to Clacton-on-Sea.'

They sat down and he brought them each a pale sherry. Davies thought of Colonel Ingate in his cascading house in Yorkshire. There was a lot of solitariness about. 'Sorry to have disturbed you,' he said.

'Not at all. It's time I was stirring anyway. It's almost March. You wanted to know something about my late father?'

Davies opened the valise and brought out Lofty Brock's wooden box. 'I was wondering if you would recognize this.'

137

Linder was astonished. 'Well, well,' he said, reaching out for it. 'Fancy. I never thought I would see one of these again.' He took it and turned it carefully. 'His wooden screw period,' he said.

'I wonder . . .' hesitated Davies, 'if you could tell us something about it.'

'Wherever did you get it?' asked Linder.

'An old man, who died last October in somewhat strange circumstances, had it in his possession. He had lived under an assumed name. I thought his box might give us some clue to his past and identity.'

'Really.' Linder looked up, his pale blue eyes cosseted by wrinkles. 'You do go to a lot of trouble in the police, don't you?'

Davies caught Mod's eye and coughed. 'We . . . we like to clear things up,' he said.

'But however did you trace the box here?' he asked. 'That's very clever, I must say.'

'All part of the job,' said Davies, swallowing modestly. 'It was the wooden screws. I discovered that your father was one of the surgeons who pioneered them in the twenties. Other aspects of the case pointed to this area – Clacton, Chelmsford Women's Prison.'

'Ah yes, I see. My father made a hobby of rehabilitating – or trying to rehabilitate – people who'd been in prison. He even employed some of them. I gather that the scheme was not entirely successful. Even as a schoolboy I was taught by the butler how to pick a lock.'

'That's very interesting,' said Davies, leaning forward.

'So is the box,' answered Linder. 'I used to have

several of these but I got rid of a lot of possessions when the hotel took over. There is just one I have left.' He rose and pedantically laid aside his sherry glass. 'When I was at school, I had a collection of insects. My father made cases for them. I have one left.' He went into the bedroom.

While he was out, Mod whispered: 'Don't you feel, Dangerous, that sometimes you are travelling down a dark road with no end to it.'

Davies nodded. 'I keep telling myself there's an end,' he whispered back.

Bernard Linder returned. 'It's been on the wall for years,' he said, holding out the small wooden frame. Davies took it and as he did so, one of the creatures pinned within dropped to the bottom of the case.

'Sorry,' he said with embarrassment. 'One of them has fallen down.'

'Don't worry,' said Linder. 'It's the damselfly. They become terribly frail. But, see how beautiful the frame is.'

Nodding, Davies turned the chamfered edges in his hands. He examined the joints. 'Wooden screws,' Linder said for him. 'I was about twelve at the time. I remember how pleased I was.'

'He always used these wooden orthopaedic screws?' asked Davies.

'And stainless steel,' added Linder smiling. 'There were lots of them around the place. I suppose he used to purloin them from the hospitals. And when the wooden screws went out of use, he came home with boxes of them.' He shook his head. 'He was a wonderful craftsman. He used to joke that being an orthopaedic surgeon was only like being a carpenter.

He made furniture, frames, all sorts of things, some of them quite exquisite, and he was always fashioning boxes of various sizes to give to people. He made writing boxes, modelled on those in Victorian times, and boxes for ladies – perfume, handkerchiefs and suchlike. Even tiny pill boxes. He said working like that kept his hand in, particularly later in his life when he suffered ill health.'

'You say that on occasions your father employed people who had been in prison,' said Davies.

'Yes, indeed. He was an old-fashioned idealist,' nodded Linder. 'He always wanted to give people another chance – a fair and square start, he used to say. Unfortunately, not all these people were as idealistic as he. There were some unfortunate results, thefts and that sort of thing. But he never lost his faith in human nature.'

'That's an achievement,' said Davies feelingly. As he spoke, he reached into his pocket, produced an envelope and from that took the prison photograph of the young woman. 'You would not by any chance recognize this person, would you, Mr Linder?' he said. He handed the picture across. Bernard Linder's pale face went tight. His hand went to his neck.

'Good God,' he said. 'Nanny.'

11

'"Prenderley, Mavis Anne. Convicted of Theft,"' read Mod. 'That's it, Dangerous.' He slammed the bulky index fiercely, sending a mushroom of dust against the low ceiling. Davies coughed and blinked, backing away against the steel racks in the basement of the County Library. 'Twenty-sixth of March, 1936,' said Mod. Eyes screwed behind his glasses, he progressed crabwise along the shelves. The newspaper files, tall, red-bound, gold-embossed, were drawn up in the dimness like an enchanted military parade, forgotten and layered with dust. 'There, this is it.'

He levered the heavy file from its slot among the others and carried it to a table beneath a low lamp. He blew the dust from the cover towards Davies, causing him to make another face and back away. Mod did not notice. He began to turn the big brown pages with a sound like the flapping of sails. 'March 12th, 19th . . . here we are, 26th. Now I can't remember which page it said.' Hopefully he regarded Davies. 'Have a look in the index, Dangerous. It's quite simple.'

'Even for me?' said Davies. He edged back along the narrow alleys between the metal shelves and picked out the tall volume.

'Got it!' exclaimed Mod from the table. 'It's all right. Don't bother. It's here.'

Davies, like a soldier in a slit trench, retraced his steps. Mod had the bound newspaper opened on the table. 'There,' he said. '"Woman's Thefts from Country Homes".' Davies edged him over and they read the two columns together, Davies aloud: 'Got herself a job, good references, sussed the place out, and left a window open – for an accomplice "as yet unknown". Now if there was anything little Lofty was cut out for, it was a cat burglar.' He returned to the page. 'Here she was found with some of the goods on her – they called it "swag" in those days, didn't they? In the *Beano* burglars always wore masks and striped jerseys and carried a bag marked "swag".'

Mod looked disdainful. 'We're reading the *Essex Chronicle*,' he pointed out.

'Jewellery and silverware. Five charges. Three different houses,' said Davies. 'She got eighteen months.' He suddenly thrust his head close to the page. 'Ah, but look, this is interesting. "The Rev. Michael Jones, vicar of Purwell-by-Sea, who said he had known Prenderley and her family for several years, spoke on her behalf and said that she had fallen into the hands of an unscrupulous accomplice who had used her and whom she still refused to name."'

'Where's Purwell-by-Sea?' asked Mod.

'Probably not far,' said Davies. His nose went up as though sniffing the brine. 'Feel like a day on the beach?'

*

A niggling force eight came in over the North Sea, buffeting everything from gulls to grass; black and silver mud stretched from the low land to the rough and bitter water. A solitary man, far out, stood against the wind and stoically dug for bait.

'Not much of a day for building sand-castles,' mentioned Davies to the landlord.

'Never is here,' agreed the man. 'Sand went away years ago. The tides changed and carted it down the coast. Purwell-*by*-Sea? Purwell-away-from-the-sea more like it.'

'Nice bit of fish, anyway,' said Davies, eyeing the white morsel on his fork as Mod nodded agreeably. 'Local?'

'Birds Eye,' said the landlord with uncaring honesty. 'The chips are too.'

'Times change,' said Davies philosophically. 'Nothing's the same.'

'That table over there,' offered the man, nodding to the other end of the bar. 'See how thick it is. The men used to get up there and dance in their clogs.'

'You been here long?' asked Davies.

'Ten years,' said the landlord. 'This'll be my last summer.'

There was only one other customer, a glancing man in a brown cap sitting by the thick table. 'I remember the clog-dancing,' he called to them. 'An' the shove-'a'penny championships.'

Davies half turned. 'Do you recall a family called Prenderley?' he asked the man before looking back at the landlord. 'Had a girl called Mavis?'

'Not in my time,' said the landlord. 'You know them, Bert?'

"Ow long ago?' asked Bert. 'I got a feeling I know the name.'

'Before the War,' said Davies. 'And a bit after, probably.'

'I got a notion they lived up by the old coastguard houses,' said Bert. 'But I don't remember 'zactly. My mind's going anyway.'

'There's not that many people living here now that would have been here then,' put in the landlord. 'It's all changed even while I've been here.' He glanced towards Bert. Both seemed glad that Davies had brought up the topic. 'Old Tommy ought to know,' he suggested.

'Aye,' agreed Bert. 'Old Tommy ought.'

'Where will we find Old Tommy?' asked Davies.

The landlord leaned across the bar. 'If you turn around,' he said, 'and look out of that window, you'll see him. A long way out, see? He's digging bait.'

'We spotted him,' said Davies, his spirits dropping. 'How long will he be out there?'

'Till dark,' put in Bert. 'Once 'e gets out there, 'e don't come back till it's dark or the tide comes in.'

'Six o'clock today,' said the landlord with a sort of fatalism. 'Soonest.'

'And . . . there's no way of getting a message to him?' asked Davies. 'Like a loud-hailer?'

'Or a boy who doesn't mind getting muddy,' put in Mod.

''E wouldn't take any notice,' said the landlord. 'Is it that urgent then?'

Davies took the risk. 'Police,' he said, taking his warrant card from his pocket. 'We have to get back to London.'

144

'I thought so,' said the landlord.

'So did I,' said Bert.

'Is there a way to get to him?' asked Davies. 'Safely?'

'There's a way across the flats,' nodded the landlord. 'That's how Old Tommy gets out there. But you'll get muddy. I've got a couple of pairs of boots you can borrow.'

Mod raised his hand. 'Only one pair,' he intoned. 'I'm not going.'

'I thought you might not,' muttered Davies. 'Thanks,' he said to the landlord. The man nodded at Bert.

'Bert knows his way out there,' he said. 'I expect he'd go with you.' Bert's creased little face had contracted further.

'Retired,' he said. 'I've retired.'

'Ten pounds,' said Davies.

'I'll go 'ome and get my boots,' said Bert.

Mod had settled himself in a public shelter facing on to the barren coast. Wandering shafts of gaunt sunshine moved over the mud but scarcely lightened the colourless afternoon.

'You're quite comfortable, aren't you?' inquired Davies caustically. 'I mean, you wouldn't like a blanket and a hot Thermos.'

'Both,' replied Mod, 'would be welcome. I'm willing, however, to undergo a certain amount of deprivation, seeing as you are doing so.' He viewed the unhappy policeman clumping towards the mud in great green waders. 'I'll wait,' he promised.

'Take us 'arf 'our,' said Bert. 'There and back.' In his thin waders he stepped stiffly but safely, like a long-legged sea-bird. The wind bit at their faces. Davies buttoned his long-serving overcoat around his neck. Bert went down the short grass and on to grey shingle and Davies followed him, with one last glance back at Mod who waved daintily. Davies cursed.

The shingle crunched like nutshells below his boots, gulls squealed and flung themselves about the sky, the wind was like a flight of arrows. Bert plodded on ahead. 'Keep right aback of me,' he called over his small shoulder. The wind whipped the words away as soon as they were spoken. 'If you get bogged, shout out loud.' He had insisted on payment in full before leaving.

Davies narrowed his eyes towards the bereft horizon. Mud – leaden, faintly glistening mud – stretched between him and it. There were channels and smooth but ominous pools of sea water, like dead eyes, and neat holes that blew inky bubbles. Far, far out, much more distant than he had seemed before, was the lugworm-gathering figure of Old Tommy.

Bert, his arms and legs at the tangents of a star, went over the mud adeptly, locating unseen firm places, rocks and parts where stones had been strung out to form a causeway. With his four points of balance and his little balaclava-covered head dodging this way and that, he progressed, leaving Davies stumbling along in his rear. The wind was raw, it scythed across the mud-flats, rifling the lapels of Davies's coat, making his eyes and nose stream and leaving his skin sore. Twice, having stumbled forward into the sucking mud, he involuntarily shouted and the wind flung away his words over his shoulder as soon as he had called them. They certainly never reached Bert who went jerkily but further ahead, like an expert cross-country skier leaving a novice far behind.

Davies was also finding it exhausting. The weight of the tall, clinging waders, the effort to make progress against the wind, his antics with the moving mud, all sapped his suburban strength. Halfway to Old Tommy, he turned and saw Mod sitting fatly in the seaside shelter. Angrily he waved his fist and Mod, mistaking the gesture at that distance, waved amiably in return.

Bert reached the bait-digger several minutes ahead of Davies and, after turning around to see where he was, stood alongside Old Tommy who showed no interest in his arrival and carried on with his spadework. Bulky and wet as a walrus, Davies paused and observed them against the wide and weakening sky.

Eventually he reached a ridge of rocks, worn flat by years of tides, and rested for the last time. One more advance across the morass following Bert's indentations and he reached the pair, panting but triumphant. No conversation was passing between the local men. Old Tommy was digging and Bert was staring at the horizon as if wondering what lay beyond it. Nor was his own advent to give cause for the merest excitement. Old Tommy scarcely glanced his way as he stood, mud three parts up his waders and thick on his coat, ribs aching, face raw, mouth opening and shutting to no avail. Eventually Davies gathered himself sufficiently to bawl against the shrieking wind, in Bert's direction: 'Did you ask him?'

Bert looked mildly offended. 'Ask 'im what?' he shouted back.

'About the Prenderley family?' Davies yelled.

'Oh, that. No, I thought *you* was going to ask him that.'

Davies glowered. 'Can he stop digging for a moment?'

'I 'spect he could,' bawled Bert. He laid his hand on the thick elbow of Old Tommy. The lugworm-seeker reluctantly straightened. He was very tall and powerful for an old man. His riven face turned away from the wind, the eyes red as furnaces.

'What you want?' he bellowed.

Davies almost staggered back but he stood his ground and yelled back at the face: 'I'm Detective Constable Davies . . .'

'What?'

'Detective Constable . . . oh Christ . . . this wind! I'M THE POLICE!' For a moment he thought he had communicated because the big old man looked towards Bert, the lines in his face even deeper. But the face then returned to Davies.

'POLICE!' bellowed Davies again into the howling wind.

'He's deaf,' said Bert in an almost normal voice which he seemed able to slot between gusts. 'Been deaf for years.'

Davies thought he was going to fall backwards into the mud. He looked aghast at the puckered Bert. 'Deaf?' he howled. 'Bloody hell, why didn't you tell me?'

148

'You didn't ask,' shouted Bert, a little shamefaced. He regarded Old Tommy, who examined the contents of his lugworm bucket, and then summed up the dimming horizon. 'Get him ashore,' he suggested. 'Ask him on shore. Got a fiver?'

'Yes . . . what for?'

'Wave a fiver at him.'

'Oh . . . I see. All right. Christ, what a performance!' Swaying in the mud he managed to extract a five-pound note from his wallet. As he held it out speculatively so the wind, apparently having been lying in wait, gusted and tore the blue note from his fingers. Davies cried out and Bert watched expressionless as it flew off across the mud. 'Bugger it!' exploded Davies.

'There it is,' pointed out Bert. 'Miles away.' He looked up with a creeping sympathy. 'Won't get that back now.'

Old Tommy, apparently not having witnessed the drama, finished counting the worms in his bucket. He straightened up, picked up the spade and the receptacle and, with no word nor gesture to them, began plodding back towards the murky shore-line. Bert jerked his head at Davies and followed. Davies turned, weary and defeated, and became the tail of the short, slow, homeward crocodile. The wind was at his back now, pushing at him like someone overdoing encouragement. He stepped carefully, resisting the force of the gusts, and was thinking that at least he was becoming more skilled when, negotiating a screed of bare rock and slimy gullies, he became unbalanced and an opportunist blast between his shoulder blades sent him sprawling forward. He fell on his knees in the icy ooze, his arms sinking to the elbows. His cry caused Bert to turn casually, but the little man made no effort to return although he waited. He watched stonily as Davies unplugged his arms and with anger and anguish eventually contrived to regain his feet.

'Looks like Old Tommy's spotted your fiver,' Bert told him chattily when he had caught up. 'Look, 'e's off over there.'

The bait-digger had taken a diversion and was youthfully stepping across inlets and flats. He bent and picked up the five-pound note which was floating in a pool, hugging a wall of rock like a sheltering ship. In almost the same movement, he thrust the note into his pocket before continuing his progress towards the land.

Bert said philosophically: 'Being deaf 'e's 'ard to argue with.'

He continued carefully across the mud, the policeman miserably in his wake. Dusk and tide were both advancing. Water began to slide about their waders. Davies looked towards the dim shelter on the shore. Mod could just be discerned. There were two other figures with him. Old Tommy had already gained the grass and Bert was almost there. As Davies got closer, he saw that the shapes flanking Mod were uniformed policemen. It was difficult for his heart to sink further. Slowly, he progressed towards them, the surface beneath his waders becoming firmer. There was a police car standing outside the pub with the driver reporting his arrival over the radio.

He was icy, wet, bruised and coated with grey

slime. He felt he could scarcely stagger another step. His teeth clattered. Old Tommy had taken his bucket in the direction of the last of the daylight. Bert walked away into the anonymous gloom. One of the policemen sitting on either side of Mod arose and ambled towards him. He was a sergeant.

'Good afternoon, sir,' he said. 'Been digging for bait?'

From within his coating of mud, Davies regarded the man with true hatred. His arms and legs felt like frozen wood. 'No,' he said bitterly. 'I've just walked from fucking Denmark.'

12

'Anyone,' sighed Inspector Joliffe of Essex Constabulary, 'who lets himself in for arranging police balls must be mad.' His arms were folded on his desk and he looked sombrely and directly at Davies, as though confident he would find sympathy. After some initial surprise, Davies was swift to offer it.

'Exactly my sentiments, sir,' he said. 'Coppers are apt to get disgruntled.'

'It was last night,' groaned Joliffe. 'Southend. And it's the final one for me. I can tell you how bloody relieved I was when they played the last waltz. Last straw more like it. Half the raffle prizes were stolen, the band was terrible, and one of the wives hit a woman PC on the jaw.'

Davies moved his head sympathetically. 'They can get rough. We've had to call the police before now.'

'We don't *have* to call them, they're waiting outside with the breathalysers,' complained Joliffe. 'Those who didn't want to go to the ball, spoiling it for others.' He bumped his forearms forlornly on the desk.

Davies said: 'You're quite right, sir. "Blow into this – and it's not a bag of chips." We've got them as well.'

The inspector shook his head and withdrew his arms from the desk. The action seemed to remind him that he was there to interrogate Davies. 'Well, what's all this then?' he asked. He picked up a written report and held it at a distance from his eyes, blocking Davies's view of him. 'Talk about coppers turning on their own,' he said from behind the paper barrier. 'We've had to bring you in.' The report sheet was lowered. The eyes were troubled. 'What's it all about then?'

'Inquiries,' answered Davies inadequately.

'Inquiries?' said Joliffe, his voice firmer. 'But you can't just come down here on *inquiries*. Not just like that. There's channels. We can't have the Metropolitan Police making investigations in Essex, in our manor, our patch, with not so much as a by-your-leave. You know about permissions and suchlike.'

'Yes, sir, of course,' said Davies dolefully.

'Who knows where it would stop? There's the old man in the hotel at Frinton, Mr Linder. You tell him you're the police but he sees you drive off in a beat-up old heap that obviously isn't a police vehicle. So he telephones us. Have you got a current MOT certificate, by the way?'

'Oh yes, I have,' said Davies. 'Somewhere.'

Joliffe wrote something in the margin of the report sheet. 'You'd better produce it,' he murmured. 'And your driving licence and insurance at your nearest police station.'

'Right. Of course. I'll take it in when I'm next working,' said Davies. 'I should be on duty this morning. I've had to phone. That's why I wanted to get the matter sorted out yesterday.' He realized he was adopting the chummy attitude of the petty criminal when cornered. 'Incidentally,' he mentioned.

153

'I know a friend of Max Bygraves. When you have the police ball next year . . .'

Joliffe looked up and regarded Davies carefully. 'Max Bygraves?' he said. 'Max Bygraves wouldn't come here, would he? You mean, if you asked him?'

'He might,' muttered Davies half-encouragingly. 'You never know with these people. Like, if he was on his way to somewhere else.'

'There *is* nowhere else out here,' said Joliffe, looking at the divisional map on the wall apparently to make sure. 'Only Ipswich. And he's hardly likely to be going to Ipswich, is he? Ipswich apart, all there is after here is mud.'

'I know,' said Davies feelingly. 'I've been stuck in it.'

'Ah yes. They were having a laugh about that at the ball last night.' He examined Davies, apparently for signs of slime. 'But they helped you to get cleaned up.'

'Oh yes. They were very decent,' said Davies.

'And they victualled you.'

'Yes. And they put me up in the section house. The cells were probably full.'

'Yes, yes. We're not a bad bunch really in this division,' said Joliffe. 'The ball brings out the worst I always think.' He sighed ponderously. 'Unfortunately this . . .' Regretfully he tapped the sheet of paper. '. . . has now gone into the works, the gubbins. Into the computer. And you know as well as I do what that means – there's no retrieving it. You could bring The Rolling Stones to Chelmsford, and we still couldn't get you off. Once it's in the gubbins, it's in the gubbins for good.'

154

'It's going to be difficult for me,' admitted Davies.

'What were you up to, anyway? Whatever it was, you weren't very quiet over it. After alarming the old boy at Frinton, you go to the pub at Purwell-by-Sea and tell them you're coppers. The landlord rang us as well.'

'He hired me his waders,' said Davies bitterly.

'Why did you want to go out on the mud?'

'To see the old man digging bait. There were some questions I wanted to ask him. He turned out to be stone-deaf.'

'What sort of questions? What's the background?'

'The inquiries are about a man called Lofty Brock,' said Davies. 'Although that wasn't his real name. And he's dead now anyway. He was drowned in a canal.'

Joliffe twirled his pencil as if the story were all too familiar. 'Why didn't you do the proper thing then, go through channels?' he asked. '*We* could have made the inquiries. We *can* ask questions, you know, just as well as the Metropolitan Police.'

'It wasn't official,' Davies admitted in a low voice. 'It was a personal sort of investigation.'

'Oh, I see,' said Joliffe, shaking his head. 'On your tod, was it? That's a bit frowned on. It would be here.'

'Yes,' nodded Davies glumly. 'It's frowned on.'

'And you went to Purwell to ask about this man Brock, who's dead?'

'Yes. A family called Prenderley. I thought the old man, Old Tommy, might know them.'

'He ought to,' said Joliffe. 'He's one of them.'

*

Staring at the rainy road ahead from behind the Vanguard's massive wheel, Davies once more began to mutter bitterly. 'He was *one* of them. The old deaf bastard was a *Prenderley*. Why didn't they say so in the pub? They must be as thick as the mud they bloody well *live* on.'

Carefully, Mod said: 'Do you remember what they *did* say, Dangerous?'

'Go on, go on. Tell me what I missed – again.'

'It's only now I think of it,' Mod said. 'When you asked about the Prenderley family in the pub there was a bit of a silence and the landlord asked the man in the corner . . .'

'Good old Bert,' said Davies, grinding his teeth.

'Exactly. And Bert said something about the Prenderleys having lived at the coastguard cottages. Then the landlord said to Bert something like "Old Tommy ought to know" and Bert agreed that Old Tommy ought to know. Of course he *ought* to know – because he was *one* of them. But they weren't going to tell you everything. If Old Tommy wanted to tell you, let him tell you himself.'

'Except there was a gale blowing and he was stone-deaf,' said Dangerous.

'He's the last of the Prenderleys?'

'In that area he is. That's where they all come from. The inspector, Joliffe, told me there were still some Prenderleys living in Southend. They're a well-known local family, or they were.'

'Even notorious, perhaps. One of the girls doing time for nicking the silver.'

Davies sighed and the sigh turned into a grunt of indignation. 'And she's the one who knew the man we call Lofty Brock,' he said. 'Or did. She may be dead now.' In his exasperation he trod on the accelerator and sent the car bouncing and skidding on the soaked road.

'Steady, steady,' cautioned Mod. 'You were way above forty then.'

'Now we'll never know,' continued Davies, managing to steady the car. 'If I ever so much as put my snout in this manor again, that will be goodbye. I'm going to be in enough bother as it is.'

'What can they do to you?'

'For undermining authority? For going into another force's territory unofficially – and getting caught? And remember, we've been to Yorkshire, Hampshire and I went to Bedfordshire to see the old prison lady. For that lot I could find myself standing next to you in the queue at the DHSS. On the other hand, they might be lenient and put me back in uniform.'

Mod was shocked. 'Oh, Dangerous,' he said solemnly. 'I didn't realize it was that serious. Is there anything I can do?'

'Yes,' said Davies grimly. 'Try not to laugh.'

He had tidied himself up, resolutely brushing his hair and getting out his blazer. Superintendent Vesty kept him waiting for half an hour and he sat grimly in the CID room, trying to interest himself in an old issue of the *Police Gazette*. Even that was a mockery. Everyone else seemed to be in the process of being promoted.

When Superintendent Vesty sent down, he was in the lavatory and there was a further delay while they shouted around for him. In his rush his braces slipped and caught him a vicious blow in the eye. He reached the office with tears streaming down his cheek.

'Took your time didn't you, Davies?' said Vesty. Propped before him was a folder with 'Police Boxing' printed on the cover.

'Sorry, sir. I was out for a minute.'

'What's wrong with your eye?'

Davies grappled for a handkerchief, failed, and wiped the water away with the back of his hand. 'Bit of a cold, sir.'

Vesty, a wide-eared, round-shouldered man, took no further interest. He bowed low over the folder. 'D'you know Wilfred Gamage?' he inquired almost absently. 'Black kid. Fancies he can box.'

'Yes, I know him,' answered Davies. 'Wilful Damage, they call him.'

'It's the Police Boxing Night,' said Vesty, tapping the folder. 'He wants to fight a policeman.'

Davies felt himself go pale. 'I'm a bit old for that, sir.' His voice came out in a croak.

Vesty looked aghast. 'Christ, not *you*, Davies. You get dented enough when you're on duty.' He appeared to recall the purpose of the interview and picked up a typed letter with several attachments. He sighed and said: 'Now, what the hell have you been up to?'

'It's the Essex thing, is it, sir?'

The superintendent's round shoulders seemed to get rounder. 'What else? Have you been up to anything else?'

'Oh no, sir. It was all a bit unfortunate.'

'Listen, Davies,' said Vesty ponderously. 'You know bloody well that nobody – *nobody* – can just traipse across another police force's manor without express permission. You know how touchy they get. We wouldn't like it ourselves. If some copper from Chelmsford suddenly took it into his head to roam around this division, there'd be hell to pay.'

'Yes sir.'

'And what, in God's name, was it all about?' He tapped the paper in his hand. 'What's all this stuff about Brock?'

'Lofty Brock,' replied Davies defensively. 'Remember, he died in the canal here, last October. But I don't think it was just an accident . . .'

Vesty banged the letter on the desk. 'Oh, come on now, Davies! You know as well as I do that you can't just take things on yourself. The Brock case according to our records which I have here – was open and shut. There was an inquest.'

'Yes, sir. Open verdict.'

'I don't give a damn what the verdict was! All I know is that you've been pissing about where you shouldn't be. Haven't we got enough to occupy you here? We had half a dozen parking meters prised open this weekend – with an axe by the look of it. Is that stuff too small for you?'

'No sir. I was doing the Brock thing in my own time.'

Again Vesty slammed his fist on the table so fiercely he winced. 'Your own time! Jesus – that's worse!' He stood and leaned over like a toppling tree. His thick fingers wagged. 'You must be potty! Drop it – drop it now, Davies! At bloody once.'

Davies eyed him nervously. 'Yes sir . . . I have. Right now. More or less.'

'More or less nothing!' exploded the superintendent. 'You are in trouble – right in the shit, believe me. This has to go further. It's out of my hands.' He looked bitterly at Davies. 'Anything else? Anything further you want taken into consideration?'

'No sir, nothing,' said Davies. 'Nothing at all.'

Vesty's sigh as he sat down was so loud it emerged like gas from a balloon. 'If this sort of thing went on all the time, the Metropolitan Police as we know it would be rent apart,' he said sonorously. 'Let's hope we can get you off lightly.'

'I hope so, sir,' said Davies. He rose from the chair. Vesty was glaring at the letter again.

'You must be potty,' he repeated. 'Isn't there enough crime without inventing it?'

When Davies went down to the evening meal at 'Bali Hi', Furtman Gardens, that day, he was discomfited to find his estranged wife Doris sitting primly alone at the table. Mod, he knew, had been summoned to a meeting with a senior employment officer and had gone with anxious heart; it was Minnie Banks's night for her grooming and personality class, Mr Smeeton had an early performance and Mrs Fulljames was immersed in culinary steam.

''Evening,' said Davies politely as he took his chair at the opposite end of the table. The off-white cloth was like a gulf between them. 'Not a bad day for the time of year.'

'You've ruined my life,' said Doris, looking down at her knife, fork and spoon. 'Ruined it.'

'Not now,' pleaded Davies. 'I've had a terrible day at the police station.'

'Every day is terrible for me,' she sniffed. She picked up the knife and laid it down again. 'You've ruined my life.'

'So you said. But why bring it up now? It's been years, after all.'

'Years,' she agreed. 'In this house. Separated. We can't go on living together like this.'

'Well,' said Davies, pondering the logic. 'It's been all right so far. It suits us both. We don't get under each other's feet all that much.'

'Don't you remember,' she said, her voice all at once hushed, 'when we were tango champions of Finchley Lacarno. Doesn't it mean anything to you? You were different then. It was when you got out of uniform – and started drinking.'

'It's difficult to go drinking wearing a helmet,' he acknowledged. 'Somebody always notices.'

'Make jokes,' she retorted. 'Go on.' She began to sob.

'Oh, don't cry, Doris,' said Davies genuinely. 'Not here.'

'Where can I cry then?' she snivelled. 'In my room?'

'I'm sorry. I'm really sorry.'

'No, you're not. You've still got that darkie.'

'That is professional. And it's my business,' he said firmly.

'It's *mine*. You're my husband.'

The reality came to him with a sort of shock. He almost said: 'So I am.' Instead he asked her: 'Would you be happier if we had a divorce?' Her expression sagged. The tears which had been suspended from her lower eyelashes splashed to the table-cloth.

'Divorce?' she said. 'Divorce? We can't have a divorce. Never. I couldn't face the disgrace.'

She blew her nose, terrifically, into her paper table napkin. Minnie Banks came in from the grooming and personality class as wan and knock-kneed as ever. She wished them a timid good evening and left again to wash her hands. Mrs Fulljames emerged from the kitchen with two plates of brown Windsor soup, carried at arms' length like smoking bombs. 'Been having a little chat, have you,' she said, placing one before Doris and one in front of Davies. 'It's nice when you can get together for a little chat, I think. It clears the air.'

Doris blew her nose violently again, sending tidal ripples over the surface of the brown Windsor.

'It's called clinging to the wreckage,' said Davies.

'Both of you,' said Jemma. They were in The Babe In Arms awaiting Mod.

'I suppose so. It's ridiculous, I know, but we've been going along like this for years. In the same house. She's been there and I've been there and we've hardly exchanged a civil word. But it didn't seem to be so difficult or embarrassing.' He looked at her deep eyes regarding him soberly. 'But it's you. That's the difference.'

Jemma put her fingers on the hand folded around his beer. 'Dangerous,' she said with great seriousness. 'There's no way we could ever get together; I mean *marry*.' She appeared unusually embarrassed. 'Even if you asked. I could never take you to Martinique.'

'No, I don't suppose you could,' mumbled Davies

as if the matter had preoccupied him over a long period. 'Not Martinique.'

Mod appeared, a wide cheery smile topping his overcoat collar. 'You won, did you?' said Davies, rising to get a round of drinks. The bar was only a yard distant. 'There's no danger then of you personally diminishing the unemployment figures.'

'None at all,' said Mod with satisfaction. 'And as from now I am not merely unemployed, I am unemployable.' From beneath his overcoat he produced a bunch of stapled papers. 'My file,' he said with some pride. 'I went back after the interview to tell the senior official something in mitigation of my circumstances. I was almost in the street when I remembered it. So I returned to the interview room and it was empty. The chap and his clerk had gone. And my file was on the table.'

'What you are about to confess is criminal,' said Davies, bringing the drinks to the table.

'It's *my* file,' pointed out Mod.

'I don't want to hear another word about it,' Davies warned, sitting down. 'And I didn't hear the words you just said.'

Mod sat quietly: 'I had to wait for about half an hour in another office.'

'What did you nick from there, the Queen's national insurance card?'

'No, this,' said Mod, burrowing in his pocket. 'They had telephone directories for every part of the country. So I amused myself looking for Prenderleys in the Essex directory. Like the policeman in Chelmsford told you, there's only a single group of them, all living in Southend. Apart from Old

Tommy at Purwell.' He found the piece of paper. 'There,' he said, handing it to Davies. 'There's four of them on the phone.'

Davies took the list. 'I've been warned off,' he muttered. 'I had a nasty few minutes with the super today and he's not all that pleased with me. Trespassing on another manor. It's got to be referred higher. I may get the heave-ho.' He smiled at Jemma. 'I may leave the country. Go to live in Martinique or somewhere.'

Jemma said: 'We've got a choral society outing to Southend next week.'

They sang all the way from Kensal Rise, the coach itself seeming to roll and roar in harmony. Davies, who knew none of the words and few of the tunes, sat next to Jemma against the window, mouthing haplessly and with increasingly weary lips. Jemma had told only Mr Swingler, the conductor of the choir, of Davies's real mission, and then in considerably altered details. As far as the other members of the society were concerned, he was a visiting tenor from Wales who sang only in Welsh. Davies made mouth movements and emitted occasional pseudo-Welsh sounds while looking resolutely out of the window at the passing suburbs and eventually the brief grey-green rural approach to Southend-on-Sea.

It was a poor day for visiting the seaside. Windy drizzle blew against the coach windows. People crouched along pavements, hoping for something better. It mattered little to Davies, nor did the oddness of his situation, the impossibility of matching the singing nor the increasing tiredness of lips and gums. None of it mattered because Mavis Prenderley, late nanny of Cape House, Frinton, and inmate of Chelmsford Women's Prison, was alive and well and he was going to see her.

The coach reached the domed hall where the choir festival was taking place. Canvas banners strung across the outside strained like sails in the wind coming from the muddy sea. The members of the choral society came off the coach like disembarking footballers, flexing their limbs, making sharp forays along the promenade while gulping in lungfuls of brined air; sounding off scales and snatches of cantata.

'Wait until they're all inside the hall,' whispered Jemma, 'and then make a dash for it. Get back by six or you'll be left behind.'

They followed the other choristers into the building. The main lighting had not been switched on and the singers moved about like shadows, complaining about flying dust and testing the acoustics by singing out from the stage to colleagues placed in strategic parts of the auditorium. Everyone appeared to be occupied. Jemma rolled her eyes to Davies to make for the door.

At an elated crouch he went from the hall into the grey afternoon. Byron Street where Mavis Prenderley lived was only ten minutes' walk; he would not even have to get a taxi. In the slack season seaside taxi drivers were inclined to be nosey and observant.

He had his collar pulled up, for both shelter and concealment, but he strode purposefully like a man with nothing to hide. A policeman came around a corner, one of those apparently aimless wandering constables who appear for no reasonable reason at inconvenient moments. Davies stopped himself crossing to the other side of the street and, burying his face deeper into the cleft of his collar, he slightly less blatantly strode on. The policeman paused and, to Davies's relief, studied the contents of a second-hand shop window.

Byron Street was terraced houses, small and old but with optimistically painted doors, clean curtains and plant pots in the windows. At number forty-three he paused, lowered his collar, and knocked. She answered so immediately that he thought she might have been waiting inside the door. He must have studied, stared at her, because she gave an elderly blush. 'Mr Thompson?' she said. 'Come in. Don't stand in the street.'

Already committed to the lie, Davies mumbled his thanks and ducked below the threshold. The door gave straight into the room, a crowded, tight, old-fashioned parlour, with covers on the backs and the arms of the two red chairs, a big ticking clock in between two petrified dogs on the mantelshelf, droplets of glass hanging around the light bulb and damask curtains suspended within the modest nets at the window. There was a decorative square of carpet, balding in places, and a heavy dark table and four chairs. Over the fireplace, above a gas fire which, judging by its sputtering, had just been lit, was a picture of a wild mountain scene and beside it a framed photograph of a small and grinning young man. He tried not to stare too closely at it. Was it? Was it Lofty Brock? He swallowed so hard the old lady heard him.

'Sorry,' he said lamely. 'I suppose that's what comes of hurrying down the street.' Almost as a diversion, he held out his hand. 'Harry Thompson, Premier Insurance Company,' he said. 'It is very good of you to spare the time to see me, Miss Prenderley.'

'Time?' she answered. 'Time's nothing. I've got plenty of time. You find you do when you get older.' She motioned him to sit at the table. 'I'll get you a cup of tea,' she said. 'George Prenderley came round to tell me you had phoned. That side of the family haven't said a dicky-bird to me for years. I suppose when they heard it was insurance they thought there might be something in it for them.'

She went into a kitchen and Davies heard her filling the kettle and lighting the gas. He got up and squinted closely at the mantelshelf photograph. 'It was the only way we could do it,' he called out to her. 'We knew you lived somewhere in the Southend district so I had my assistant call all the Prenderleys in this area.'

'We're all here,' she called back. 'All in a couple of miles of each other. But we're not much of a family. Hardly anyone talks to anybody else. There's only Tom, my brother, who lives away, and that's only at Purwell. I suppose he's still alive. When they die is the only time you get any news of them.'

She returned with the tea on a tray with a teapot in the shape of a cottage and the words 'A present from Clacton' on the side. 'It's a bit of excitement anyway,' she said, putting a small embroidered cloth on the table and placing the tray on that. 'You

167

coming here. I don't get many strangers. When they do come they either want to buy my old furniture and bits for next to nothing, or they're people gassing on about God.' She poured the tea. Davies pointed to the photograph on the mantelshelf.

'Who is that gentleman?' he asked as casually as he could.

'Billy,' she said. 'Billy Dobson. He died in the War. At least he was never found. He was . . .'

She stopped and looked into his face. 'It's not about Billy is it? He's not turned up?' The teapot was frozen in her hand. 'I always thought he would.'

'What makes you say that?' asked Davies carefully.

'Billy? He could wriggle out of a milk tin.'

'He actually did,' said Davies.

Her puffy face paled. 'I knew he would,' she whispered angrily. 'I knew the bugger would.' Her expression hardened. 'So he wasn't dead,' she muttered. 'But he never got in touch.'

'Tell me about Billy,' said Davies. 'Would you mind?'

'I don't mind,' she told him slowly. Her eyes showed that she was thinking of long ago. 'Why should I?' Davies thought how odd it was that she had not asked him why he was there, what his business was; it was as if she had been waiting for years to tell him. Her voice was slow but there was a change taking place in her eyes. 'A holy terror if ever there was,' she said with a suspicion of eagerness. 'All the girls loved him. But I was the only one he wanted to marry and I turned him down.'

'Why was that?'

'Too short,' she said emphatically. 'For one thing.

For another, the way he lived was not very steady. Burglary. You'd never know when, or if, he was coming home. That's what I said to myself. Billy had been through the windows of half the big houses in Essex, and outside. He was reckoned to have got into Sandringham, you know, where the King lived. And the King was *in* at the time. Edward the Eighth, the one that resigned.'

'He had aspirations?' said Davies, adding: 'Billy.'

'I don't know about that,' she replied, still almost dreamily. 'He liked a better class of thieving. He always worked the same. He'd get to know one of the girl servants. He was only dinky, as I say, but he knew how to get around girls. With his wicked eyes and his bright little teeth, full of jokes and flattering nineteen to the dozen. Off he'd take them for the day at Clacton, on the roundabouts and side-shows, walk along the front, fish and chips on the bus coming back, and that was that. He could sing too. They'd do anything he'd ask them. I know, I was one who did. The next thing you know, you'd be leaving a window open for him.' Abruptly, she came out of the reverie. 'I'm telling you all this,' she said guiltily, 'and I don't know why. What's it for? Tell me about him not being dead.'

'He is now,' said Davies sombrely. 'He died last October. In a canal in London.'

'He couldn't swim,' she said, shaking her head. 'He wouldn't even go in up to his knees at Clacton. He could climb but not swim.'

'He lived his last years in a men's hostel,' continued Davies carefully. 'Nobody knew much about him. He reappeared after the War with a different name – he called himself Brock. Wilfred Henry Brock. Known as Lofty.'

A soft smile settled on her pink face. 'Lofty,' she said. 'Fancy that.'

'When he died,' said Davies, 'the hostel people went through his belongings. There wasn't much, but this was there.' He took from his pocket an envelope, and from it produced the picture of the girl in the tin frame. At once she reached out for it as an eager child might reach for a toy.

'Oh,' she breathed, looking into her own youthful face. 'My Chelmsford jail picture.' She looked up, her eyes happy. 'And he had this still,' she said.

'It was in an envelope with your name on it, Mavis Anne Prenderley,' he said. 'But no address or anything. That's why it has taken me so long to find you.'

'Just to give it back?' she said.

'Not really.' He had to tell his lies carefully now. 'There were some other things.'

A delayed embarrassment seized her. 'Oh,' she said, her pink hands going to her mouth. 'Now you know I was in Chelmsford. In prison. I just told you. I've never told anybody.'

'Don't worry,' he said, patting her hand as she lowered it. 'It was a long time ago and all this is confidential.'

'They sent me in because it wasn't the first time,' she admitted. 'I'd been leaving windows open for Billy before that. We'd worked together for quite a long time. I'd get a job in the house and then he would pinch the silver. It was while I was inside Chelmsford that he started working with other girls.'

170

She looked fondly at the photograph. 'They took these in the chapel,' she said. 'They only used it for prayers on Sunday so it was empty the rest of the time. The man would tell you to look at the Cross and then he'd take the photo. That's why I'm staring like that.'

Feelings of guilt and worry moved within Davies. When there were steps and voices from outside the front door, he found himself glancing in that direction as if he believed that Inspector Joliffe and a posse of Essex Constabulary were about to burst in. 'There was also this,' he said to the woman. He took out the bag containing the single pearl.

Once again she sounded a small exclamation of recognition. 'Now, look at that,' she said. 'I never thought I'd see that again!'

'It was the only thing of real value he left . . . among his possessions,' said Davies.

Diffidently her fingers came across the table and she took the pearl. 'Billy always reckoned he'd give me this.'

Hurriedly, Davies held out his hand. 'I'm afraid,' he flustered, 'I can't let you have it just yet.'

'Oh, I know that,' she said reasonably, handing the pearl back. 'I wouldn't want it. *I* know where he got it. It might be years ago, but it's still stolen.'

'That was all he had,' said Davies, putting the pearl away. He glanced at the photograph in the frame which lay between them on the table. Without seeming to catch his look, she picked it up and handed it to him.

'It's all ancient history,' she said. 'Me included.'

'What did he do with the other stuff?' Davies asked

her. 'The proceeds of the robberies? He didn't appear to spend much.'

'Not even on girls,' she agreed. 'Fish and chips on the bus coming home from Clacton isn't what you'd call high living, is it?' She regarded him steadily. 'He tucked it away somewhere. Hid it. I don't know where. I bet nobody else does either, not now Billy's gone. He never believed in trying to get rid of stuff too early, too quick. That was how you got found out, he used to say. And the prices were bad. His idea was to tuck it all away, for years if necessary. When he was called up for the army, he thought it would give him a couple of years' break before he went back for the stuff he'd hidden.'

'Then he thought of coming back under another name,' suggested Davies. 'Starting again and just picking the odd bit of jewellery out to sell? But it didn't work out like that. He apparently never went back to it. He lived in near poverty.'

'Could be that somebody got there before him,' said Mavis Prenderley. 'All I know is it wasn't me.'

He knew it was time to go. 'I'll let you know what happens,' he said, rising and shaking hands with her. He hesitated again over the fabrication. 'About the insurance. You may well benefit.'

She smiled at him. 'You're a policeman, you are,' she said.

Davies was shocked. His mouth opened but only disjointed words emerged. 'I'm . . . me? Police?'

'I can tell a copper from here to the sea front,' she said. 'But it's all right. I'm in the clear. I haven't done anything wrong for years.'

'I'm sorry,' Davies mumbled. His face was hot.

'It's all right,' she repeated. 'I was expecting you anyway. Inspector Joliffe from Chelmsford said you'd probably be along.'

Davies's lips still hurt from all the pretence of singing aboard the choral coach. He could feel how sore they were against the edge of the beer tankard. 'All the way there,' he complained to Mod, 'and all the ruddy way back. And they sang the two hours in the middle as well. They must have mouths like rhinos.'

'Except Jemma,' suggested Mod, looking up expectantly.

'Except Jemma,' he agreed. 'She only sings the solo bits.'

They drank up and headed towards 'Bali Hi', Furtman Gardens. The evenings were a touch lighter now. Soon the clocks would be changing. Soon Davies would be shedding his long johns. They had left The Babe In Arms at an unusually early time so that Davies could give some attention to his dog which had thrown a mad mood during the day his master was absent at Southend, bolting from the garage and colliding with a Greek-born bookmaker's clerk in the street. The man had been toppled, his small change had rolled away and his betting slips were scattered to the spring-time wind. The early prostitute, Venus the Evening Star as Davies had always called her, had witnessed the affray and had hardly stopped laughing since. The dog had allowed himself to be captured by her, thus saving further mayhem.

Kitty was sitting in the back seat of the Vanguard with the door open like a soldier in a sentry box. He growled, as was his habit, when he saw Davies but then, to the man's intense pleasure, the dog rubbed his tangled head against him and even performed a token lick with his damp salmon tongue.

'See that,' said Davies proudly to Mod. 'See, he likes me.'

'It's taken him six years to make up his mind,' pointed out Mod. 'I think he's just ashamed of all the palaver yesterday. He very nearly brained the Greek.'

'I'll be getting complaints then,' said Davies. He patted the dog while he had the chance, while the animal's contrite mood prevailed.

Mod said he did not think so. 'The girl, Venus, has got some sort of hold over the Greek. I hate to think what it might be. When the dog ran to her, the matter was over.'

'Did the naughty Greek get in your way then?' Davies said, bending close to the dog. Kitty had come to the end of his period of good temper and emitted a slow growl. Davies apologized and went to prepare his dinner.

'Why do you think the Essex police told the Prenderley lady that you were coming?' Mod called to him.

'It was Joliffe, not the Essex police in general,' said Davies. 'And he only told her I *might* turn up. And he didn't tell her why. It was just a notion of his.' He brought the large bowl to the door of the car and Kitty stepped down regally to meet his dinner.

'Joliffe,' continued Davies, 'is a notion-copper.'

'Like you,' suggested Mod.

'Only he's got the clout to follow up his hunches,' said Davies. Mod had filled the dog's water bowl and they left the garage, solemnly wishing the animal good night. He did not glance up from his dish.

As they walked from the yard and into Furtman Gardens, Davies said: 'In the back of Joliffe's mind I think he believes there might just be something in all this. I only went over the basic facts and, whatever his notion is, it's not directly concerned with the death of Billy Dobson, alias Lofty Brock. But a good copper has a sort of small section of his nose that smells out possibilities. The Prenderley family have been around for years in his division and I wouldn't be surprised if their name hasn't come up at times during the course of police business.'

'Smoke and fire,' said Mod.

'Yes. I'll bet you that once I'd gone, Inspector Joliffe called for all the records on the Prenderley family. He probably knows some of them pretty well if he's spent all his police service on that patch. I'm sure he knew Mavis Prenderley previously. She sounded as if he was no stranger.'

'So he thinks he might let you burrow around just in case you might turn up something. But he doesn't know what.'

'The outside busybody,' agreed Davies. 'After all, from what Mavis Prenderley said, the proceeds of half a dozen pre-War country house robberies might well be waiting to be found. That could have been the motive for Lofty Brock's murder. I can't get used to calling him Billy Dobson. He'll always be Lofty to me.' They had reached the door of 'Bali Hi'. 'Maybe one of the Prenderleys gave Lofty the final push.'

'Maybe Mavis herself,' suggested Mod.

'Maybe her,' shrugged Davies, giving the girl in the stained-glass door her evening kiss.

They went into the hall. Mod sniffed. 'Curry,' he said. 'Oh, God, she's trying to cook curry.'

Davies picked up a letter from the hall-stand. 'It niffs a bit,' he agreed.

'A bit? This is the sort of thing that lost us India.' Davies was reading the letter intently. 'What is it?' asked Mod. 'From a fan?'

'Sort of. It's from Colonel Ingate in Yorkshire. He's, after all, decided to come down for his ex-prisoners-of-war dinner. He wants to have a word. He says he might have come up with something.'

Not for many years could Davies remember being in a crowded room where he was the youngest person present. He was also keenly aware of the absence of medals on his hired dinner jacket. All along the tables they glinted like silver moons.

'Did you serve?' asked the thin and ancient officer on his left. Colonel Ingate had introduced him as Captain Barrett.

'National Service,' admitted Davies.

'Ah, of course. I'm afraid one thinks of everyone having served in wartime. Too young, eh?'

'Only by four years,' Davies assured him. 'I was called up in 1949.'

'Pity. It wasn't the same.'

176

'No, I suppose not really. I never got out of Aldershot.'

Captain Barrett looked genuinely upset. 'Good God. How dreadful,' he said. 'What bad luck.'

'You had to go where they sent you,' said Davies. Colonel Ingate was on his other side. He wished the conversation would change.

'Damned bad luck,' said the old man again. 'Which regiment?'

'Pay Corps,' said Davies miserably. 'Royal Army Pay Corps.' He attempted to forestall the next inquiry with a joke. 'I rose to lance-corporal.'

His neighbour looked as if he were making an effort to pull himself together. 'Pay Corps,' he repeated. 'Not much chance of seeing action.'

'Not in Aldershot. I fell off the desk once.'

The old man laughed. 'Hard luck,' he said, suddenly good-humoured. 'Not everyone strikes lucky. Lance-corporal eh?'

'Acting, unpaid,' admitted Davies.

'Well someone had to be. Pity to miss the War though. Quite an experience.'

'I imagine. I was in the air raids on London. Our school was bombed.'

Captain Barrett nodded: 'Probably saw more action than some of us,' he said. 'I spent the last two years behind wire. With Robin Ingate in fact. That's why he put us together tonight. You have some interest in the events of those days, I believe. I was the medical officer of the prison camp.'

Davies shook hands with him, although they had already done so. 'I understand now,' he said. 'He wrote that he had something that might concern me.'

The old officer said: 'I probably knew more and remember more about individuals from those days than anyone else. You get to know a bit more as a medical officer, of course. When you've seen a chap with his trousers down, there's not much he can hide. And they used to come to me with all their problems, trouble with the wife and that sort of thing, even though she was back home in England. You'd be amazed at the capacity of people to indulge in domestic quarrels by letter.'

'Nothing would surprise me about husbands and wives,' said Davies feelingly. 'So you remember Lofty Brock in the prison camp.'

'The big fellow. Oh yes. He's one of the people you would certainly remember. When they went off to Silesia I had to stay behind. I can't honestly say I was sorry. Brock died there, so I understand.'

'And somebody else took his identity,' said Davies.

'Good God, did they? Well, I suppose that sort of thing happened. Who was it? Do you know?'

'A man called Billy Dobson. A little chap.'

Captain Barrett stared thoughtfully at his soup. 'That,' he said, 'does undoubtedly ring a bell. I have my records at home and I will need to check them. But, unless I'm mistaken, he was the little fellow who went around muttering to himself, picking up odd bits of paper and putting them in his pocket.'

'That,' breathed Davies, 'sounds like him.'

'He was Lofty's pal. It was quite a joke because they used to walk around together, one tall, the other so small. He was brought to the camp with a bad case of what they used to call shell-shock, Dobson. He'd gone completely. He couldn't *remember* his name half the time. I spent a lot of time with him but I didn't get far. He couldn't remember where he came from or anything. The Germans put him in hospital for a while, but with a war going on around you and getting closer every day, there wasn't much opportunity for psychiatry. There was nothing much physically wrong with him. He was just sadly batty.' He ate his soup in a studied way. 'You say he assumed the name of Lofty Brock?'

'Yes. After the War. He ended up in a hostel for homeless men. Walking about, as you say, muttering and picking up pieces of paper. And he was known as Lofty Brock.'

'He'd probably forgotten his real name,' said Barrett. 'He was a very bad case. Sometimes they never regain any sort of recall, nothing whatever. What do you know about him?'

Davies took a deep breath. 'He was drowned in a canal last October,' he said. 'Perhaps murdered. Before the War he was a successful burglar. He stowed away what could be a huge amount of stolen jewellery but never went back for it. Now, after what you've told me, I think I may know the reason. *He couldn't remember where he had hidden it.*'

13

It was somebody's birthday and Shiny Bright had got off with a suspended sentence; much had been consumed in The Babe In Arms that night.

'Shiny,' said Davies. 'You told me the truth, didn't you? About what went on that night on the tow-path?'

The small criminal's eyes had clouded into a profound hurt. 'Dangerous,' he said. 'Would I lie to you?'

'He would,' said Davies to Mod as they walked home below chimneys and moonlight. 'But I don't think he did.'

At the door of 'Bali Hi', Furtman Gardens, they each waited for the other to produce a key. Neither did. It had happened before. 'God, that's done it,' said Davies. 'If we get her up at this time . . .'

'And with the beer and everything,' continued Mod. He tried to smell his own breath by breathing on his hand.

'She'll go mad,' said Davies. 'She'll have only just gone to bed. She'll hardly have taken her teeth out.' They backed away from the door. 'We'll go to Harry's,' decided Davies. 'And think.'

They retraced their way along the street and turned two corners into the ghostly shopping area, lit and vacant except for Harry's All Night Refreshments, a glow of habitation in an empty world. Only Venus, the Evening Star, was there.

'Finished, love?' asked Davies.

'Didn't start it tonight,' sighed Venus. Her dyed red hair was hanging like a damp mop. Her eyes were smudged. 'Don't suppose you'd like a quickie, either of you, would you?'

'You're way beyond my price range,' said Mod. He nodded at Davies. 'And he's going steady.'

'So I've seen,' said Venus. 'She's all right too, for one of them.'

'Thanks for sorting out my dog,' said Dangerous. He handed her a five-pound note. 'He sent you a present.'

Venus simpered gratefully as she took the money. 'Never had a present from a dog before,' she said. 'It'll help me out. Give him a kiss for me, will you, Dangerous. On the lips.'

'I will,' he promised. 'On the lips.'

She said a subdued 'Ta' and stretched down from the stool, her tight, cheap skirt riding up her thin thighs. ''Night, 'night,' she wished them. ''Night, Harry.'

She clipped away on her stilted heels. 'Poor little cow,' said Harry.

'She should get a proper job,' said Mod piously.

Davies glanced at him sideways and said: 'You should talk.'

They finished their coffee and wished Harry good night. Mod was about to move in the direction of 'Bali Hi', Furtman Gardens, when Davies caught his arm. 'She'll have hardly started snoring yet.'

'What are we going to do then?'

'Why don't we go and have a chat with that little chap who's supposed to be the security guard at the trading estate,' suggested Davies. 'He'll probably be glad of the company.'

Mod sighed and turned with him. 'If you solve this case,' he said, 'providing, that is, there *is* anything to solve, you won't know what to do in all the spare time you're going to get.'

They plodded towards the canal bridge, turned clumsily down the silent steps, and went alongside the buildings and the moping water. Even the moonlight, now clear and widespread, made only a vapid impression. The lamps glowed sullenly. Davies stood on the bank and looked down for a few minutes. 'There's always a chance that we've overlooked something,' he said to himself. Mod waited until he had finished his rumination and then joined him as they continued along the tow-path and up the inclined alley. A right turn at the top brought them to the main gate of the trading estate. They could see the low head of Curl, the small security man, in his lit gatehouse. Davies banged his hand on the wire mesh of the gate several times without attracting the watchman's attention. Mod settled it by heavily pressing a large white bell-button. The result was resounding.

Curl turned to view them suspiciously through his window, but then put on his elevating cap and came to the gate. 'Mr Davies,' he said in his pleased way. 'It's you.' He unlocked the door set into the gate. 'Bit late to be abroad, isn't it?'

'The police, Edwin, never sleep,' recited Dangerous,

taking the boy-sized hand and shaking it. 'Neither should you.'

'Just cat-napping,' said Curl. 'I have to while I can.'

'This is Mr Lewis,' said Davies. 'He walks with me by night.' With the same enthusiasm Curl shook Mod's hand.

'Like a little bevvy?' he asked. He took an almost full bottle of Scotch from his shelf. 'A present from a well-wisher.'

'One of your several women?' asked Davies. 'He's got three women,' he explained to Mod.

'Four now,' corrected Curl, looking coy. 'Well, one's on the way out and a new one's on the way in. She's a fourteen-stone blonde.'

He poured generous measures of the whisky into three cups and they toasted each other and drank soundly. 'Not from my women,' said Curl. 'From Blissen Pharmaceuticals. She brought it back from somewhere.'

'A thank-you perhaps,' suggested Davies.

'Oh no. Just a present.' He pointed a finger at Davies. 'You're still trying to catch me out, you are, Mr Davies. You're still making those inquiries of yours.'

Davies tried to look unconcerned. 'Oh, that. Well it's always at the back of my mind, Edwin. What time are you going on your rounds?'

Curl looked at the clock. 'I ought to be now,' he said. 'But we'll have another drink first.'

'We'll come with you,' said Davies. 'Keep you company.'

Curl looked half-shocked. 'Oh, all right,' he said

eventually. 'There's nothing much to it. You've had a good look before. By yourself. But come if you like. After all, you *are* the police.'

He poured them further generous measures and since there was only a quarter left in the bottle, he poured that out too. 'Well,' he said. 'If you can't have a bit of pleasure, I always say, what can you have?' They carried their cups with them. Mod began to walk like a polar bear on hind legs, one heavy foot planted after another, as he often did when he had taken a lot of drink. It had been a considerable night. Davies also felt his eyes were sticky and his steps uncertain. Only Curl seemed light-footed.

They walked with him down the road between the trade premises. He recited their names as he went. 'Pax Papers . . . Hally's Cast Iron Fittings . . . Bell's Exhausts . . . Blissen Pharmaceuticals . . . you know them . . . Security Plus Safes . . . Shurrock Clocks . . . what a state he gets in, that Mr Shurrock . . .' The recitation continued as they followed him through the dark ways of the estate, the beam of his torch bouncing before them. 'All locked up, tight as a virgin's legs,' Curl said cheerfully. Mod grimaced towards Davies.

'This is my favourite,' announced Curl as they trudged up an incline towards a tall windowless shed. 'Iverson Theatricals. It's only a warehouse, a store really, so there's hardly ever anyone here. But . . . come and have a look.'

'I came here before,' said Davies. 'When I had a look around. But it was shut.'

'Like I say, it nearly always is,' said Curl. From his cluster of keys he selected two and turned the door

184

locks. 'They turn up now and again and take some of their stuff, or bring it in.' He pushed the tall door and, as it swung inwards, turned on a powerful light. Davies and Mod stopped in astonishment. The copious building was hanging with coloured figures, dummies, some of them huge: Humpty-Dumpty, Pinocchio, a snarling giant, a massive duck; row upon row of rag figures, their legs and arms hanging bonelessly.

'Blimey,' said Davies, 'what a pantomime.'

'Exactly right,' enthused Curl. He threw out his small hands as though presenting the extravaganza to a great audience.

Mod said: 'One of the Seven Dwarfs is missing.'

'Sleepy,' agreed Curl, moving towards the bright, bug-eyed group in a corner. They were hanging over a rail, their outsized heads propped up. The security man bent down into the dark part of the wall and pulled up the figure of Sleepy. 'He seems to really doze off,' he said, putting the head beside the others.

'Where's Snow White?' asked Davies.

'Ah, now you're asking,' answered Curl. 'She used to be here and I used to come up and see her. Almost every night.' He looked suddenly abashed. 'I liked to give her a cuddle,' he said.

'I see.'

'They took her away somewhere. I miss her.'

Mod coughed to clear his embarrassment and began to wander into the interior of the amazing shed. Some of the figures were gigantic, suspended like airships from the ceiling. 'They supply people all over the world,' said Curl, following him with some relief. Davies stood for a few moments studying the

185

dwarfs and then followed them into the central aisle of the warehouse.

Curl was throwing his hands about. 'Carnivals, Hallowe'ens, Mardi Grasses, all things like that. The big heads are very popular. They have huge special vans to collect them because they don't collapse or come to pieces. Some of them do, but not many. Look . . .' He strode out enthusiastically. 'Look at Humpty-Dumpty . . . now you won't tell, will you? Just watch.'

As they watched, he lowered the gigantic head by a pulley, manoeuvring it like an attendant with a balloon until he had it hovering above him. Another relaxation of the pulley and the great, grinning head dropped over his. Curl's small body became even smaller under the monstrous shining cranium, his legs danced grotesquely. Davies and Mod laughed wildly at first as Humpty-Dumpty began to bounce around but then they stopped. The huge smiling egg had come to a standstill, and the small uniformed lungs underneath were panting. 'All right,' shouted Davies, not sure whether Curl could hear. 'You can come out now.'

'I can't,' came a wistful echo from within. 'You'll have to help me. I can never get out of this one.'

Davies looked at Mod. They moved in together and, to Curl's hollow-voiced instructions, they manoeuvred him below the pulley, turned the massive egg to the right and then half-left. Three tugs on the pulley and, like a swiftly rising moon, the head ascended leaving a perspiring, smirking Edwin Curl below. 'I always get jammed in that one,' he explained bashfully. 'I was in here for hours one night, trying to get out.' He

186

looked at them, almost a plea. 'It's good fun though, isn't it?'

'Terrific,' said Davies flatly. 'Have you tried all these others, then?' He began to walk deeper into the cavern. Painted faces grimaced and laughed from shelves and rafters. There was a line of trousered dummies hanging from a rack.

'Death Row, I call that,' said the little security guard. 'It's creepy, isn't it?' He opened a locker and produced another bottle of whisky. 'I keep this in here in case it gets me down,' he explained. 'We'll have to drink from the bottle, though.' He handed it to Davies. 'You first,' he offered.

Davies took the Scotch. 'From another well-wisher?' he asked as he raised it. Curl shook his head. 'I'm not sure whether that came from,' he said. 'In the security business you often get stuff and you can't remember where it turned up from.' After he had taken a swallow, Davies passed the bottle to Mod. He kept his eyes on Curl. 'You're a bit of an actor, Edwin,' he said. 'In secret.'

'A thwarted one,' said Curl, looking down at his uniform. 'I'd rather have a packed audience than a packed lunch any day. But I never will, not now.'

Davies patted him on his slight shoulder. The friendship immediately revived the little man. 'Want to try?' he asked. 'Would you like to have a go, Mr Lewis?'

They had replenishments from the bottle and then Mod agreed to try one of the heads, and chose a wizard. The head was not as large as some, but was pinnacled with a tall, pointed hat. Davies and Curl helped him into the aperture and lowered it to his shoulders. They stepped back and Mod assayed a few clumsy and drunken steps. 'Magic,' said Davies. 'Bloody magic.'

'Now you,' encouraged Curl. The whisky and the game had heightened his voice and his miniature face was earnestly pink. 'There's a big old policeman around here. He's ever so funny. I've put him on before now.' They walked down a wide aisle, leaving Mod incanting and making wizard movements in the background.

'There,' said Curl pointing up. 'Police Constable Fuzz. Isn't that a lovely helmet he's got.'

Davies looked up. The giant policeman looked down. It was like a threat of things to come. Curl handed him the whisky as if in encouragement. 'All right,' said Davies hazily. 'I might as well get used to it.'

Curl lowered the head and demonstrated how Davies should manoeuvre himself into it. Still doubtfully, but egged on by Curl and the whisky, he pushed his head up into the massive head of PC Fuzz. He almost panicked. It was close, smelly and dark in there. But his eyes found the observation holes and he peered out into Curl's gleeful face. 'This way, this way, Mr Davies,' enthused Curl. 'Let's go and see the Wizard.'

Relentlessly the liquor swilled within Davies's stomach. He staggered a few steps, feeling the head wobbling over him. 'We're *off* to see the Wizard,' he began to sing unreasonably. 'The Wonderful Wizard of Oz.'

He could hear Curl chortling with delight. 'Come on, come on!' He rolled down the aisle towards the open area inside the entrance to the building. Mod was meandering under his disguise and Davies danced in to join him. It was as though the pantomime had given them a new and novel inebriation. They circled each other jovially and were joined by Curl wearing the gross features of Mrs Spratt, Jack's wife who would eat no lean.

The swollen trio circled each other, letting out toots of laughter, stifled by their encumbrances. Mod and Curl collided and it was Mod who staggered back, tripped and was flung backwards on the boards. Davies and Curl gathered to view the felled Wizard whose seemingly small arms and legs kicked desperately. 'Trust you,' Davies called at him. 'Spoiling the game.' He struggled out of his head and was annoyed to find himself streaming with sweat. It was running down his face, his neck and down the front of his shirt to his stomach. Curl divested himself of Mrs Spratt and they went to Mod's aid. They succeeded in righting him and then eased the carnival head from his shoulders. 'God, I thought I was done for then,' he trembled. His face was wet. 'It's just like drowning.'

It was four in the morning before they returned to 'Bali Hi', Furtman Gardens. They had accepted more of Curl's Scotch to assist the recovery from their exertions in the theatrical warehouse and were now convivially and unsteadily carrying a square suitcase between them.

'Not a sound,' warned Davies. 'Not a snort. All right?'

'Not a sound,' agreed Mod. He looked about them. 'Good job they keep the street lights on.'

'If anything goes wrong,' said Davies. 'Just scarper.'

'Scarper,' confirmed Mod.

They paused outside the hushed silhouette of the house. Davies put his hand over his mouth. His eyes were shining like a boy's. They carried the case below the window of Mrs Fulljames's bedroom. Mod fumbled with the fastenings. Davies took over. The top of the container opened like two trapdoors and there slowly emerged a mechanical top-hatted clown. The head was on an articulated extension. Davies pulled a lever and it rose, two feet from its box, until he pressed the control again and it stopped. Another touch and it rose a further three feet so that its head was on a level with theirs, its fixed grin in their faces. The two drunks looked at each other and smirked. 'Now,' said Davies. He pulled the lever further and the clown's garish head began to rise on its long mechanical neck. Entranced, they watched it ascend until the painted, grinning, top-hatted head was directly outside the landlady's window. Their cheeks were puffed, their ribs shook.

Davies made a tapping motion with his hand and Mod pushed the supporting apparatus forward so that the brim of the clown's hat knocked on the curtained glass. Three times they did it, and then withdrew the head until it was a foot clear of the window. The clown was looking directly at the curtains. Nothing happened. 'Again,' whispered Davies.

At that moment they saw the bedroom light go on above them, and then the curtains were fiercely pulled aside. There was a second's pause and then the most terrible echoing screech, followed by a second. 'Christ!' exploded Davies, staring up. 'Run!'

Taking the wildly wagging head with them, they scampered around the corner of the house. Mrs Fulljames's screams still rent the night. Lights were going on in the house and in others in the street. Around the corner, Davies pressed the lever which lowered the toy head back into its case. 'Hurry up, hurry up,' he pleaded. Mod was already running, down the short garden and through the back gate into the narrow alley. Kitty began to howl hollowly in the garage. Windows were banging up and heads appearing. 'Wait for me!' gasped Davies. 'This thing is heavy.'

He caught up with Mod and, both carrying the case, they lumbered along the alley and out into the main street. Everywhere was deserted. Panting and howling with mirth, they reached the shops and Harry's All Night Refreshments.

'Back again, Dangerous,' said Harry, rising from behind a newspaper.

'Take this, will you, mate,' puffed Davies, offering the case across the counter. 'It's not nicked or anything.' He had to wipe his eyes. Mod was doubled up over a stool. A police car siren was sounding easily in the streets.

'You're sure?' said Harry.

'Would I pass hot property on to you, Harry?' asked Davies. 'Two coffees, please.' Still doubting, the stallholder took the case. 'As it's you, Dangerous,' he said. He regarded Mod. 'What's so funny?'

Davies leaned forward and opened the flaps.

191

'Look,' he invited. 'It's only Topper the Clown.' Mod again became convulsed.

Harry peered down at the clown's hatted head. 'How long do I have to keep him?' he asked solidly.

'Only till tomorrow,' said Davies, breaking up again. 'We'll collect him then.'

Harry put the case at the rear of the premises where he cooked the food. 'Anything else, gents?' he called.

'Two bacon sandwiches,' Mod called. He was still wiping his eyes. He looked at Davies apologetically. 'You don't mind buying me breakfast, do you?' They both began to laugh again. Harry looked over his shoulder and shrugged. Gradually they subsided. They drank their coffee. Mod picked up Harry's newspaper and began to scan it idly. He put it down and then leaned over and re-read something closely. Glancing towards the back of Harry, busy at his frying pan, he carefully tore a small square from the newspaper. Davies was listening for noises from Furtman Gardens and did not see what he did.

'And may I inquire where you persons were last night?' Mrs Fulljames said between taut lips; pronouncing 'persons' so tightly that it emerged as 'poisons'.

Having just entered the room, Davies and Mod looked innocently at each other and then at the occupants of the evening table. 'Us persons?' inquired Davies eventually. Cautiously they took their seats.

'Indeed, *you* persons,' repeated Mrs Fulljames.

'You weren't in your beds,' put in Doris spitefully.

'Mrs Davies,' said Davies, leaning towards his estranged wife. 'I hope you did not enter my room, or Mr Lewis's.'

'It wasn't necessary,' retorted Mrs Fulljames. 'You didn't appear when all the noise was going on. It was *I* who went to your rooms.'

'What noise was this?' asked Davies. He looked only briefly towards Mod.

Mrs Fulljames dabbed her eyes and paddled the ladle around. Steam joined her tears. 'It's disgraceful,' she trembled.

'Disgusting,' put in Doris fiercely. She nodded her head like a hammer. 'Look, you've made Mrs Fulljames cry.'

'No he hasn't,' rejoined the landlady. She wiped the vapour from her face. 'Take more than *him*. Terrorizing women.'

Davies appeared stunned. Mod held out his hands. 'Terrorizing which women?' asked Davies.

'Us,' replied Doris briskly.

'Me, actually,' said Mrs Fulljames with a short, hard look at Doris. 'I was the one in terror.'

'Screaming,' said Minnie with a sort of satisfaction. 'In the passage.'

'Why?' asked Mod. 'I'm afraid I don't understand.'

'Nor me,' protested Davies. 'What's it all in aid of?'

'You understand right enough,' said Mrs Fulljames. But now a little doubt sounded in her voice. 'Don't tell me *you* didn't put that terrible thing up at my window.' Emotion engulfed her again and she half missed the next plate with a ladle-load of lamb stew. 'Oh,' she seethed, scraping it up. 'Oh!'

Davies rose chivalrously and procured a cloth

from the kitchen. 'Here,' he said with solicitude. 'Let me do it.' He passed the cloth to Mod who made one or two ineffectual dabbing movements over the spilled stew before it was forcibly reclaimed by Mrs Fulljames.

Uncertainty, Davies could see, however, had set in. 'Do you swear to me, on your honour as a police officer, and as a man, that you had *nothing whatever* to do with what occurred in the night?'

'I do,' answered Davies blatantly. 'I still haven't been told *what* indeed did occur.'

Doris said tartly: 'Somebody put a head, a head and a hat, up to Mrs Fulljames's window. At four o'clock this morning.'

'A head?' inquired Mod. He looked askance at Davies. 'A hat?'

'Whose head?' put in Davies. 'What hat?'

'Don't, don't,' pleaded Mrs Fulljames. 'Please start your meal. I don't want to remember it.' Sharply, she turned to Davies. 'Never in my life have I been so upset,' she said. Her voice began to vibrate again. 'Not even when that horse somehow got into the house.'

'Ah, that horse,' said Davies, nodding at Mod.

'That was a business,' said Mod.

Mrs Fulljames, spoon poised, gave each of them an edged look. 'Exactly,' she said. 'And so was this a business. A painted face . . . like a mad clown . . . tapping at my window.'

Davies appeared aghast. 'Really,' he remarked inadequately. '. . . a mad clown eh?' His concerned eyes travelled to Mod. Mr Smeeton, the Complete Home Entertainer, had said nothing and was minutely trying to extricate a morsel of lamb from a bone.

194

'Clowns,' said Mod. 'Sounds more like Mr Smeeton's line of country.'

The entertainer raised profoundly injured eyes. 'I was in my bed, Mr Lewis,' he replied. He resumed his quest. 'Asleep.'

'So were most of us,' said Doris with her sniff. 'But you two weren't.'

'Indeed,' agreed Davies. 'We were absent.'

'Where?' asked Mrs Fulljames.

Davies finished a piece of gravied swede and slid a carrot down his throat like a magician swallowing a goldfish. 'Mrs Fulljames,' he eventually told her. 'I am sure you will appreciate that as an officer of the law I am unable to inform you about many things. Where I was, and indeed where Mr Lewis was last night *should* be one of them . . .'

'*He's* not an officer of the law,' pointed out Mr Smeeton spitefully. 'Not Lewis.'

'Last night,' reiterated Davies, '*should* be one of them. However, since my whereabouts, *our* whereabouts, seems to be so crucial to this matter, I think I would be permitted to tell you that I was at an all-night drugs party. Mr Lewis was with me.'

'Drugs?' whispered Doris. Her eyes bolted about the table.

'I was the undercover man,' said Mod, attempting to appear mysterious.

Davies added hurriedly: 'It was necessary for a witness to be present who was not a policeman.'

There was silence, apart from spoons and forks striking plates. 'Are you sure?' said Mrs Fulljames. 'I *could* ring the station.'

'That would *not* be advisable,' said Davies quickly

again. 'If you so much as intimated that you knew something about this matter, the drugs squad would be turning this place over before we'd finished our pudding.' Mrs Fulljames gasped. Davies pushed aside his plate, the bone of the single piece of lamb crouched on it like a skeleton in a desert. Reflectively, he knocked it about with his fork. 'A mad clown,' he murmured. 'I don't think I've ever come across a mad clown.'

Edwin Curl was sitting in his gatehouse, his head just visible over the sill, when Davies unloaded the box containing the clown's head from the Vanguard.

'Ah, you've brought him back,' he enthused, getting up and going to help. 'I'm glad he's come home. I can't imagine why you wanted to take him.'

'Nor me,' admitted Davies. 'It was the Scotch. I'm afraid.'

'Oh yes, the Scotch. We drank quite a drop, didn't we? Up there.'

'It's certainly an interesting place,' said Davies. He sat on the edge of Curl's table. 'Never seen anywhere quite like it.' He had fixed Curl with his eye. Curl tried to look away but was not strong enough.

'Go up there more or less every night, do you, Edwin?'

The little security man looked abashed. 'Now, Mr Davies,' he said like a plea for fair play. 'I don't know how much I talked last night. It all got a bit out of hand. The drink and that . . .'

'Do you go up there every night?' repeated Davies. 'To that store?'

'No, not every . . . Not now.'

'Not since they took Snow White away?'

Curl looked sulky. 'Now you're taking the piss,' he said in a hurt voice. 'That's easy. I might have said something I shouldn't have said but . . .'

Leaning towards him, Davies gently took the collar of the uniform shirt between finger and thumb. 'Edwin,' he said remorselessly. 'You *were* up there, weren't you, with Snow White on the night last October when that man died in the canal? Lofty Brock.'

Misery crowded into the security guard's miniature face. The little head nodded. 'All right,' he answered throatily. 'I was up there with her. Nearly all night.'

Thoughtfully, he drove back to The Babe In Arms. Rain was coming down steadily but it lacked the discomforting edge of winter rain for the season was moving on. Mod was established at their table. Jemma came in from her choral practice.

When he had sat down with a drink before him, Davies said slowly: 'Edwin Curl, the man who was supposed to be guarding the gate of the industrial estate, had absented himself on the night of October 6th last year.'

'What was he doing?' asked Jemma.

'Embracing Snow White,' said Davies simply.

Her expressive eyebrows arched, but before she could ask questions, Mod took a ragged portion of newspaper from his overcoat pocket. 'I'd overlooked this,' he said, leaning across the table. 'I seem to

197

remember taking it from a paper at Harry's last night.' He looked up. Their faces were only half-expectant. 'I'll read it,' he said.

'Please,' invited Davies. 'I'm on edge.'

Mod put his unwieldy glasses on his face. 'It's only a paragraph,' he said. 'It says: "Dorset Police have identified a body washed ashore at Chesil Bank, near Weymouth, on October 7th last year, as Sigmund Dietrich, an executive of the Becker Pharmaceutical Corporation, of Zurich, the resumed inquest at Dorchester was told yesterday. An open verdict was recorded."'

'October 7th. The same day as Lofty was found,' breathed Davies. He reached for the scrap of newspaper. '*And* a pharmaceutical executive.'

'It needn't mean a thing,' said Mod, but obviously pleased. 'But it may.' He wagged a fat and none-too-clean finger. 'You know we've always thought of Frau Harrer, who *also* works for a pharmaceutical company, as German. But she could easily be Swiss. After all we call her the Jungfrau but where *is* the Jungfrau?'

'In Switzerland,' said Jemma.

14

Spring was edging its green way through the countryside. Even the ancient Vanguard seemed to know this, for it produced several roaring spurts which, at times, swung the speedometer beyond the fifty-miles-an-hour mark.

'Steady,' cautioned Jemma. 'If this falls to bits, it's going to cost a fortune to have it cleared from the motorway.'

'Hampshire,' enthused Davies. 'Look at the catkins.'

A great bruised cloud moved across the sun and soon it began to rain briskly. She held on to his arm above the elbow. 'We're on holiday,' she breathed. 'Just think, we're on our first holiday together.'

'Compulsory leave it's called,' corrected Davies. 'In my case. Only one better than being suspended. Compulsory leave while the Metropolitan Police makes up its mind whether or not to kick me out of the force.'

'If they do,' she said decisively, 'then I'll pack up as well.'

'We could come down to Hampshire,' he said. 'And grow catkins.'

She looked at her watch. 'Eleven o'clock,' she said enthusiastically. 'What shall we do when we get there?'

'I'm treading carefully,' he said. 'I can't go around asking too many questions, acting like a copper. The Dorset police could really cook my goose, providing there's a goose left.'

She pouted. 'I didn't mean that,' she said. 'I meant like walking together on the beach or sharing a bottle of wine.'

'Ah, that as well,' he said. 'Both in fact.'

They reached the end of the motorway where the road by-passed Winchester and curved gradually west. The Hampshire fields with their reappearing rivers gave way to the New Forest brushland. They crossed into Dorset. Jemma said: 'You'll be very disappointed, won't you, Dangerous, if none of this works out?'

'Very,' he nodded. 'If there was no crime then I'm never going to find one, that's for sure. I could go on raking old ashes for ever.' They drove in silence until they reached Wimborne. 'We keep finding disjoined pieces, don't we?' he said eventually. He was trying to reassure himself. 'Every time something turns up, it adds something to it. Lofty Brock, for example, is now Billy Dobson.' He looked at her sideways, beseechingly. 'Don't say that doesn't mean he was murdered.'

'I wasn't going to,' she assured quietly. 'But it doesn't.' She half turned, consolingly touching his hand on the steering wheel. 'You've been finding things, Dangerous,' she said. 'But they're bits of history. Bits of crimes long ago, secrets and everything. But . . .'

'But what? *But* I still haven't discovered whether it *was* a murder much less *who* did it, if it *was* in the first place. Nor the motive – if there ever was a motive.'

'That's the nearest thing to double Dutch I've heard, even from you,' she laughed.

He grinned at her. 'When sober that is,' he said. He looked out at the low, old Dorset roofs. 'Let's have a drink,' he suggested. 'They seem to keep sensible opening hours down here.'

The car was turned into the courtyard of a white-washed inn with a powerful tower of a church rising beyond its roof. The engine died with a sigh of relief. Davies hurried from the driving seat and with massive courtesy opened the passenger door for Jemma. She was wearing a green sweater and slim white trousers. As they went into the bar, Jemma first, a man who was balancing across the floor with a full tankard let it slip in his fingers and slop over. The barman, his attention also fixed on Jemma, kept pulling the pump handle long after the glass beneath was brimming over. There were three other men in the room and they sat entranced. 'They don't see many girls in green sweaters down here,' suggested Davies in a whisper.

'Especially black girls,' she whispered.

They advanced on the bar. ''Morning,' said the barman, still looking at her. 'Nice day for travelling.'

Jemma ordered a glass of wine, Davies had a pint of beer. 'How did you know we were travelling?' asked Davies.

'I knew you weren't from around here,' said the barman. 'I'd have noticed.' He looked up uncertainly. 'Deduction,' he said. 'I used to be a policeman. In London.'

'Retired to peace and quiet, have you?' said Davies easily. He took the drinks. 'Not a lot of crime around here, is there?'

'We have our share,' said the man. Davies asked if he would like a drink and he accepted. 'Across the back here . . .' He nodded over his shoulder. 'In the graveyard, there's one of the great unsolved mysteries.'

'What's that?'

'The burial place of the man they reckon was Jack-the-Ripper. The prime suspect. Montague John Druitt. Nobody will ever know now, of course. It's too far gone.'

'Some things are like that,' said Davies.

In the late afternoon, they walked over the coastal hill, a chapel at its summit, the airs of spring all around them, puffing freshly as they climbed. Soon they were looking down on the humped roofs of the village and the yard of the inn where they were staying.

'Did you see the lady's face when we walked in together?' laughed Jemma.

Davies was panting from the climb. He sat down clumsily on a shelf of rock protruding like old teeth from the hillside grass. 'You *are* a bit of a pioneer,' he told her.

She sat beside him, nudging him along the rock. 'And see what I've found,' she said. Again she laughed and they kissed, their arms flapping about each other. Then they sat and surveyed the distance. The far flank of the valley ascended to a newly leafing copse; a dog and a man walked towards it. 'We should have brought Kitty,' said Jemma.

'We should,' admitted Davies guiltily. 'But he'd

have had to share the room. And you know how he gets jealous.'

The sunshine was intermittent, sweeping over the vale and the village. They could hear a stream. Davies sniffed deeply. 'Lovely,' he said. 'Sea air and cow dung.'

'It's beautiful,' she agreed seriously. 'I'm glad you brought me.' She stood up and he did also.

'Brought *you*,' he said, wrapping his overcoat arms around her again. 'You've brought *me*. I used to spend my holidays in the Cricklewood Snooker Hall.' She laughed with him. Her arms encircled his waist and their faces sidled to each other, his red nose touching the tip of her black nose. They both squinted inland as if to make sure no observer was far below. 'Nobody looking,' reported Davies. They kissed again deeply.

They walked up the short remainder of the hill, past the stark chapel, and found themselves looking out over widespread sea and land. Windy sunshine patterned the long sea, ruffling it, illuminating its corrugations. Waves rolled with heavy indolence against the remarkable landfall, the ten-mile curve of Chesil Bank. It travelled in an amazing arc, diminishing to a point miles east. Below them, the pebbled beach stood with casual confidence against the blunt rollers, breaking each at its final assault.

'Listen,' said Jemma. 'You can hear the pebbles from here. Rattling as the sea comes in.'

Davies said: 'I wonder where they found the body of this Swiss chap.'

*

At evening lights were lit at dispersed parts of the horizon and, only a little higher, there appeared a loitering star. 'You can still hear the waves washing against the pebbles,' said Jemma. They stood at the small upstairs window at the inn. Davies had his arm about her waist, rubbing his hand against her hipbone like a gun in a holster under her robe. She leaned languidly against him, her head lolling against his neck. A lamp burned behind them in the room, amber across the bed.

'I think we've been noticed hereabouts, Dangerous,' she said.

'I wouldn't be surprised. People tend to be nosey in these places.'

'If you want to attract attention, take a black girl to the English seaside off-season,' she murmured.

'Especially if you're the wrong side of fifty, and the wrong side of twelve stone, and the aforementioned black girl is excessively beautiful,' he added. He turned towards her and kissed her. She reached and drew the curtains. 'I'm not doing a show for the fishing fleet,' she said.

She had brought him a present, a striped silk dressing-gown, in which he now stood before the mirror in the door of the dark old wardrobe that leaned towards him with the list of the ancient floor. He posed first one way then another, pushing his thick white leg through the divide in the garment. Jemma lay across the bed.

'There's no doubt,' smirked Davies, 'that I do have a modicum of style.'

Smiling she said: 'You're sensational.'

'On the other hand,' he went on, striking a further

attitude. 'How this is going to look with the flannel pyjamas remains in doubt.'

'You're not wearing any,' she told him firmly. 'I'm not coming away with a man who packs flannel pyjamas.'

'No such conditions were mentioned before we set out,' he said, studying the slim brown leg that had slipped naked from below her robe. 'I know your sort, miss . . .' he advanced on the bed. 'Get a man to take you somewhere exotic and then play hard to get.' He sat on the edge of the bed and began stroking her stomach.

'I'm not hard to get, Dangerous,' she told him peacefully. 'You know how easy I am.'

Her long fingers went up his thigh below his robe. He regarded her seriously. 'You're going to spoil your dinner,' he forecast.

'It gives me an appetite.' She moved over on the big dimpled bed and he lay beside her. 'This place is probably haunted,' he said, looking at the beamed ceilings.

'You'll be haunted if you don't stop fooling about,' she threatened quietly.

He rolled against her, feeling her long, soft form fold into the knots and crevices of his everyday body. ''Tis a night for smugglers,' he muttered hoarsely in a grating dialect. '"Brandy for the parson, baccy for the clerk."'

'You know that?' she said, opening her eyes.

'Only one I do know,' he confessed. '"Five and twenty ponies trotting through the dark" . . . I had to write it out a hundred times at school for letting off in the literature class.'

She pushed her nose under his armpit. 'Do you want a fuck or a pantomime?' she asked.

'Some of both if you've got them,' he answered. He kissed her on the shoulder and around and about the breasts.

'That's more like it,' she said. 'I was ready to go home.'

'Don't,' he said gently, 'go home.'

He was getting much better at it. After years of neglect and indifferent company, he had rediscovered the uniqueness. She had also taught him the fun. He eased the robe away so that the glowing stomach and soft pubis lay exposed. 'You're like an animal,' she smiled as he put his mouth on her skin again.

'A tortoise,' he mumbled.

'Perhaps,' she said into his eyes which at that moment had risen in front of her face. 'There's a lot to be said for taking your time.'

He took his, and hers. As they lay against each other she said, her eyes closed: 'There are times, Dangerous, when I feel that I'm just not decent.'

'Thank God for that,' he muttered.

It was an hour before she left the soft, lumpy bed, sliding out to go to the bathroom. He was dozing but he knew it would be rewarding to open his eyes to watch her walk naked across the room. It was. She returned and arranged her robe loosely about her. He half levered himself up in the bed. 'I can't sleep without my flannel pyjamas,' he said.

'It's a sort of flannel pyjamas place,' she admitted, looking around the shadowed room, the ponderous and lopsided furniture, the flowered pitcher and bowl on the wash-stand. She touched each of them. 'Even having a bathroom seems to spoil it.'

She took the jug to the bathroom and, with mounting pleasure, he heard her filling it. She had a studied expression when she returned and set the jug on the stand and the bowl on the floor. 'Out you get,' she ordered quietly.

Davies left the bed. 'Kneel down,' she added without looking at him. 'I even found a flannel.'

As she washed him, never lifting her head from what she was doing, she said: 'Do you think the people here think it's odd you being with a black girl?'

He touched her dark and lovely head, running his fingers from her hair down to her ear and on to her neck and shoulders. 'I'm trying to keep it quiet,' he said throatily. 'They'll all want one.'

They had dinner at a rocky table near the window of the inn. It was so unstable they played a game of see-sawing it from one side to the other. The plump woman who served them said: 'He was meaning to fix that afore he went and died.' She frowned, apparently annoyed at the omission, then said: 'Where you be coming from then?' An hour before, as she served the soup, she had spent a measurable time noticing Jemma's lack of a wedding ring.

'London,' answered Davies amiably. 'North-west.'

'Oh,' said the woman, looking at Jemma. 'You as well, miss?'

'London, north-west,' confirmed Jemma sweetly. 'It was a wonderful dinner.'

'We do our best,' said the woman. 'He's been gone five years, but we do our best.'

She served them coffee and went away. Davies rocked the table again. 'I think he's trying to get a message through,' he said.

'That's why he never fixed it,' she smiled.

After the coffee, they went under the low beams into the bar. It was crowded. As they went in, fifty faces turned on them. ''Evening,' said Davies, genially and generally. Someone made space at the bar. Many of the faces were red with weather, eyes blackened but bright, heads apparently balancing on roll-neck jerseys. 'A brandy,' said Davies to the girl behind the bar. 'And a Cointreau.'

He heard the word 'Cointreau' being passed about the room. They stood at the bar and the room settled to its former conviviality, the men, however, moving at short intervals, one taking the place of another, like a country dance, so that each could have an uninterrupted view of Jemma. With her customary, professional ease she fell into conversation with them. A reddened man with cracked lips and a curtain of whiskers stood next to Davies. 'Sun went down a bit early today,' he remarked.

'Oh, did it? How was that?'

'Too early for I, believe me.' His voice was broad Dorset. 'This season you keep looking for the light dusks. Get more done.' With a touch of surprise he looked at his empty beer glass. 'You don't start on the drinking so early,' he said.

'Like another?' asked Davies. He began reaching for his money.

'That be very civil,' said the man. He held up a

hand like a placard. 'But I won't . . . until we been rightly introduced.' He jabbed his hand towards Davies. 'Jim Fisher,' he growled. 'Fisher by name, fisher by trade.'

'You are?' said Davies, accepting the handshake. 'In that case, my name ought to be Agent, but it's Davies.'

'A secret agent?' asked the man, his gnarled eyes widening. 'Is that it?'

'Insurance,' corrected Davies. 'Insurance agent.'

'I see.' He swung his glass towards Davies. 'Ale is mine,' he said.

'I think I'll go on the ale too,' said Davies. 'One brandy is enough.' He asked the girl, who was eyeing Fisher uncertainly, for two pints. He leaned sideways and asked Jemma who was at the centre of a clutch of fishermen.

'No darling,' she said over her shoulder. 'We're discussing single-parent families.'

'Where did you come on her?' asked Fisher innocuously. 'Africa?'

'North-west London,' said Davies.

'Don't see many dark ones in these parts,' said Fisher regretfully. 'I likes 'em myself.' He accepted the drink. 'Is it marine?' he asked.

'Marine?'

'Insurance.'

'Oh, I see. Well in this instance, yes, I suppose. But not generally.'

'What is this instance then?'

Davies took a deep drink while he thought about it. Eventually he said: 'It's about a Swiss chap whose body was found on the beach here.'

'I reckoned it might be. Don't often go an' get drowned, the Swiss, do they?'

'You don't associate them with water,' Davies agreed. 'Unless it's in Lake Geneva. What made you think that might be the reason I'm here? I could have come down to collect sea shells.'

Fisher laughed mysteriously. 'There's nothin' folks around here don't know afore long,' he said. 'When you was up on chapel 'ill this afternoon, you was speakin' about it to your dark lady. The wind carries voices easy in these parts. The old woman dustin' in the chapel, she 'eard you.'

'It's certainly a funny business,' said Davies sagely. 'Six months before the body was identified.'

The fisherman shook his head. 'By the time the sea 'ad swelled him up and he'd been thrown on the Chesil Bank back and fore, 'is own mother wouldn't 'ave knowd him.' He leaned over the bar. 'Nance,' he called. 'Get the *Gazette* there.'

The girl paused in washing glasses and passed the newspaper to him. ''Tis all in here,' he said, un-folding it. 'The Inquest. Still, I 'spect you know all about that.'

'Yes, yes, of course,' said Davies leaning forward. 'But I'd still like to see what it says. You never know . . .'

'There,' said Fisher. 'And the picture of 'im. Sigmund Dietrich. What a name.'

'Swiss,' shrugged Davies, taking the newspaper. 'Well-known Swiss name.' He studied the picture. 'He looks like a Swiss.'

'Sounds more German.'

'Well it does. But there are subtle differences.' He

had spread the front page. 'Mystery of the Chesil Bank Body Solved,' Davies read aloud. He sensed Jemma's half-turn before she prudently turned back to her discussion group. 'No papers, no identification,' murmured Davies. 'Well, we knew that.'

'How come they didn't miss him in Switzerland?' asked Fisher shrewdly. ''Is family?'

'Oh, they did,' said Davies, reading quickly. 'But everyone thought he had gone to the Far East. His family and the firm he worked for.'

'They was looking in the wrong part of the world. So I remember now.'

Davies looked up. 'How do you think he got to be here?'

'Washed up on the Bank, you mean? I don't know what 'e was doin' 'ere in the first place, naturally. Nobody does, do they?'

'I mean washed up on the Bank,' said Davies.

'Well, 'tis for certain he didn't swim from Switzerland,' said Fisher. 'So I reckon he went over the side of the Weymouth ferry.'

'Ah, of course. They run across to the Continent from Weymouth. How far is it?'

'Weymouth from 'ere? Oh, seven, eight miles. But anyone going overboard a mile or two off-shore, from the ferry like, is going to land up on Chesil Bank. That's how the currents run.'

'They think he was in the water only twenty-four hours,' said Davies, knocking the newspaper with the back of his hand. 'That,' he added hurriedly, 'confirms our information.'

'That's enough,' said Fisher. 'The sea water and the throwing him upwards on to the pebbles and

back again and up again. It makes a mess of a man.'
He glanced up. 'You want to see where he came
ashore?' he inquired. Fisher's eyes almost disappeared into his own wrinkles.

'I wouldn't mind,' said Davies. 'Is it far?'

'Ten minutes along the Bank,' said Fisher. 'Your
lady ought to be staying here while we go on.'

Jemma turned, her expression doubtful. 'I won't
be long,' said Davies. 'Half an hour at the most. Go
on up if you feel like it.'

'I'm all right,' she replied quietly. 'We're now on
the subject of AIDS.'

She kissed him on the cheek as he turned towards
the door. A mutter of approval came from the men.
As they went out into the starlit night, with the salt
smell and the sound of breakers coming from the
pebbled shore, Davies said: 'It might be helpful if I
could have a few words with the man who actually
found the body.'

'You have,' said Fisher. 'It was I.'

It was one in the morning when Davies returned.
The inn was closed and locked and he stood in the
dark and the wind calling up to Jemma. There was a
subdued light in the window but his exhortations
went unheard. Eventually, he tossed up a half-
handful of shingle and her face immediately came to
the window. She opened it. 'What do you want?' she
inquired.

'I'm locked out,' he said.

'How do I know you will do me no harm?' she
asked.

'I won't. I'm too bruised. I kept falling down on the pebbles.'

She disappeared from the casement. A few moments later, she pulled the bolts from the sturdy door. 'You look like the old man from the sea,' she said.

'Yo, ho, ho,' he grumbled. They went in. She restored the bolts and followed his complaining figure up the grinding staircase.

'Oh, my shins and knees,' he moaned, rolling up his trouser legs. 'Those pebbles are killers. I'm black and blue. Look at the bruises coming out already.'

Her nose was working. 'You've been drinking rum,' she said accusingly.

'Rum and shrub,' he acknowledged. 'I think it's rum with all the impurities put back.'

'I've been waiting for you,' she said. She took off her robe and he saw she was wearing his flannel pyjamas. 'I got cold,' she said.

He kissed her after protecting his shins and knees with his hands. Painfully, he began to undress. 'I should have kept the long johns on,' he grumbled. He looked at her. 'Can I just have the bottom bit?' he asked. 'To protect my legs?'

Jemma slid out of the heavy pyjama trousers. Still groaning, he put them on, patting them gingerly over his shins. She pulled the bedcovers back for him and he carefully got into bed. She followed. They lay on their backs. 'Those pebbles are twenty feet high in some places,' he muttered. 'They're like shelves. I kept falling down them.'

'Did you find anything?' she asked. 'Solve any mysteries?'

'It was Fisher, the man I went off with, who found the body. These people never tell you everything at once. They're like the lot at Purwell. It must be the salt in the air or something.'

'In the end it's all the same coast,' she pointed out.

'I suppose it is. Well, he took me to the place where he found the body. He went straight to it in the dark. Do you know how they can tell which part of the Bank, as they call it, they're on even at night – and remember it's ten miles long?'

'The pebbles are different sizes,' she said. He turned his head. 'I've been with the locals too, remember,' she told him. 'At one end of the Bank the pebbles are as small as a pea, and they gradually get larger until at the other end they're huge. Right?'

'Right,' he acknowledged. 'That's how he knew the spot where the body came ashore. He said it was knocked about by being thrown upon the pebbles, probably several times.' He rubbed his legs. 'And I can understand that.'

'How did the man get in the water?' she asked. 'Did he have any ideas?'

'Well, he's pretty sure he didn't go in from the beach. It's not difficult to drown that way because you step straight off the pebbles into a twelve-foot trough with a terrific undertow. But Fisher says that strangers walking along the Bank at this time of the year tend to be noticed, and we know that's true. Also poor old Sigmund Dietrich was not wearing an overcoat or anything protective. Only a city suit. Fisher says he thinks he must have gone overboard from a boat a couple of miles out, and most probably one of the ferries that ply between Weymouth and the Continent.' Davies paused. 'And there was nothing in his pockets.'

'Fisher had a look, did he?'

'It's an old custom down here. If he's speaking the truth and he didn't empty the pockets himself, then it points to some person or persons dumping Sigmund in the Channel and not wanting him to be identified. Even if Fisher helped himself to valuables, he's hardly likely to have taken papers or what-have-you from the body.'

'I don't understand why it's taken six months to identify the body. Didn't anybody miss him at home in Switzerland?'

'Apparently he was thought to have gone to the Far East. They'd been looking for him in the stews of Bangkok and he was in Weymouth Mortuary all the time.'

'You're still fairly certain he had some link with the Lofty Brock business?'

'He's Swiss, like Frau Harrer, he's in pharmaceuticals, and he apparently went overboard on October 6th, which was the day before Lofty's body was found in the canal. Two drownings on one night. And remember Shiny Bright said he heard a kerfuffle outside Blissen Pharmaceuticals and actually saw a man being struck down. What better than to take the victim back in one of the vehicles and dump him over the side from the ferry.'

'His photograph was in the local paper,' she said. 'I saw you looking at it.'

'Yes, it was obtained by the police from the Swiss authorities for identification.' He had closed his eyes but now opened them to study the old brown ceiling.

'There's a man in Weymouth, the owner of a hotel near the ferry landing, who, according to Fisher who seems to know everything, has told the local police that he recognized the photograph of Sigmund. He says he has stayed in the hotel on occasions. I'm going to see him tomorrow.'

'It's turning out to be a lovely holiday,' she sighed. 'How are the shins?'

'I'm sorry,' he said. 'I had to go to Fisher's cottage and that's where the rum and shrub is located. It's terrible stuff, especially if you have to walk back over mountains of pebbles.'

'It's a great smuggling coast,' she said. 'In the bar there's an account of the goings-on around here. The smugglers knew where they had come ashore on the beach by the size of the pebbles. There was a book called *Moonfleet* written about it. It was quite a thriving industry.'

'It still is,' he told her.

15

The Seashore Hotel, Weymouth, bore the scars of its name. Its façade, looking out on to the promenade and the blunt Channel, was pitted by spray and gales, its windows crusty with salt. It faced the Continental Ferry Terminal.

'He'd been several times in here,' said the manager, Sam Sealy. He gazed from the window as if he expected to see the drowned man arriving for another stay.

Davies said: 'And he stayed here on October 6th last year, but only for a few hours. The day before his body was found.'

'Right. Normally he and the other men, the drivers, would come off the six o'clock ferry and put up for the night, starting out again in the morning. I took it they did it because the place where they were delivering the goods in London, or wherever it was, would be closed for the night if they drove on.'

'But sometimes they would drive straight to London?'

'Yes. Every few weeks or so. The last time – October 6th – was a bit odd because they came over on the midday boat and just hung about. They had two cars that time, two station wagons, Japanese, not the bigger trucks like usual.'

'They were killing time?'

'I suppose they must have been. They had a meal and lasted that out. Then they must have gone for a wander in the town, or gone to the pictures or something. They came back after five, had a drink and another meal and eventually drove off about six-thirty.'

'Where did they park the vehicles?'

'Well, normally they just left them in the ferry lorry and car park, across the road, but this last time the man who drowned, what was his name . . .'

'Dietrich. Sigmund Dietrich.'

'That's him. On this occasion he asked if he could park the two station wagons in the hotel car park, around behind. It's only a small space but only my car was in it so I said all right. But then . . . ah, now I come to think of it . . . he asked if it was possible to lock the gate. It can be locked but I couldn't find the key.'

'Did he seem concerned about that?'

'Sort of, now you mention it. He had me looking around for it for quite a long time. But I couldn't find it, so he had to put up with it. I wouldn't have gone to all the trouble normally, but you have to look after regulars in the winter, even if they're only occasional regulars.'

Davies was drinking coffee. He could see Jemma walking noticeably along the sea front, a bright spot against the grey English sea. Far out in the bay, a large vessel was growing larger. 'Noon ferry,' said Sealy. He looked at the clock enclosed in a steering wheel above the bar. 'Good weather, good time-keeping.'

'Where do they sail from?' Davies asked. 'I know they come from the Channel Islands, but where else?'

'Yes, Jersey and Guernsey. Also France, Cherbourg.'

'What were the other men like?'

'The two with Dietrich? Well, they were different types. More lorry-driving types. Wore sweaters and leather jackets, but when he came here he was always in a suit and tie and he had a good overcoat. Expensive, I'd say.'

'An overcoat. What colour?'

'Dark. Navy blue. Must have cost a bit. There was a label inside and I remember seeing it once, when it was hanging up here. But I can't recall much about it, except it seemed good stuff. Paris or somewhere.'

'He wasn't wearing his overcoat when he was found on Chesil Bank,' said Davies. 'Nor did he have anything in his pockets.'

'So I hear.' He looked distantly out of the window. 'But things fall out of your pockets when you get drowned,' he said. 'Especially in these parts.' His eyes came down to Davies. 'It's the currents.'

Davies said: 'They're pretty powerful.'

'There's no man or vessel has a chance along the Bank,' said Sealy. 'In the old sailing days ships would be driven in-shore and they'd jettison every single thing they could, guns and everything, to make less weight. But they'd never get off the Bank. Whole crews were drowned twenty yards off-shore.'

'Would you be expecting to see the other two men who used to come here with Dietrich? What time of the month would they arrive?'

'Early in the morning,' said Sealy. 'About now

really. During the first week. They've been here since, just as usual, but it's not the same two men every time. In fact, when Dietrich stayed here in October, the last time, I'd never set eyes on the other two before.' He pointed towards the ferry terminal. The noon boat was nearing the jetty. 'See that man there, the one sitting down wearing the brown duffel? He'll be able to tell you more about the times they might arrive. He's been sitting there for days, checking in every ferry, noting the vehicles as they leave. He's some sort of government chap, I think. Ask him.'

Davies went out on to the breezy promenade. The man in the duffel coat, square as a cardboard box, was seated on a public bench facing the harbour. He had a clipboard on his knee. Davies strolled along the causeway, watched the approaching ferry, and then retreated to the promenade until the first vehicles were driving ashore from the vessel.

Sniffing the air to give him a casual appearance, he sauntered back towards the ferry landing and this time sat next to the duffel-coated man on the public seat. The man had a ginger beard and glasses. As the commercial vehicles came ashore, he checked them off on his clipboard list.

'Counting them in and counting them out, are you?' said Davies amiably.

'Are you a policeman?' asked the man, scarcely looking up from his task.

Davies was shocked. 'Me? Why do you ask?'

'You move about like a policeman,' said the man. 'I've been watching you. Little bit here, a little bit there, then you go back to the promenade, then you come and sit down here. You couldn't be more obvious if you had a flashing blue light on the top of your head.'

'Thanks very much,' muttered Davies. 'As a matter of fact, you're only half right. I'm an insurance investigator.'

'Oh, really. What company?'

'I'm not at liberty to discuss that. What are you doing, if I may ask?'

'Counting them in and counting them out, as you put it,' answered the man. 'Askew, Department of the Environment. We do a check on vehicles entering the country. Various ports. And this is one of them.' To Davies's surprise, he smiled through his stiff beard and held out a hand backed with ginger hairs. He was a big man and the hand was hard.

'Davies,' said Davies, 'Insurance. How long have you been counting them in and counting them out here in Weymouth?'

'A few months now. Generally they move us about but I seem to have been stuck here for a while.'

'Since October?'

'Since August. Came here straight after my holidays last year. I got more sun here than I did on holiday.'

Davies said: 'I've got an interest in two vehicles which regularly make deliveries of pharmaceuticals and they come ashore in Weymouth. Becker Corporation. Sometimes they're small trucks, other times two cars, station wagons. They usually come over once a month – about this time of the month.'

Askew gave him a sharp look and flicked over the top sheet of the paper on his clipboard. 'Due tonight,' he said. 'Nine o'clock ferry. I don't remember checking them specifically, but I've obviously seen them if they're regular.'

'Thanks,' said Davies. He stood up to go. Jemma was waiting by the Vanguard on the promenade. 'I may see you tonight then.'

'I'll look forward to it.'

'Nine o'clock,' said Davies. 'That means, if they go straight through, which means they're on their special run, they ought to be at Blissen Pharmaceuticals at about one o'clock in the morning.' They were sitting on the beach in the brisk sun. Jemma threw pebbles into the growling water. 'Look how deep it is, right against the shore,' she said. 'When the wave goes out you can see that the shingle dips down like a chute.'

'I'm going to need someone at the other end,' he said. 'At Blissens, to see what happens there.'

'Ring the police,' she smiled ironically. She tossed another pebble.

'Imagine me phoning Vesty,' he pondered. 'Hello, superintendent old man, how's Mrs Vesty and all the little singlets? Oh, good. Listen, super, why don't you get a couple of hundred coppers to surround Blissen Pharmaceuticals tonight. I'm expecting a big drug smuggling consignment at about one o'clock. Yes, it's Detective Constable Davies down in Dorset. Still following up the Lofty Brock murder. What? Oh, thanks, super, I'll take some leave while I'm down here and then get back in time for my promotion party. No, of course I won't forget my expenses!' He wiped his hand across his eyes. 'Jesus, can you imagine it,' he sighed to Jemma. 'I'd be going back to face the firing squad.'

'It's clever,' said Jemma. 'Smuggling drugs in with pharmaceuticals. Drugs with drugs.'

'It was clever until poor old Lofty happened to pass by and disturb the arrangement.'

'And Dangerous Davies looked in,' she mentioned.

'We shall see about that. With my sort of luck the Jungfrau Harrer is working on a secret mercy mission for the International Red Cross.'

'You don't think Harrison, the boss, is in on it?'

'I doubt it. He may be but in that case he's a good actor. And it's all done after hours. If he were in the know there's no real reason why consignments of heroin, cocaine, and whatever else they're trading in, shouldn't be trundled up to the front door of Blissen Pharmaceuticals in broad daylight.' He looked pensively out to sea. 'I still need somebody to watch the other end.'

'There's only Mod,' she said.

'Unfortunately that's it.'

'Unless you'd like me to go.'

'No. Thanks just the same. I think you ought to be here.'

'Do you think they're on to you?'

'I wouldn't be surprised. You couldn't break wind along here without them knowing in Penzance. This run could be their last. The Jungfrau must know the game is almost up – now the body of Dietrich has been identified. She also knows that I've been making a nuisance of myself. Adding the ones and twos shouldn't be too hard for a Swiss mind. She's probably got her bags packed for Buenos Aires as soon as this consignment of drugs is distributed.'

'Are you going to ring Mod?'

'I can't think of anybody else.' He looked at his watch. 'He's on his lunch break now at The Babe In Arms. I'll get him there.'

Her face was turning away, watching the long waves swelling on to the beach. 'You'll be very cautious tonight, won't you,' she said.

'You don't know how much,' he assured her.

'If you don't get back by a certain time do you want me to call the police?'

'The very word sends shivers down my spine,' he said. 'But if I don't turn up after, say, three hours, I think you could.' He checked his watch again, and they walked back to the inn. In the room he picked up the receiver and gave the girl in reception the number. She rang him back quickly.

'Hello,' said Davies, 'is that The Babe In Arms? Ah, Patrick, is Mr Lewis there? Mod, yes, Mod. Thanks.'

He sat on the bed and waited. Jemma was framed by the midday light of the window, looking out to the pale blue of the sea. His eyes went down from her hair piled above her slender brown neck, to her shoulders, her arms loosely held behind her backside with her fingers hooked, her tight waist and long brown legs. While he waited for Mod he wondered, a little sadly, what was to become of her and him.

She seemed to feel the thought because she turned from the sunlit window and smiled wistfully at him. She could make even a single pace graceful and she took it and sat on the bed beside him. The telephone was still against his ear but she manoeuvred herself around it and kissed him quietly.

Mod came on the line. He sounded breathless. 'Oh, Dangerous, it's you,' he said, apparently relieved. 'I thought it was my brother in Wales, with bad news about my mother.'

'I didn't know you had a brother or a mother,' said Davies.

'I don't tell you everything,' said Mod. 'My family is better left unsaid.'

'Oh, I see what you mean.'

'Are you having a nice holiday?'

'I'm sitting here in my bathing costume. Now, Mod . . . there's a favour I need.'

'I thought so. What is it?'

'You know little Edwin Curl, the security man at the trading estate? . . .'

'Snow White's fiancé.'

'Yes. Well, tonight will you trundle over there, tell him you're working for me, and get yourself into some place where you can observe the comings and goings at Blissen Pharmaceuticals. . . .'

'I don't like the sound of this, Dangerous.'

'You'll be all right. Keep out of sight, that's all. See if you can see what the Jungfrau is up to.'

'What time is all this?'

'After closing time. Get there about midnight.'

'That's very late for me.'

'Mod, I think there's going to be some drama there tonight. . . .'

'What sort of drama?'

'Cars turning up and that sort of drama.'

'The last time there was that sort of drama, Lofty ended up dead in the canal.'

'I know, but it won't be like that. You keep well out of sight but make sure you can see what's going on. If there's any danger I'll make sure the police will be there.'

'Why can't the police be there anyway?'

'You know as well as I do. Because they won't believe me and if it goes wrong, if I've got the whole scenario wrong, I'll be for the biggest high-jump since the last Olympics.'

'I can't say I like the sound of this at all,' muttered Mod. 'It's way past my bedtime. But . . . as it's you . . .'

'Good old Mod. I'll buy you a pint when I get back.'

'It may cost you more than one.'

Davies put the phone down. 'That's that bit done, anyway,' he said.

'He'll go, won't he? He'll not let you down?'.

'He'll go. He'll probably be so well hidden he'll see nothing, but he'll go.'

Jemma regarded him solemnly. 'Don't you think it might be a good idea if you threw yourself at the mercy of the police,' she suggested.

'I *can't*! You know that.' His hand touched her face. His voice dropped. '. . . They'd throw the book at me. Maybe nothing will happen. Maybe the cars will arrive and the drivers put up cosily at the Seashore Hotel in Weymouth, like they do on their legal run.'

'Not even a call to the drug squad?'

He shook his head. 'It won't be any good. As far as the Metropolitan Police are concerned, I'm a marked man.'

226

The telephone sitting on his lap rang so sharply that he threw it in the air like a bomb. It landed on his knees again and he picked up the headset. 'Hello.'

'Is that Mr Davies . . . Insurance?'

'Yes, Davies, Insurance speaking.'

'This is Askew, Department of the Environment. We talked at Weymouth quay . . .'

'Yes, Mr Askew.'

'The parties you're interested in are definitely booked on the ferry to arrive here at nine this evening. I checked for you.'

'Oh, you did. That's very kind.'

'I thought I might be of further help. Naturally I don't know the nature of your investigations . . . business . . . but I think I can help. I'll show you a few short cuts. I can even get aboard the ferry before she docks, while she's out in the bay. We can go aboard the pilot cutter. Are you interested?'

'I think I might well be.'

'Right. I'll pick you up at eight.'

In the late afternoon a dusky rim appeared on the western horizon, moving quickly and within an hour darkening the whole sky. The wind which pushed it convulsed the sea, and rain began to drop in heavy pellets. By seven o'clock a storm was in full voice. The shutters of the inn rattled and the curtains in their room were agitated. 'It's no night to go adventuring,' grumbled Davies.

'Great dramas are played out on nights like this,' said Jemma, lying beside him. 'Ask Shakespeare.'

Askew arrived promptly at eight, and with his

overcoat up to his ears Davies hurried across the front yard and climbed into the waiting Land-Rover. 'How did you know I was staying here?' he asked when they were driving east.

'I saw your car in the front when I came by, after I'd been talking to you,' said Askew.

'It's not easy to miss,' conceded Davies. 'I keep going to change it but my dog likes it. Are we going to be able to get out to the ferry before she docks? I'd like to get a good look at these characters before they get ashore.'

The rain was thick against the windscreens, the wipers swinging frantically. 'You *are* a policeman, aren't you,' asked Askew. It was scarcely a question.

'Since you ask, yes,' said Davies. 'You spotted my funny walk, didn't you.'

'What is this? Drugs?' asked the man.

'Yes.'

'It makes it easier that you are a policeman because it gives us more elbow in getting on the pilot boat. An insurance man might be difficult to explain.'

'I don't want this getting too official,' said Davies, alarmed. 'It's a bit of an undercover effort.'

'I see. Well, just to get on to the pilot landing and to go out on the pilot boat is always difficult. They're naturally security conscious like everybody else these days. God, you ought to see it at the Department of the Environment. On the other hand, if somebody wants to get out to the incoming ferry, the pilot cutter may well pick them up off-shore. Then it's not so official, nobody has to sign things or know the reason why.'

'That sounds more like it,' said Davies. 'The more unofficial the better.'

'I'm enjoying this,' said Askew frankly. 'A bit of skulduggery. Checking vehicles on and off ferries gets incredibly dull.' He laughed. 'One day I'll be able to boast about it. There's a rumour that it's tied up with that chap who was found drowned on the Bank last year, the Swiss. Is that true?'

'That's true,' agreed Davies. 'Everybody around here knows so much, I'm beginning to feel like a tail-ender.'

The storm was unabated when Askew turned the vehicle on to a concrete platform overlooking the Chesil Bank. Gusts of rain blew straight in from the unseen sea. 'You'll need to run,' said Askew. 'We go down the beach to the fisherman's landing. There's a hut there, so we can shelter. I've fixed for this chap to take us out to the pilot cutter in his boat. I'll lead the way. Don't fall on the pebbles. They hurt.'

He jumped from the Land-Rover. Davies followed him. The rain was pounding and he ducked his head and began to run after the big crouched figure ahead. Now, even above the wind, he could hear the growl of the breakers and the rattling of the stones as the sea fell back to gather itself for a further rush.

Despite the warning he stumbled and swore a couple of times. The lights of Weymouth were shimmering as though through water on the horizon ahead. 'Are you all right?' shouted Askew.

'Fine. It's just a broken leg,' called back Davies after once more tripping over the slanting pebbles.

Askew waited for him. 'He's not here yet,' he said. 'The chap with the boat. He shouldn't be long.' As he said it, he himself stumbled forward and tripped.

Something fell on to the pebbles and bounced with a metallic clatter. Davies knew it was a gun.

'Damn, my lighter!' exclaimed Askew. He began feeling about in the dark, almost on his hands and knees.

'You must smoke heavy cigarettes,' said Davies. He moved towards Askew and the big man, with a surprisingly agile spring, came up from ground-level and punched Davies on the side of the head. It would have been the chin but Davies was slithering sideways. He fell down a slope, the small pebbles avalanching after him. Askew was still frantically searching for the gun in the pitch-darkness. Davies got up and charged up the slope at him. The man hit him again and knocked him into the next trough. Now he abandoned his search for the gun and came down powerfully after the policeman. Davies saw him looming above him and flung a handful of small pebbles in his face.

Askew cried out and staggered back, the moving slope causing him to tip backwards. Davies jumped up and flung himself on him. They rolled, hugged together down the incline to the edge of the sea. A powerful roller, black as the night itself but breaking into clouds of dull white, crashed up the beach and engulfed them. Still clutching each other, they felt themselves being torn away from the Bank by the huge undertow. Davies's overcoat wrapped itself around him like an octopus. He hung on to Askew.

'Let go, you stupid bastard!' bawled Askew. 'We'll both drown.'

They released each other simultaneously and each managed to crawl on slipping, sliding hands and knees up the cascading shingle to the first platform of pebbles. Panting and soaked, they faced each other. As though by tacit agreement each pulled his encumbering overcoat off. They then closed with each other again.

Jemma had watched from the streaming casement as the Land-Rover had picked up Davies and driven into the stormy dark. Uneasily she finished dressing then went down to the dining-room. She sat with the gale shaking the window at her elbow, the rain flung with the fury of the sea itself. The girl from behind the bar brought her the pencilled menu and she sat, troubled, with a glass of wine, watching the storm. As she ate she saw the knot of lights out to sea that she guessed was the approaching ferry. She wondered if Davies would be seasick. He probably would.

'How far out does the pilot boat go to meet the ferry?' she asked the girl.

'That I don't rightly know,' she answered. 'I'll find out.'

There were only half a dozen people in the bar at that early hour. In one of the corner benches sat an old couple, solidly sipping Guinness. The woman nudged the man as if to stop him saying something, but he nevertheless called over to Jemma whom he could just see under the arch formed by the old beams.

'What did you ask, miss? About the ferry?'

'I wondered how far the pilot boat had to go out to meet it. I know someone going out there tonight and it's bound to be rough.'

The man seemed in no hurry to reply. He took a drink from his glass and, having swallowed it, said: 'There ain't no pilot boat, miss.'

Jemma got up from the table and went towards him. The couple were startled. 'How do you mean, no pilot boat?'

'There ain't,' insisted the man. 'Because there's no pilot. The ferry comes and goes without one. The captain knows these waters like 'is own garden path. They don't need no pilot.'

Jemma made for the door, calling 'Thanks' over her shoulder. She went to the bedroom, pulled on her coat and picked up Davies's car keys from the dressing table. Briefly she touched the telephone but then took her fingers away. It might still be all right. It might have been a mistake. She hurried down the creaky stairs and went straight out into the gusting night.

She had never driven the old Vanguard and she had trouble backing it out of the inn yard. She kept thinking she ought to tell someone. But who was there to tell? Only the police. She decided to go alone.

The rain suddenly eased and a trace of moon came out, running between torn clouds. She drove determinedly along the coastal path, bordering the beach at one point, turning inland and curling through streaming lanes by stiles and cottages for another mile and eventually touching the beach again. A prolonged cloud space suddenly flooded the whole of the seashore with moonlight. She could see the galleries of silver waves ploughing against the shingle of Chesil Bank. She stopped the car once and hurried to the top of the Bank, looking along the length of the illuminated amphitheatre. The coloured lights of Weymouth shimmered in the distance.

Back in the car she drove straight and fast until, rounding a curve hung with a clutch of low, wind-bent trees, she saw the Land-Rover parked clear of the shingle. She turned out the Vanguard's head-lights and pulled up against the other vehicle. Briefly she looked inside and then took off her shoes. Carefully she trod over the soaking pebbles, until she was in a gallery looking down to the next layer and the breaking sea. At once, immediately below her she saw a man on hands and knees. He was picking up something from the pebbles. In the wide moonlight she saw the silver glow of a gun. He was only yards away and she heard it click in his hand. He began to walk carefully, below her elevated place, and she saw he was advancing on a huddled mass on the beach.

Jemma crouched and crawled along her pebble gallery until she was ahead of the man. She could hear him cursing as he stumbled along the lower stage of shingle. Now, she guessed, they were both within feet of the heap on the Bank. Bent double she heard the man advancing. Then there was another stirring and Davies's blurred voice saying: 'So you found it.'

'I found it,' answered the man.

Jemma knew he was almost below her. She waited until he had stumbled past and then half rose from her concealment. He had his back to her now and Davies was another few paces in front, still half lying. Her stockinged feet moved swiftly over the small pebbles. She briefly wondered if he would hear her over the pounding of the breakers, but it was too late now anyway. Ahead of her Davies was struggling to his feet. The man lifted the gun.

'Excuse me, Mr Askew,' she said quietly from immediately behind his back.

He whirled around and she brought a heavy pebble in her hand down on to his forehead. He dropped at her feet, the gun clattering away on the stones.

'Oh, Dangerous,' she sobbed, stepping over the man and running to him. 'You're all wet.'

'Christ,' he breathed against her neck. 'I was very nearly all dead.' He kissed her, keeping one eye on the prostrate Askew. 'I think it's time someone called the police,' he said.

'We're both going,' she told him firmly. 'God knows where the gun went. Leave him here. The police will find him.'

Arms about each other they staggered up the beach to the cars. Davies opened the vent and let the air out of one of the front tyres of the Land-Rover. 'Try blowing into that,' he muttered.

His neck and nose were bleeding, his nose copiously, his face was bruised, and there was a cut on his head. He began shivering with the wet cold. 'I'll drive,' she said, helping him into the Vanguard. 'We'll go back and ring the police.'

She started the heavy engine and backed out on to the road. 'Thanks for turning up, darling,' he said fervently as he lay back against the head-rest. 'I thought that was goodbye.'

'Anything for you,' she said, heading the car back to the inn.

234

'That stone you hit him with was like a housebrick,' he said. 'I couldn't find anything larger than a marble on that bit of the beach.'

'I brought it with me,' she said.

16

'Nice havin' a while in London,' said the young police driver conversationally over his shoulder. 'I got an auntie at Shepherd's Bush. I can go and see 'er.'

The older man in the seat beside the driver was on the radio. 'Car H for Hardy T for Tess. Dorset Police, special escort. We're just approaching M3. Location of suspect's car, please. Over.'

He turned to his colleague. 'You've not got no auntie in Shepherd's Bush,' he said mockingly. 'It's that old slag you met when you was on Miners' Strike duty.'

'She's my auntie,' insisted the driver primly. 'I ought to know.'

The radio crackled. 'Hello, Dorset Police, special escort, car H.T. . . . Your suspects have just passed our check at Basingstoke, heading for London. Speed seventy.'

'That's very law-abiding,' said Jemma.

'They'll not want to be nabbed for speeding,' said Davies. His nose had begun to bleed again. She handed him a pillowcase. The inn had been short of bandages, but had been generous with substitutes. 'Does your eye ache?' she asked gently.

'Like hell,' he replied. 'Both. He had the biggest fists I've ever known and I've known a few.'

236

The radio came through again. It was eleven-thirty and there were few cars going towards London. 'Hello Dorset special escort, H.T. Over.'

'Dorset H.T. here. Over.'

'Can we check the registrations of your two suspect vehicles? They're Continental. Over.'

'Right then. First one – 2765 J. O. That's J for Jude, O for Obscure. Over.'

'Got that. Over.'

'Second one. 8965 N. G. That's N for Native, G for Gabriel. Over.'

'Got that one too. Thanks. Over.'

Davies, his injuries throbbing, dozed against Jemma in the back. 'What's for C?' she asked. 'Casterbridge?'

'How come you know our codes?' the policeman said over his shoulder.

The next check was at Sunbury at the end of the motorway. The two estate cars were ten minutes ahead. Davies awoke and blinked at the white lights arched like luminous trees over the road. 'Nearly there,' said the driver. 'I recognize this section. 'Tis a bit different from Piddlehinton, ain't it, Percy?'

'More like Bere Regis,' said the other policeman. 'Can't wait to see how these London coppers spring the trap. They'll all be ready now.'

'If I know anything,' said Davies wearily, 'they'll be strung three abreast across the road stopping all traffic entering the area, including the two cars we're supposed to nab.'

They drove over the elevated sections of the road on to the suburban carriageway and turned north. Davies sat up expectantly as he gave the driver final

237

directions. 'I wonder how Mod managed,' he said to Jemma.

When they reached the trading estate it was flooded with light. People were standing on the opposite pavement and leaning on their forearms in the upper windows of their houses. The Dorset car was stopped by a road block but after some discussion was permitted through. The gates of the estate were wide open and guarded by further police. 'They've certainly sat up and taken notice,' said Jemma.

'Sometimes they tend to go over the top,' said Davies. 'They've probably got a warship patrolling the canal. There are the cars.'

Two estate vehicles, surrounded by police, uniformed and in plain clothes, were parked directly outside the gaping service doors of Blissen Pharmaceuticals. An ambulance was drawn up on the road and the attendants were loading a stretcher on which was a substantial mound. 'Mod,' said Davies.

They got out as soon as the Dorset car stopped. Police were chattering into walkie-talkies. Davies and Jemma hurried to the ambulance. By now Mod was inside groaning on the stretcher. They went in after him. He was lying, head padded and bandaged, eyes closed, his cheeks blowing like bellows. He opened his eyes and saw them. 'God, Dangerous, what you let me in for,' he moaned. 'That woman, the Jungfrau, she caught me. She beat me up something terrible, Dangerous. Both fists. I've never been so battered. She hit me a glancing blow with a fire-axe.'

Davies said: 'Thank God it's not serious.'

'It was quite a soft fire-axe,' muttered Mod. 'I hope I can claim compensation.'

They left the ambulance to take him to hospital. 'Poor old Mod,' said Davies. He looked at Jemma. 'Fancy being mugged by Frau Harrer.'

They saw Harrer immediately they entered the Blissen warehouse. She and three men from the estate cars were handcuffed, scowling, and sitting on some cardboard cartons, half-surrounded by police. Superintendent Vesty appeared. 'The drug squad are livid, Davies,' he said with gritty satisfaction. 'Their guv'nor, Berry, is after your skin. They've been watching this set-up for months and now they reckon you've fouled up the whole operation.'

'We've got them in handcuffs,' said Davies, nodding towards the prisoners. 'What else do they want?'

A stranger in a blue raincoat appeared. 'I'll tell you what, laddie,' he said, strongly Scots. 'About forty others. I'm Inspector Berry of the drug squad. You've screwed up months of surveillance. The others have taken off by now. All we've got, Mr Davies, is the wee fry.'

Angrily he strode out through the warehouse doors. 'They call him Logan Berry,' said Vesty conversationally. 'Good nickname, isn't it?'

'I wouldn't call Mrs Harrer wee fry,' muttered Davies.

The huge woman seemed to hear. She rose from a cardboard carton and, despite the timid efforts of two constables to persuade her to remain seated, she advanced on Davies, her handcuffed hands held out in front of her.

'So,' she sneered. 'You again have ballsed up it!'

'Seems like it,' shrugged Davies.

'You balls up it for me also,' she grunted. She strode towards him and before any of the dithering officers could move, she brought up her handcuffed hands like a shaft on a beam engine. She dealt Davies the most fearful blow under the chin and sent him staggering back towards the door. He collided with an engrossed constable, and they both tipped to the floor. With a great Teutonic cry Mrs Harrer plunged forward through the gap created, and pounded out into the night. Shouts and whistles rose and a posse of police went in pursuit, some further treading over the prostrate Davies.

Screaming and swinging her handcuffed hands before her like a battle-axe, she bounded on her mighty legs down the sloping road towards the canal. The gate in the wire mesh fence was open. She charged at it with every pound of frenzied force in her enormous body, ramming the duty constable and sending him spinning on to the tow-path. With a shrieking Valkyrie cry, she ran a last few unhesitating paces and threw herself into the black water of the canal. She hit the surface with a gigantic splash. Her pursuers poured out through the mesh gate and halted, looking at the cold, grim water and the widening circles under the light of the old lamps.

As the growing crowd of policemen stared from the bank, so the woman came to the surface. She had changed her mind. 'Help!' she bellowed. 'I order help!' Once more her large body sank.

'There's no fucking way I'm going in there,' muttered a constable. Others shook their heads.

Two others took off their boots and jackets and jumped, holding their noses, into the foul, dark water. Frau Harrer once more came to the surface, her handcuffed hands beating the water.

She resubmerged, this time not to reappear. When Davies, helped by Jemma and PC Westerman, who had stumbled to the edge of the canal, arrived they were towing her body ashore with boat-hooks. 'There goes my witness,' Inspector Berry of the drug squad complained. 'And mine,' muttered Davies.

They turned away from the tow-path. Westerman went to another ambulance whose obliging crew tried to stop his nosebleed while they waited to receive the body of Mrs Harrer. Jemma put her arm around Davies. Then a further commotion rose from between the dark walls of the industrial premises. Another few yards and they rounded a corner to see three stunned policemen backing away while down the sloping path from Iverson Theatricals came the little-legged figure of Pinocchio, the great head swaying from side to side, the body staggering, hands clutching two Scotch bottles. 'Hi diddlee dee,' sang Edwin Curl. 'An actor's life for me!'

Mod was lying in the hospital bed looking large and pale, his head plastered, a saline drip inserted into his wrist, and a disgruntled expression in his eye. 'We've changed places,' he mumbled through his thick lip when he saw Davies. 'I tried to get your regular bed, but there's somebody in it.'

'It doesn't have much of a view,' said Davies. 'How are you feeling?' Jemma patted Mod on the arm and he winced.

'Battered,' replied the philosopher. 'Severely

battered. God, that Jungfrau is a size. And she was mad as hell. I never thought I'd be beaten up by a woman. I was just creeping to look into the window of the Blissen premises. She caught me and before I knew what had happened, she was thumping me all over the place. Naturally, I couldn't retaliate. She's a woman, after all, despite evidence to the contrary. She would have killed me, Dangerous, if the police hadn't arrived.'

'She jumped in the canal,' said Davies simply. 'There was a hell of a splash.'

Mod's bruised eyes opened. 'She's dead?'

'Drowned. Like Lofty.' He felt his face. 'She gave me both handcuffed fists. She was certainly no featherweight.'

Mod moved his feet over and Jemma and Davies sat on the edge of the bed. It was nine in the morning. The sky was insipid outside the window although there were shades of green on a bush that brushed the panes. 'So it's all over,' said Mod. 'Everybody's satisfied.'

'Nobody's satisfied,' corrected Davies. 'The drug squad are livid because we spoiled their ambush by having one of our own. According to them or their guv'nor, Mr Logan Berry, if you can believe it, the Harrer woman was only part of a bigger scene and all the others have now done a runner.'

'So you're still in it.'

'Right in it.'

Jemma said: 'But now, at least, you know what happened to Lofty.'

'Indeed. That's easy now. There he was trundling his pram along the tow-path, still trying to remember what he'd done with all that pre-War loot, and he chances on the end of the latest drug run. Not just that, but he arrives at the very moment when they're clobbering poor old Sigmund Dietrich, breaking something over his skull – the scene that Shiny Bright also witnessed.

'The Jungfrau and her mates can't allow Lofty to see that sort of thing going on, doors open, cars unloading, man floored with a fire-axe . . .'

'Don't,' pleaded Mod. 'Not with the fire-axe.'

'Pardon. It was just a case of thieves falling out. Perhaps Dietrich wanted a bigger slice of the profits, perhaps they had discovered he was untrustworthy. Whatever it was they had parted his hair rather spectacularly. When his body was washed up the cleft skull was there for all to see, but it was concluded that it was caused by being thrown up repeatedly on to Chesil Bank.'

'Did you have a nice time down there?' asked Mod.

'It was lovely,' said Jemma. 'You must go some time.'

Davies said: 'I was just about to be slaughtered by their watchman, a gent who said he was Askew of the Department of the Environment. He nearly did for my environment, I can tell you. Fortunately, this lady, despite her slight appearance, wields a nifty rock, so that bit of blood and thunder we eventually won.'

'You think he was waiting for you?' asked Jemma. 'Not just linking up with the smugglers.'

'He counted them in and out,' said Davies. 'But this time he was waiting for me too. Once Dietrich's body was washed up, they must have known their time was limited. That last run was the biggest consignment of heroin ever to be brought into this country. There was enough there to keep the entire addicted population smiling quietly for a long time.'

'Smuggling drugs in pharmaceuticals is not a bad idea, is it,' mumbled Mod. 'Was the boss of Blissen, what's his name, Harrison, in on it?'

'He knew nothing about it until some copper got him out of bed in the middle of the night. The late Jungfrau was the operator. The consignments which left Zurich were legitimate enough, and those that arrived by trucks in normal trading hours were above board. That's when the drivers stayed overnight in Weymouth and came on the following morning to London. The dodgy ones came off the boat and straight to London, except for the October consignment which, because fog delayed the previous day's ferries, arrived in Weymouth at midday on October 6th, and the drivers and Sigmund Dietrich had to kill a few hours at the Seashore Hotel until it was all right to proceed after dark.'

Jemma said: 'Why did they come through Weymouth?'

'It's quieter than Dover or the other entry ports,' said Davies. 'But they also picked up the drugs somewhere in France, Paris or perhaps even Cherbourg, where they joined the ferry. There's no way they would have been processed through Switzerland, although the whole thing was obviously financed and organized there.'

'Will I get a reward or a medal?' asked Mod practically.

'I'd recommend it, but I think I'm on the verge of getting the elbow myself,' said Davies. 'Mr Logan Berry is after my head.'

'He can have mine,' moaned Mod.

'We'd better go,' said Jemma. 'We'll come and see you tonight.'

'It must be murder lying there with a bottle just out of reach,' said Davies, nodding at the drip.

'Salt water,' said Mod.

They left the ward and the hospital and walked out into the street. It was quietly raining. She put her arm in his as they walked. 'You're still not happy, are you,' she said.

'Not really,' he answered. 'What we've done is to solve the wrong mystery.'

On the night, a week later, that they let Mod out they went to The Babe In Arms.

'Is your promotion through yet?' Mod asked.

Davies shrugged moodily. 'As far as the Metropolitan Police is concerned, I'm still in limbo,' he said.

They had been there an hour when a tall thin man came in at the distant end of the bar. He began to look around.

'That's the diver,' said Jemma, who saw him first. 'The one that went into the canal after the pram.'

'Tennant,' said Davies. At that moment the man saw them, waved and moved through the drinkers towards them. He was wearing an overcoat and had another over his arm. Davies bought him a drink.

'I've been thinking of coming to see you,' he said.

'I've been in here once or twice but you weren't here.'

'We've all been on holiday,' said Mod, feeling his head. 'These two at the seaside, me in the Central Middlesex Hospital.'

'Sorry about that,' said Tennant but not asking why. He shifted the second overcoat on his lap. 'It was this,' he said. 'This coat.' He handed it across to Davies whose hands were already halfway to accepting it. Davies opened the collar and looked at the label.

'Raoul Susini, Paris,' he said. He looked at Jemma and then at Tennant.

'You recognize it?' said Tennant.

'I think so. It belonged to a Sigmund Dietrich, deceased, formerly of Zurich.'

'It's been hanging up in the subaqua club,' said Tennant, embarrassed. 'I thought it might be something important. I read in the papers about the police at the Blissen place by the canal, the raid, and the woman dying and I guessed this might be something to do with it. You remember Archie, one of my divers that day we brought up the old pram? Well, he found it.'

Davies said: 'In the canal?'

'Right. He saw it there, a bit downstream when we were looking for the pram. He didn't think much of it, so he said, but he went back afterwards and lugged it out. He could see it was a good coat, so he dried it out, had it cleaned . . .'

'And kept it,' muttered Davies.

'Right. It was just his size.'

'Where is Archie now?'

'Saudi Arabia,' said Tennant. 'He left it on the coat hangers in the club. It's been there ever since. Is it important?'

Davies shrugged. 'It might have been. The owner was murdered.'

'Christ! I'm sorry.'

'So was he,' said Davies. He rubbed the material. 'Lovely bit of cloth,' he said. His hands went around the coat. 'Was there anything in the pockets?' he asked.

'I don't know. There was nothing when I found it on the hanger. No clues, eh?'

Davies was staring into his beer. Mod looked over to see if a spider or some other insect had fallen in. Davies looked up. 'There are times,' he said very slowly, 'when I think I'll never make a copper.'

'Now you tell us,' said Mod.

'What is it?' asked Jemma, leaning towards him.

'Lofty. Right at the very beginning of all this. God, we've wracked our brains enough, but I'd forgotten to ask if he had *anything in his pockets* when he was found. He had trousers, a jacket and an overcoat.' He stood up. 'I'd better hang on to the coat,' he said to Tennant. 'I'll make sure the Met. Police don't sell it.' He looked around at them. 'I'll just wander down the nick,' he said. 'I'll be back in twenty minutes.'

He walked quickly towards the police station muttering under his breath. It was a light, damp evening. Children were playing games in the side-streets. Venus was patrolling on the over pavement. She waved a hand. 'Busy?' Davies called to her.

'Nothing moving, Dangerous,' she called back.

He went into the police station. Lewis Emmanuel was on duty behind the desk. 'Lew,' he said. 'I'd like to have a look in the lost property cupboard.'

'What've you lost, Dangerous?'

'I don't know yet. We still put stuff in there found on corpses, don't we? It's the same place?'

The sergeant produced a key. 'Stiffs' lost property is in the cabinet on the right,' he said. 'How's your lady friend?'

'Fine, thanks,' he said, taking the key. 'She sends her love.'

'I wish she'd bring it herself,' said the sergeant. 'I can never understand how you got locked in there at Christmas.'

'It's a mystery,' acknowledged Davies. 'But we deal in mysteries, don't we.' He went down a corridor, opened a door and turned on the light switch. It was a small room, little more than a cupboard, green-painted and smelling damp, hung with coats and hats, umbrellas, and other mislaid personal belongings, including – he was briefly intrigued to see – a red flag, three pairs of heavy boots and a box of fireworks. The cabinet on the right had a key in its lock. He turned it and opened the door. Everything in there was contained in plastic bags. On each bag in thick ink was a name. Davies searched. Many people had died leaving little personal bits and pieces behind them. Most of the packets rattled with small change, there were the shapes of several pairs of glasses and the ghostly outlines of false teeth. He had turned over half a dozen before he came to a plastic envelope with the inscription 'Wilfred Brock'. He picked it up. There was only one thing inside it. He could feel its shape. A single key.

They were waiting at The Babe In Arms. Mod was professing embarrassment that financial circumstances had ruled that Jemma had provided the last round of drinks. 'When I get my police reward,' he promised, 'we'll have a party.'

Davies sat at the table and took out the plastic bag with the key. He held it in the palm of his hand, an old-fashioned, yellowed key with a ragged luggage label attached to it. 'No. 134. SRCB,' he read from the printed label. He looked around at them and sighed: 'The clues don't get any easier.'

They had a guessing game as to what the letters might mean. Tennant had gone but, as an apology for the coat, had left five pounds with the barman for Davies to disburse as he thought fit. 'He didn't mention it to me,' grumbled Mod.

They all had drinks. Shiny Bright came in looking prosperous: a new suit, a flower in his lapel and a twinkling pair of brown shoes. 'All honest, Dangerous,' he assured before Davies had asked the question. 'I found a dog that runs with six legs. You should have backed it yourself. It's called Dangerous Moonlight.'

He bought all three of them a Scotch, and then Davies bought another round and the evening went swiftly. They left The Babe In Arms and walked along the main shopping street towards Harry's All Night Refreshments. There were stars caught in the rooftops; the air was bland.

"'On such a night as this,'" quoted Mod, looking at the sky.

"'When the sweet wind did gently kiss the trees . . .'" Jemma laughed. "'On such a night, did Thisbe fearfully o'ertrip the dew . . .'"

Davies said: 'Oh, God, don't start all that now.'

'How about this?' chortled Mod. On the corner was a white Barclays Bank. He struck a pose. "'How sweetly sleeps the moonlight on this bank . . .'"

They groaned and laughed and went on to Harry's. 'You're still worrying about it,' said Jemma like a mild accusation.

'Well it's not finished, is it,' said Davies. Moodily he drank his coffee. He took out the key and recited the message on the label again. 'No. 134. SRCB.'

They drank their coffee, said good night to the illuminated Harry and walked home. Jemma had another social worker, who had been thrown out by her husband, staying with her. Davies kissed her on the doorstep and turned home. The moon had cleared the house-tops and was running like a river through the empty streets. As he passed the bank, Davies tried to remember what Mod had quoted. 'Moonlight on Barclays,' he said to himself.

He went to bed, lay thinking in the dark and then slept. He woke at three. 'Bank,' he said to himself. He sat up abruptly in his bed. 'Bank.' He believed it; he knew it must be right.

The Simmonds, Rowe and Campbell Bank of Brightstone-on-Sea, Essex, had, like so many of the small pre-War banks, been absorbed in 1940 into the more widespread East Anglian Bank and this, in turn, had found itself taken under the arm of Barclays after the War. 'We have, however, remained under the same roof since the early thirties,' said the manager, Harold Buss. 'In the nineteenth century Mr Simmonds, Mr Rowe and Mr Campbell all had their separate banking houses, so we go back quite a long way.'

'And the safe deposit is still the same, intact, since before the War?' said Davies cautiously.

'Indeed, as I told you on the telephone. We've modernized of course but the old cellars are still much the same and some of the safe deposit boxes there go back to the beginning of the century. The number, I believe you told me, was 134. You have the key?'

Davies took a deep breath and handed over the key. 'Ah, yes,' said Mr Buss. 'Quite a museum piece. It's certainly one of ours. This way please, gentlemen.'

Mod and Davies followed him through the lime-green office, nodding at the girls working at computers as they went. 'Banks don't smell of money any more,' whispered Mod.

'Did they ever?' whispered Davies.

'Here,' said Mr Buss as they entered a glassed inner office, 'we keep some of the old registers. It's not often we have to consult them now. And even these have found their inevitable way on to a computer.' He took down a worn red leather book from a high shelf. 'No. 134.' He glanced at the label on the key. 'Nor these days would you have the pleasure of dealing with such a simple, uncomplicated number as 134.' He turned the ledger pages. 'Yes, here we are. Mr Augustus Bryant.'

Davies saw Mod's face drop and felt his do so also. But he quickly said: 'Yes, that's the chap. He had various names, but that's him all right.'

'Well,' said Mr Buss. Prudently he looked at the letter of authority with the heading 'Metropolitan Police'. Davies swallowed heavily. 'Well, that seems to be in order.' He glanced up with a professional smile which Davies returned timidly and Mod scarcely at all. 'Let's go down to the depths,' he invited.

Some of the girls looked up from their keyboards and the men from their telephones and papers as the two bulky men followed the manager through the airy office. Spring sun was drifting through the windows. Mr Buss unlocked several doors, the third one opening on to a set of stairs. 'This is the oldest part of the establishment,' he said. 'Some of the safe deposits down here have not been disturbed for seventy years.'

'*I'd* be tempted to have a peep,' admitted Mod. 'Come down here with the master key and open them up.'

'Banking,' said Mr Buss a little reprovingly, 'is not that sort of business. Fantasy is frowned upon.' He paused. 'Here we are. Box No. 134.' He handed the key back to Davies. 'If you would like to open it, Mr Davies, I will leave you.'

'No,' said Davies hurriedly. He caught the manager's arm. 'If you didn't mind . . . if it's allowed . . . would you like to hang around? I may need a witness . . .'

Mr Buss looked secretly pleased. 'Yes, of course, if you wish,' he said. 'There's nothing that says I shouldn't be present. It's merely that we imagine people want privacy.'

'Not,' answered Davies, 'in this case.'

He felt the key had become warm in his hand. The box was shallow, about eighteen inches long and twelve wide. It was made of sturdy wood which, as his fingers disturbed the dust, was revealed as veneered, not unlike the lunch-box of Sergeant Emmanuel. There was a cobweb over the keyhole. Davies brushed it away with his hand. Mod and Mr Buss looked on with silent expectation. Davies inserted the key and felt it turn. 'It still fits,' he said quietly. He took the weight of the lid, easing it up. It squeaked softly, like a mouse. A dusty smell came from within. A creased piece of red silk was revealed, covering the contents. Davies, hardly breathing, pulled it away. Underneath was a crumpled copy of the previous day's *Daily Mirror* and a personal note addressed to Davies from Inspector Joliffe of the Essex Constabulary.

'Just look at that,' said Inspector Joliffe. 'Have you ever seen a nicer haul?'

The jewellery was spread on a baize-covered table in his office. There were diamonds, emeralds, opals, zircons, mounted on silver and gold and platinum; necklaces, brooches, rings, chains and chokers.

'It's very nice,' conceded Davies.

Joliffe came around the table and put a senior officer's friendly arm around him. 'Mavis Prenderley has been able to identify quite a lot,' he said. 'Some pieces came from Sandringham. She's got an amazing memory for an old dear. Still, I suppose she helped to nick some of it.'

'People around here,' observed Davies begrudgingly, 'are very co-operative with the police, aren't they.'

'They're well-trained,' agreed Joliffe. 'People tend to come to us when they're "not sure". Mr Buss, the bank manager, gets a letter with a Metropolitan Police heading and the first thing he does is dial 999. Then you telephone him and give him the number of the safe deposit box. They have a master key, you know, even when they go back to the year dot. So we opened it and this is what we found.'

Davies said: 'You even put the cobweb back.'

'Over the keyhole! Yes, we did. Sorry to take the glory from under your nose, Davies.'

'The carpet from under my feet,' mentioned Davies sombrely. 'The second time this week.'

'Ah, yes. We know all about that. We've been keeping a general eye on you, of course, since you first put in an appearance on our patch.'

'When Mr Linder and the landlord of the pub both shopped me,' sighed Davies.

'Well, you do rather trudge around.'

'I suppose I do. I've got a talent for causing small hurricanes. And I'm usually the one who's shipwrecked. You know all about the drugs thing then?'

'We had a full summary. You did pretty well there, Davies, and of course it all followed on from this Billy Dobson case.'

'Lofty Brock,' muttered Davies. 'That's right. But all I got was trouble. I fouled up a master plan of the drug squad.'

'Never mind,' said Joliffe. '*We're* pretty pleased about the whole business. I'm afraid the headlines will say: "Essex Police Recover Million-Pound Proceeds of Pre-War Robberies". They'll quote me, my chaps will get the credit but, since you were, shall we say, *ex officio*, you won't get a mention. But you'll have the satisfaction of knowing the truth.'

Davies shrugged: 'I'll still be in the mire about trespassing on your territory, I suppose. I'm on compulsory leave now. I'm expecting to be back on the beat any day, if I'm not thrown out.'

'It's in the gubbins,' said Joliffe, shaking his head. 'And, as I told you before, once it's in the gubbins it's in there for good.' He patted Davies on the shoulder once more. 'However, I'll do what I can,' he said. 'A few words here and a few there, and things can be erased from the gubbins. It's difficult but it can be done.'

'Thanks very much,' said Davies. 'I don't look good in uniform.'

Joliffe laughed. 'It'll be all right, I'm sure,' he said jovially. 'But don't forget that chap you know who knows Max Bygraves. When we get around to arranging next year's police ball, we might take you up on that.'

'Oh, that . . . well, yes. Just contact me. I'd better go, I suppose.'

Joliffe shook hands firmly with him. 'You're not a bad copper, Davies,' he said. 'You've got a lot of good points even if you're not very careful. If you weren't so old I'd say you had a promising future.'

'Thank you,' said Davies again. He turned to go.

'There was one more thing,' said Joliffe. 'The pearl. The one you showed Mavis.'

'Oh . . . oh right. Yes, *that* pearl.' He fumbled in his pocket desperately hoping he had not lost it. With relief he located the ring box. He opened it. Joliffe smiled and took out the pearl. 'Last bit of the jigsaw,' he said. He stepped to the displayed jewellery and placed the pearl as a pendant at the bottom of a fine necklace. 'Fits perfectly,' he said. 'Mrs Simpson lost that. The Duchess of Windsor.'

He had his arm around Davies's shoulder all the way to the door and then offered his hand for a final shake. As Davies went out, Joliffe called after him: 'I'll contact you about Max Bygraves, Dangerous. I'll know where to find you, won't I?'

'Yes, usual place,' answered Davies. He turned and walked alone into the streets. 'In the shit,' he said quietly.

Jemma went into The Babe In Arms and saw Mod sitting at their table, wondering how long he could eke out half a pint. It was just after midday. The bar was otherwise empty. 'I thought he'd be back by now,' said Jemma.

'An essential part of the third-degree torture,' said Mod, 'is that it takes a long time.' He looked cornered. 'May I buy you a drink?' he asked discouragingly.

'No thanks. I think I'll walk down to meet him. He may need some comfort.'

'Very probably,' answered Mod. His deep eyes unfolded. 'He had another development this morning, you know. In the post.'

'What . . . how do you mean?'

'A note which said merely: "We killed *both* Lofty Brocks." It was signed: "The Silesia Survivors."'

She looked at him, astonished. 'You mean . . . It's not finished? I can't believe it . . .'

'Far from finished, apparently,' said Mod. 'It's going to keep Dangerous occupied for a long time yet, I suspect.'

She left the bar and turned down the spring-time street. He was coming towards her, coat hanging negligently, hat on the back of his head, hands in pockets. She hurried along the pavement and embraced him. He folded his large arms about her. Several people stopped to watch. 'It's all right,' he said. 'They've let me off – *everything*.'

'That's wonderful! I should think so, as well.'

'Breaking up a drug smuggling ring, solving a murder and finding the bloody crown jewels helped a bit,' he said. 'But there were a few things on the debit side.' He grinned at her. 'Askew, the chap you clobbered with the big pebble down at Chesil Bank – he was a Customs and Excise man.'

'Oh God. Why didn't he say so?'

'They often don't mention it,' he shrugged. 'Apparently we threw another spanner in the works there. He was watching for the two cars with the stuff and suddenly we turn up. He had to put me out of action and quick.'

'But you told him you were the police.'

'That might be the reason. Apparently the Customs

257

were mounting their own operation on the Jungfrau and her mates and were trying to get in before the police. It's all kudos, you know. Nobody told anybody what was happening. The drug squad and the Customs are not exactly in love. And we clobbered Askew, who is now probably collecting VAT arrears somewhere. It apparently brought a rare smile to the face of Mr Logan Berry, until I wrecked his bit of the action.'

They turned and walked away from the direction in which Davies had been progressing. She regarded him seriously. His lip was taking longer to heal these days. 'What about this new note? Mod told me. From the Silesia Survivors?' she asked. 'Don't you think you ought to drop the whole thing now?'

He stopped, took his arm from around her waist and produced a creased sheet of paper from his inside pocket. 'I am,' he said. He handed the single sheet to her. 'One thing which is not completely obvious about this note, without examining it too closely, is that the paper was stolen from the local public library. Look, see, on the reverse side, if you care to turn it over, at the bottom it says: "Brent Library Services".'

'Mod!' she exclaimed.

'He'd never make a forger,' Davies grinned. 'He thinks something to worry about, like Lofty, keeps me happy, busy, lively.'

'Does it?'

'Yes, I suppose so.' He looked at her. 'But now there's you as well.'

They stopped and kissed in the street. 'Do you

want to come for a walk with me and Kitty?' Davies asked. 'We could go and get him. He needs a bit of fresh air.'

'So do I,' she laughed, taking his arm. 'Come on, Dangerous, let's go down the cemetery.'